Praise for Roger Croft

Operation Saladin

Croft's world of double-dealing and treachery, with a suggestion of indifferent, manipulative bureaucrats, confirms the dour observation of a veteran spymaster that loyalty among spies verges on being an oxymoron. Croft's moral wilderness and compilation of treachery ring far truer than the glamour of a James Bond. And the clash between romance, personal loyalty and institutional duplicity bears the unmistakable tone of one who knows.

—*Publishers Weekly* (Starred Review)

Croft once again intrigues his reader with this fast-paced sequel...Tightly written and laden with dramatic tension, Vaux's quest for truth and freedom is constantly tested, especially when his own friends become less and less trustworthy and his own safety is further compromised. Surprises lurk behind every character in this original storyline fraught with suspense...A suspenseful, behind-the-scenes look at espionage and politics through the eyes of a British journalist. A web of secrets and betrayal, sure to grab spy novel fans.

—*Kirkus Reviews*

Operation Saladin is an amusing read and may please fans of the spy genre, particularly those who take the professionalism of the secret services with a pinch of salt. One thing Croft does well is character study.

—*Daily Star,* Beirut

The Vaux in this book is more confident and more experienced in the ways of espionage. There are Israeli and Syrian professional hit men hunting for Vaux. He is moved from safe house to safe house and finally sent to a remote military base in England. There is humor for those who are familiar with the spy genre. When an MI6 staffer suggests at a top level meeting that Vaux 'has come in from the cold,' the head of MI6's Department B3 nearly chokes on his digestive and blurts out: 'We'll have none of that silly talk, thank you.' Alena, Syrian-born and beautiful, and the love of Vaux's life, returns in this sequel and appears much more complicated than originally thought [as] Vaux becomes her prey. This novel is a terrific follow-up to Mr. Croft's first spy novel and I highly recommend it.

—*Portland Book Review*

Operation Saladin is a fast-paced fascinating sequel to *The Wayward Spy*. Author Roger Croft has created a series of suspenseful novels that will leave readers mesmerized by the storyline, the characters and the action. Highly recommended and truly enjoyable.

—Amenda Kerr, Goodreads

The Wayward Spy

Our protagonist Michael Vaux is not a career intelligence officer—he's a retired journalist, independent-minded, and seemingly never without a drink in his hand...The plot is elaborate and takes the reader down countless blind alleys. But the reader would be hard-pressed to foresee the final outcome.

—*Egyptian Gazette*, Cairo

Croft deserves credit for building his story line on an unusual foundation.

—*Publishers Weekly*

'The Wayward Spy' takes the best of spy novels from the likes of Le Carré and kicks it up a notch...Wayward this spy might be, but I couldn't put the book down.

—*San Francisco Book Review*

Fun read, like the great spy novels, but with added humor.

—Cybergwen.com

This is not your James Bond–type of spy thriller. Croft is more the John le Carré–writer with a heavy mix of

Graham Greene. International intrigue, twisted plots, and spycraft, all make for an interesting read...Michael Vaux is a likeable character that readers are pulling for from the start—and there is just enough humor to keep this book a fun read.

—*Portland Book Review*

The Maghreb Conspiracy

The Third Spy Story in Croft's Mideast Trilogy

Roger Croft

The Maghreb Conspiracy

The third spy story in Croft's
Mideast trilogy
The Wayward Spy
Operation Saladin
The Maghreb Conspiracy

To Maria Mills-Farinas
With love and thanks

Other Books By Roger Croft

Swindle!
Bent Triangle
The Wayward Spy
Operation Saladin

Cassio Books International

ISBN: 1500823325

EAN: 9781500823320

Author's Note

This book is fiction, not history. But the actual events around which the plot pivots—the terrorist outrages in Casablanca, London and Madrid—are historical facts. I have taken some literary license with the chronology of this tragic period.

I used to wish the Arabian tales were true.
                          —Cardinal Newman (1801–1890)

London, May 2005

A shabby, gray building on Gower Street in the storied Bloomsbury district of London, with five floors, dusty Georgian sash windows, and a shaky, ancient elevator, serves as home base for an obscure subgroup of Britain's Secret Intelligence Service, more widely known in the postmillennial era as MI6. Department B3, an offshoot of MI6's Middle East and North Africa desk, is located on the third floor, and the few cramped rooms of the office suite look out to the gloomy white-tiled inner well of the old building. The tarnished brass nameplate by the side of the main door informs the curious that the occupiers of the suite ply their trade under the name of Acme Global Consultants Ltd.

It had been a long, harsh winter and cold spring, but the weather forecasters were saying that May and the early summer looked promising. On this particular morning, the weather, unusually, was not on Sir Nigel Adair's mind. Only yesterday, Sir Nigel, a deputy director at the spy agency, had been given a top-secret briefing on a new project—tailor-made, according to the special operations directorate, for his small team of specialists. It was early days, but Sir Nigel figured that the successful outcome of this new mission could only buttress his long-running argument with the power brokers at Vauxhall on the pressing need for additional staff. If his small team of what his persistent detractors called 'lone wolf operators' were to be totally effective, the numbers would need to be increased to the levels deemed necessary by a classified government green paper, published in 1998, that had been filed away to gather dust in the vaults at Vauxhall Cross.

Sir Nigel hung his trench coat on an ancient oak coat tree in the small lobby, stepped into his office, sat down heavily on his scuffed leather swivel chair and bellowed, 'Craw!'—a loud and clear invitation to his hovering deputy to enter his sanctum.

Alan Craw, a lean and hungry man in Sir Nigel's unchangeable view, was his long-serving deputy and, like many second fiddles, would probably stay in that position until his longed-for retirement. Craw sat down on the highly polished seat of a 1940s vintage Windsor chair. The two men nodded a good morning to each other and remained silent while Anne Armitage-Hallard, Sir Nigel's tall, blond secretary, placed an ancient, battered tin tray on the desk with two bone china cups of instant coffee and four chocolate digestive biscuits.

'Thank you, Anne,' said Sir Nigel as he scribbled something on a notepad. Craw had learned to read upside-down prose in his short intelligence training course many moons ago, and so he was not completely taken off- guard by the two questions.

'Very well, Craw. I have two main questions, the answers to which we must come up with this morning.'

'Yes, sir,' said Craw, whose long manicured fingers began to stroke his prominent Adam's apple. 'We should first of all christen the operation. Second, we must nominate our chief operative.'

'That's exactly what I had in mind. So what do you suggest?'

'Well, sir, Chris Greene remains on sick leave—'

'What the hell's the matter with him? He's a young man. I thought he had the flu and would be back by now.'

'No, sir. It's something they call H1N1, that new flu-like infection that can at times prove fatal. He's at Charing Cross Hospital, and I'm sure he'll pull through.'

'I should jolly well hope so. He's one of our best men,' said Sir Nigel.

'So I don't think we have much option in the matter. We'll have to use our new man—Sebastian Micklethwait.'

'Good God, man, he just joined us—he's still wet behind the ears. We can't suddenly throw him in the deep end like that—'

'He's been through the Portsmouth training course, sir. Learned the basics—from assassination techniques to telecom interception and coding technology, physical self-defense, dead-drop strategies, small arms—the works.'

'Never had that sort of training in *my* young days,' said Sir Nigel with some nostalgia. 'Just threw us out in the big, wide world to pick up things as we went along.' Craw decided not to review his own sparse training background. 'Well, all right. We'd better see him now. Where's he housed?'

'He's occupying Greene's desk at the moment, sir. While we work out where to put him. We don't have much space, as you are well aware. He may have to commandeer one of the empty deputies' offices.'

'He'll have to move out quickly if we are ever to be favored with another deputy,' said Sir Nigel with a sigh.

'As to naming the project: what about "Operation Maghreb"?' suggested Craw.

'Bit general, isn't it? It looks as if the focus will be on Morocco…'

'Yes, but its tentacles could easily spread to countries east— Tunisia, Algeria, Libya, and so on.'

Craw then observed a fat pigeon flutter down to the narrow sill of Sir Nigel's sash window and drop a dollop of black-and-white excrement as if to concur with his chief's lack of enthusiasm for the suggested title of the operation.

Sir Nigel said, 'Let's call it "Operation Apostate." The man's losing his faith, after all. He's coming over to our side, undergoing a sort of conversion. So he's a man without a faith—until and unless he finds another one.'

'Well, I'm sure he's still a Muslim. He's just anti all this terrorism nonsense, that's all. Anyway, I'll agree with you.'

Sir Nigel sipped the bitter coffee. He winced and then opened a small carton of low-fat milk, dribbling it into his cup. 'Poor Anne. She's hopeless in the refreshment area. Can't make a decent cup of coffee to save her life. Talking of which, Craw, this could be a very dangerous assignment we are about to send young Micklethwait on. Anything, literally anything, could happen. Are you sure we want to risk a probationer on what could turn out to be a disastrous mission?'

Craw had witnessed his share of disastrous missions. The most renowned had been Operation Helvetia, in which the leading protagonist was one Michael Vaux, an ex-journalist, who wound up falling in love with an Arab-speaking staffer who turned out to be a mole within Department B3. She had worked for the GSD—Syria's spy agency. The cataclysmic result was Vaux's quasi-defection and the collapse of the operation whose main goal had been to filch the dope on a then pending Russia-Syria multibillion-dollar arms deal. 'We all have to start somewhere, sir.'

'I suppose so. But I've just had a brilliant thought.'

'What's that, sir?'

'Our Michael Vaux is very familiar with the lay of the land out there—Morocco, I mean. Do you remember his highly successful debriefing of that Syrian defector who fled Damascus for self-exile in Tangier?'

Craw didn't like to be reminded of Vaux's successes. They had sent Vaux to Tangier with the latest monitoring device in MI6's arsenal of secret weapons: the eavesdropping chronometer (a large, round, high-tech wristwatch) to record his wide-ranging conversations with Ahmed Kadri, formerly Syria's chief arms negotiator, and a friend of Vaux's since their university days in Bristol.

Some years later, when Vaux worked for a semiofficial Syrian newspaper in Cairo, the young Bashar el-Assad's regime arrested Kadri on suspicion of spying for Britain's Secret Intelligence Service. The new Syrian regime knew of Vaux's earlier entanglements with MI6 and suspected Kadri of collusion. Vaux was ordered to return to Damascus and face an official inquiry.

Alena Hussein, Vaux's lover and then deputy chief of station for GSD in Cairo, warned Vaux of his dubious fate if he went back to Damascus to face the music. So he decided to flee Cairo. MI6, who had always kept surreptitious tabs on Vaux, then offered to help him quit Egypt under cover—on condition that he became the chief player in Operation Saladin—ultimately, after several setbacks and fiascos, a success and a feather in Vaux's cap.

'Yes, I do indeed remember, Sir Nigel. But we all know he's a bit of a loose cannon—unpredictable. Volatile, shall we say?'

'Where is he, anyway?'

'Retired somewhere in Hertfordshire, I believe.'

'Near Watford, wasn't it? Close to where old Arthur Davis used to live.' Arthur Davis, a veteran case officer and talent spotter at Department B3, had died suddenly after only two years of retirement. 'Get in touch with Vaux, will you? I think if we could persuade him to chaperone, as it were, our Mr. Micklethwait, then we could have a very effective setup. In other words, Vaux could be Micklethwait's handler—low profile and all that, but a facilitator in the mystifying lands of the Arab world...'

Craw, impatient with some of Sir Nigel's more imaginative flights of fancy, got up and looked businesslike. 'I'll see what can be arranged. Meanwhile, I'll fetch Sebastian Micklethwait.'

***

Anne's cerulean-blue eyes were concentrating on the computer monitor as she typed one of Sir Nigel's stern missives to Vauxhall HQ demanding quick action regarding the vital necessity of building his staff numbers—what he called B3's 'establishment'—to the levels recommended by the now-shelved 1998 green paper. She had just added 'cc: the director-general, Sir John Livermore' to the bottom of the rather officious and whining internal memo when Craw loomed over her with his usual lustful eyes and seductive smile. 'Anne, darling—get Vaux for me, will you? I'm sure you know the number.'

This last assertion was testimony to the suspicion that Craw had nursed since Vaux's 'retirement': that Anne and Vaux were an 'item.' It hurt—particularly as his divorce a few years back had freed him up to play the field as loosely and enthusiastically as he suspected Vaux had been doing since he had left B3 at the peak of his reputation for having secured the Syria-Saladin dossier.

'Michael's in Tangier, right now. I could either phone him direct or send an e-mail to our man in Rabat requesting early contact,' said Anne.

Craw's heart sank. Anne's total awareness of Vaux's movements only confirmed his suspicions. 'Really? How very extraordinary. I thought the fiasco with that Kadri fellow would have persuaded him to stay away from that snake pit of a city for as long as possible.'

'It's a long story,' said Anne wistfully. 'Kadri's niece now owns the villa where he and Kadri stayed together. And he's known her a few years now.'

'You mean Vaux and she are living together?' Craw found it difficult to suppress his feeling of relief and triumph. Suddenly, the road was opening up for him to make a decisive move.

'Not what it sounds like,' said Anne, a note of satisfaction in her voice. 'Safa, poor Kadri's niece, is married to a doctor, and they're all over there having an early summer holiday. That's all.'

'Whatever—get him for me, will you? There's no time to lose.'

***

Sebastian Micklethwait, in a dark-blue suit and white shirt, his long auburn hair hanging over his starched collar, sat at the large mahogany table that would have been commandeered by the second deputy (after Craw) if B3 were staffed to the now-defunct green paper's planned levels. He had heard that Chris Greene was due back any day now, so he took it upon himself to take over the last available office. On the shiny surface sat two phones, a large blotter, and a thick jam jar that housed several pencils, half a dozen ballpoint pens and rubber bands.

Micklethwait was scanning the *Daily Mail*, his tabloid of choice, when he looked up to see who had just entered without knocking. It was Craw, whose attitude toward him always reminded him of his housemaster at his old public school. He knew that to greet his senior colleague with a 'good morning' would not produce anything like a polite reply, so he remained silent, smiled wanly, and lifted his eyebrows to show that he was willing to help if asked.

'Sir Nigel has summoned you, my boy. First serious job of your budding career. I trust you are prepared for active duty,' said Craw with a feeling of relief that the young man at last had an opportunity to make himself useful. Craw sat down in a leather, buttoned armchair, about the only piece of furniture in the entire office suite less than thirty years old. 'Do you feel ready to take on a very serious job?'

'Yes, of course, sir. As a matter of fact, I was beginning to wonder why the office was so quiet. I've been here six months now, and there's really been nothing to do except clean the files up—the few you gave me. They're getting transferred to the computer people at Registry right this minute, and I think that just about does it...'

'Good man. These small jobs may seem trivial, Sebastian, but it's essential to get all our old files on the central computer. I don't have to tell someone your age that, do I? Now, as to the job at hand: I understand that Sir Nigel is going to rely on you as the chief operative on a top-secret and highly delicate venture that will involve travel, a lot of fieldwork in quite dangerous circumstances—and super-efficient tradecraft. Are you up to it, my boy?'

Micklethwait chose to ignore Craw's pompous, housemasterly exhortations. His pulse was already quickening at the thought of some action, some real bloody action, at long last. 'Absolutely, sir. I'm as ready as I ever will be...'

'That's my boy. We Oxbridge types have to stand together, you know. I understand you went to Lincoln College. Did you learn any Arabic there?'

'No, sir. I read modern history and English.'

'Oh, well, can't be helped. I took PPE, of course. Warwick.' Micklethwait translated the shorthand: Craw had graduated from Oxford's Warwick College in Philosophy, Politics and Economics. Craw then added: 'A first, by the way. And you?'

'A good second,' muttered Micklethwait.

'Ah,' murmured Craw, as if the information about his junior's degree status had some real but obscure significance. Then he remembered: Micklethwait had got on to MI6's short list as a favor to his revered grandmother, Mavis Butler—now in her mid- eighties—who in the Second World War had been one of the anonymous geniuses who broke the German and Italian intelligence codes at GCHQ's headquarters at Bletchley Park. 'Well, let's get to it, my boy,' said Craw. 'Sir Nigel is waiting in the inner sanctum—that's what everyone here calls his office.'

***

Sir Nigel asked Anne to bring in the manila folder that he had placed in the overnight safe in the small room that housed several battered filing cabinets, a fax machine, a photocopier and a gas ring for the kettle. In one of the upper cupboards sat the office supplies of instant coffee, tea bags, sugar, biscuit tins, and various office aides like boxes of paper clips, Scotch tape, ancient typewriter ribbons, and small paperweights with obscure corporate logos—all accumulated over the past decade and longer back still.

Sir Nigel looked at his Girard-Perregaux gold watch (a gift from Lady Adair to celebrate thirty years of marriage) and realized he would be late for his lunch appointment at White's, the exclusive club in St. James's favored by spymasters and fellow spooks. He was to meet with Murray Sinclair, the CIA's London station chief. He made a mental note not to even hint at the promising breakthrough that he had decided would go under the rubric of 'Operation Apostate.' Murray was a sociable and garrulous man, and he would have to be on his guard—especially after the inevitable martinis Murray considered de rigueur before a good lunch.

Craw entered without knocking, placed the manila folder on Sir Nigel's desk, and beckoned Micklethwait to follow him into the inner sanctum. Sir Nigel got up, shook Micklethwait's hand, gave the folder back to Craw and declared his imminent departure for a very important lunch date.

During the following hour, Sebastian Micklethwait learned of his imminent departure for Morocco in the company of one Mokhtar Tawil. Tawil, explained Craw, was the key man and facilitator in the mission he was to undertake. He would find the main outlines of the operation in the manila file, and he should aim to leave

London shortly—pending instructions from Tawil. Tawil himself would fill him in on the delicate and vital tasks that lie ahead. Anne would arrange a new passport. He would need to memorize his given alias and sign for a handgun at the armory at Vauxhall Bridge.

When he got back that evening to his small but elegant basement flat on the King's Road close to fashionable Sloane Square, he took the manila file from his briefcase—and wondered what all the fuss was about. For inside the folder was just one sheet of A4 typing paper plus a small passport photo of the man he was to meet. With TOP SECRET stamped boldly across the crown logo of the Foreign and Commonwealth Office, the note read:

We will rendez-vous this coming Friday May 20 at the INTERCONTINENTAL HOTEL, Rue Scribe, Paris. At reception, ask for Dr. al-Zubaidi from Cairo. Please arrive between 3pm and 4pm. Thank you.

Micklethwait then went through to the bathroom, mussed his hair for the casual look, examined his perfect white teeth, and stuffed the note in the inside pocket of his leather bomber jacket. He'd decided to celebrate his first active-duty assignment with a couple of pints at the George, his local watering hole.

2

The motion of the train, the jerky rhythm and resonant clangs when the carriages sped over the steel rails and sudden switches at busy, ill-lit junctions, the silvery moonlit landscape reeling by that showed quick, dim images of farm houses, cow sheds, small leafy copses, and broad fields bordered by hedgerows and narrow country lanes—all helped induce a delayed, deep sleep for B3's novice secret agent.

Micklethwait had climbed into the top bunk in the small compartment on the *Francisco de Goya*, RENFE's luxury night train that would take him and Tawil, a.k.a. Dr. al-Zubaidi, to Madrid by 8:00 a.m. They had met in the lobby of the InterContinental Paris, where they had had a quick drink in the ornate lobby bar. Tawil said he had reserved two separate cabins for the overnight journey. They would then go by rented car from Madrid to Malaga and on to Tangier by ferry. Mickethwait had still learned nothing about his assignment, and Tawil asked him to be patient—all would be revealed on the morrow.

They had dinner in the opulent, crowded dining car—reminiscent, suggested a dreamy Micklethwait, of the Orient Express—at least as it had appeared in the Peter Ustinov movie—and Tawil slowly drank Coca-Cola as he watched his new companion finish off a bottle of Rioja Santiago. They shared a big, silver platter of paella, bought cigars from the sullen, white-coated barman and went to bed just before midnight.

Micklethwait sat on the edge of the lower bunk as he pulled off his underwear and socks. Mokhtar Tawil, middle-aged, short with a well-fed paunch, seemed a pleasant chap, spoke English well, and he was confident that his assignment had got off to a good start. But Micklethwait was still none the wiser about what the task ahead was all about. Tawil had banned what he called 'shop talk' until a scheduled briefing in Madrid.

He took two steps on the ladder to the upper berth, pulled the crisp white sheets up to his chin and listened to the squeaks and groans of the train. He pulled the window curtain aside and guessed the shunting, the whistles and the shouts indicated they were crossing the French-Spanish border. Once the train again picked up speed, he dropped off. But during the night—he had no idea at what time—he heard a loud thump from Tawil's adjacent cabin and then a scuffling sound and an audible, long sigh of breath. Then the cabin door was slammed shut. He turned over to face the wall. Tawil, he thought, must have had a bad dream. He quickly fell back to sleep.

Three loud, peremptory knocks on his compartment's door woke him up with a start. Tawil was hardly the sort of man who would wake him so rudely. He looked at his Cartier tank watch (a gift from his grandmother on learning he had landed the job with the Secret Intelligence Service) and saw that it was only 6:00 a.m. He jumped down from the bed and quickly released the security lock to open the door. In the corridor stood the genial, overweight conductor and a short, wiry man in an ill-fitting, creased blue suit. 'Senor, please to come to the dining car immediately. It is of the utmost *urgencia*,' said the thin man in mufti.

The conductor, who the previous night had collected his passport along with Tawil's, looked apologetic and perplexed. Micklethwait searched his eyes for some immediate explanation but was answered with a shrug. 'Why? What's the urgency?'

'Never mind. You come please,' said the other man.

Micklethwait pulled on some jeans that he had fished out of his leather holdall and shook on a bulky woolen sweater. The two men waited for him at the open door. As they passed Tawil's compartment, he saw another guard standing in front of the closed door.

'Hold on, old boy. I want to talk to my colleague, Dr. Zubaidi.' He wondered whether Tawil was getting the same rough treatment and figured two remonstrators were better than one. But the thin man pushed him along the corridor toward the dining car. The conductor followed.

They sat down at the first table in the corner of the long carriage. The car was empty, with the chef and an assistant fussing about in the narrow galley, preparing for the breakfast rush. They could hear the jingle of cutlery and the occasional tinkling of china and glass as the train sped south. 'I'm Deputy Inspector Alberto Oliviera of the *Policia Nationale*. Sorry, my English is poor,' said the thin man. 'But we have some bad news. Your traveling companion, the man you had dinner with last evening, no?'

'Yes,' said Micklethwait, more bewildered than anxious.

'He—how you say in *Ingles*—he is *muerto*, dead. Killed last night in his compartment.'

As if fearing the young man's reaction, the conductor had got up and left to talk to the chef. Micklethwait was stunned. He was presumably a suspect—the last man to have been seen with the victim. 'My God, this is terrible. Have you found a doctor on the train—or anyone who can confirm your theory?'

The Spaniard shook his head. 'It's no theory, senor. The man's throat was slit'—he passed his forefinger across his throat—'and there were signs of a struggle. I think your friend put up a brave fight but in the end bled to death. There is a lot of blood.'

'But how did this assailant get into his compartment? The locks look pretty secure to me.'

'Perhaps a gentle knock at the door—your friend thinks it has to be you, his travelling companion.' The inspector lit a Fortuna, inhaled deeply. He looked accusingly into Micklethwait's green eyes. 'And perhaps it *was* you.'

'Absolutely not, my friend.' Micklethwait decided nothing would be lost if he adopted the indignant, 'Englishman abroad' attitude. 'What exactly is your jurisdiction here? This is an international train that started off in Paris.'

'Please, senor, don't make things complicated for yourself. Drug trafficking, illegal immigration. I'm sure you are aware of some of the big problems we face in Spain.'

As he spoke, Inspector Oliviera scribbled indecipherable words in a small black notebook while Micklethwait, determined to remain cool, looked intently out of the big window as the dry and sparse landscape flashed past. Then a question surfaced in his bewildered mind. 'But how did you discover him?'

'The gentleman's door was unlocked. During the night, the conductor comes round to check that all the doors of the compartments are locked—for security reasons. When he discovered the door was not locked, he knocked first and then opened the door. He discovered your dead friend in a pool of blood on the floor.'

Micklethwait knew nothing much could happen until they got to Madrid. He had about an hour to get in touch with home base.

Back in his compartment, he searched his holdall for the handset device that, thanks to a special built-in chip, could send encrypted text and voice messages to Vauxhall where around-the-clock monitors would, he hoped, promptly send the disastrous news on to Gower Street.

3

He had come to them through a secretive, serpentine route that twisted and turned via Rabat, Tangier, Madrid, Melilla and London. Mokhtar Tawil was a messenger, a secret envoy sent on a delicate mission by one of the top members of a Moroccan offshoot of the notorious Al-Qaeda in the Islamic Maghreb (AQIM) terrorist cell.

He had been gently and politely conducted through the labyrinthine corridors of secret intelligence outfits, pushed, in his view, from pillar to post, and then to end up in the hands of a small, specialist team that promised to handle the matter with appropriate speed and gravity.

Mokhtar Tawil finally sat face-to-face with Sir Nigel in B3's shabby, rundown offices on Gower Street, a far cry from the dazzlingly contemporary MI6 headquarters on the south bank of the Thames where the clandestine emissary had spent many days that ran into weeks in attempts to see 'someone senior'—as he always put it—anxious as he was for the speedy resolution of his top-secret mission.

Sir Nigel had expected Tawil to hand over some sort of report or dossier, the vital importance of which would be self-evident. After all, here was a virtual defector from a known terrorist outfit. But, as it happened, the vital communication was verbal: a key member of the executive committee of one of AQIM's several offshoots was keen to give the goods on the planned activities—mostly bombings and kidnappings—of all the active terrorist cells in the Maghreb, especially Morocco, his home territory. He would also supply the locations of the major players and how AQIM's tentacles spread eastward to Algeria, Tunisia and Libya. But nothing had been written down.

Sir Nigel promised safe asylum to 'this personage' in return for such invaluable intelligence. Then he learned that there were certain conditions. The potential defector first required a visit from a senior UK intelligence official who would not only re-assure him of his future in the West but also help plan his safe getaway. There were several conditions: no deadline—escape planning and timing were delicate and would be left to the defector to finalize; and no Special Forces in the mix—the last thing they needed was a shootout and the subsequent mayhem. No; the exit strategy had to be quiet and subtle. Last but not least: the UK government would be expected to guarantee a lifelong stipend to ensure a reasonable standard of living and/or offer a secure job in counter-intelligence or academia.

Sir Nigel readily agreed to such understandable conditions. He had told an anxious Alan Craw to get the mechanics of the operation underway. The escape route from Morocco to London would have to be planned with the utmost secrecy and caution. And thus, Sebastian Micklethwait was, somewhat reluctantly due to his probationary status, assigned to accompany this man Tawil—under cover. 'Just make sure he has an alias, false passport and all that. I don't have to tell you how to arrange these things.'

'No, sir. Will do,' said Craw. But he wondered how long it would be before Sir Nigel needed him to clean up Micklethwait's mess.

***

Micklethwait stood in the train's corridor while Inspector Alberto Oliviera rifled through his holdall. Socks, T-shirts and underpants flew through the air to land on the lower berth; toiletries were sorted; a diary with many blank pages and a few London telephone numbers examined closely. A Hugo Boss garment bag was unzipped. It contained one lightweight Austin Reed suit and several linen shirts in anticipation of Tangier's hot, early summer.

The inspector turned toward the door and Micklethwait's pulse quickened when he realized Oliviera was about to pat him down. The inspector found the handset in the outer pocket of his bomber jacket. He looked at it closely. His son was a cell phone fanatic. 'A Nokia N70. I see you buy the best,' said the inspector as he handed the encryption handset back to Micklethwait. The young man felt a surge of respect for the SIS's quiet technical teams, who worked in thankless anonymity. But then Oliviera put both hands on Micklethwait's shoulders and, with some pressure, lowered them gently down the sides of his body. Miraculously, he did not feel the shoulder holster that housed Micklethwait's Glock 32. Micklethwait breathed easier. 'What is your relationship to Dr. al-Zubaidi, senor? I see by his Moroccan passport he is—was—a private banker. Are you his *secretario,* bodyguard?'

'Hardly a bodyguard, Inspector. No, I work for an agency that helps business executives to find traveling companions. You know, older men who because of their health condition like someone around to look out for them. This assignment ends as soon as we get to Tangier.' Inspector Oliviera looked skeptical. But he did not pursue the matter.

The heavily built conductor steadied himself with the help of the carriage's handrails as he approached the two men. He had both passports in his hand and gave them to the inspector. 'Well, Mr. Knight, we are almost there. When we reach our destination, you will be taken to immigration at Chamartin station, and I'm afraid from there, you will be in custody for further questioning. The rest of the passengers will have to remain on the train for a full investigation. The doors will be sealed pending the arrival of the investigative team. Meanwhile, the body of Dr. al-Zubaidi will be taken immediately to the morgue, pending an *autopsia,* no?'

'I understand,' said Micklethwait. He had no idea how long it would take for Department B3 to react to his predicament. It was his first foray into what Craw had called 'the real world,' and it had been a disaster. He could only wait and see.

4

Michael Vaux lay under a parasol on a sunlounger by the mosaic-tiled swimming pool at the Villa Mauresque, a white stucco cubist building perched on a high cliff that overlooked the Mediterranean to the north and the Atlantic Ocean to the west. He told himself he was living in splendid isolation, and he rather liked it. He missed beautiful and sexy Anne, but if he was true to himself, he had to admit he wanted a cooling-off period. The age gap had always worried him, and his absence could induce her to meet an eligible man her own age.

Safa, Ahmed Kadri's niece, had inherited the property from her mother, who had died of old age at the health clinic on nearby Cap Spartel on the west coast. Vaux had met Safa through Ahmed when, like him, she was a guest at the house in the early nineties. They had a brief fling (Vaux had always claimed she started it), and then she had left to further her studies. While at Durham University, she met a young man who was studying medicine, and they got married.

Safa was happy. Paul, her young husband, started out as a GP in a country practice near Aylesbury. She was now working on a PhD program at Queen Mary College in London. She always had fond memories of Vaux, and she knew that he had been very close to her Syrian diplomat uncle since they were at university together. They had lost touch over the years, but Vaux renewed the friendship, with MI6's enthusiastic blessings, when he was hired on the strength of that old relationship to spy on Kadri's diplomatic mission in Geneva. British intelligence was eager to learn the details of a suspected multibillion-dollar arms deal that was being hatched between Syria and Russia in Geneva behind the smokescreen of yet another Middle East peace conference then underway.

But what had been planned as an almost impromptu vacation with Vaux was cut short by the sudden death of Safa's husband's medical partner. Paul had to leave and return to England and Safa, remembering the delicate past, had decided that her duty was to be with him. So Vaux was alone—except for Mahmud, the house-keeper and general factotum, a pool boy and gardener, and the daily cook (when requested).

He put down the latest Cara Black crime mystery and looked through the tall eucalyptus trees to the calm, blue-gray Atlantic. On the horizon, a big oil tanker was making its slow progress north-ward. He heard the phone ringing in the house and wondered whether Mahmud was around to answer it. Then he heard the familiar shuffle of Mahmud's slip-on leather babouches as he made his way toward the pool.

He reached out for the heavy white telephone. Mahmud plugged in the pool extension line, made a quick bow, and retreated. Vaux was expecting no one to call. But perhaps Safa was anxious about his supposed loneliness. In which case, he would assure her he could stay put in these beautiful and balmy surroundings until the earth froze over or burned itself up. But it wasn't Safa.

A female voice, businesslike, English upper-crust accent. 'Mr. Vaux? Please hold. It's the embassy in Rabat.'

A lengthy pause. 'Hello, Michael?'

'Yes,' said Vaux cautiously.

'It's your old mate, George Greaves. Remember me?'

'Of course I do. I thought you'd be retired by now.'

'No such luck. I'll probably be here until I drop. Can't all be rich ex-journalists, you know.'

'Ex-journalist is right, but not rich,' said Vaux. 'Anyhow, you've got a good decade or two ahead of you.'

For some years, Greaves had been an undercover MI6 operative who worked out of the British embassy in Rabat under the guise of second commercial secretary. He had recently been promoted to chief of station. They had met back in the nineties when Vaux supplied him with surreptitious recordings of conversations he had had with then-exiled Ahmed Kadri: they included a slew of economic and top-secret military data (including the ongoing manufacture of a whole armory of chemical weapons), an inside view of Hafez al-Assad's regime, other facts and figures, and anything of intelligence value about his beloved Syria that had now jilted him.

'Thanks for that bit of compassion. Look, Vaux, we need your help. I'm coming up there tomorrow and it's imperative we get together...'

'But how did you know I was here?'

'That's a silly question to ask a type like me.'

'OK. Well, you know the villa. I'll expect you when I see you.'

'Done.' The phone clicked. No more niceties required. Vaux knew he'd swallowed the bait.

***

Carlos Miranda of the Centro Nacional de Inteligencia, Spain's intelligence agency, sat in a small office whose internal window looked over the large and leafy atrium of Madrid's main rail terminus. Sebastian Micklethwait, disheveled and unshaven with soiled shirt and baggy traveling jeans, sat opposite the neatly suited CNI operative whose sleek black hair matched the long, curled lashes of his deep brown eyes. On the table as Exhibit One lay the small Glock 32, finally detected in a strip search. Miranda flipped through the pages of Micklethwait's passport, noted it was brand new, looked at the small photo and then up to the man purporting to be Edward Knight, British citizen.

'I'm here to tell you you've had a break. You are to be released forthwith—I think that's how they say it in English. Our agencies cooperate well together—especially since last year's terrorist attack.'

Micklethwait had had no sleep for twenty-four hours, and his thinking was slow, his mind numb. But he recalled the bomb attack at Madrid's Atocha station the previous July—an outrage that killed nearly two hundred commuters. The perpetrators were first thought to be ETA, the Basque separatist outfit. But it was later confirmed that Islamist terrorists had carried out the operation.

Miranda slid the pistol across the table toward Micklethwait and then handed over his passport. Micklethwait checked the chamber. The thirteen nine millimeter bullets were intact. 'On instructions from your London people,' said Miranda, 'we have reserved a room at the La Reina Victoria on the Plaza Santa Ana. It's quite close to the Prado—in case you get bored. You are to stay there until you receive further orders. Is that clear, Mr. Knight?'

'Yes, perfectly.' Micklethwait had noticed his holdall and garment bag in the corner of the room behind a door. He stuffed the Glock in the holdall, grabbed the hotel reservation slip proffered by Miranda and left the stifling hot room. A good listener would have heard his huge sigh of relief as he skipped down the escalator to the sun-filled, semitropical grand concourse and then to the taxi rank.

***

At about the same time as Micklethwait got out of the taxi that brought him quickly to the Plaza Santa Ana, George Greaves was embracing Michael Vaux like an old friend. Mahmud had brought him to the pool where Vaux had just had a midmorning swim. Mahmud quickly offered Vaux a white terry cloth bathrobe and hovered for further instructions. 'George, it's past eleven. So what will you have to drink?'

'No, it's still too early for me, old boy. I'll just have an orange juice, if I may.'

Vaux said he'd have a screwdriver and Mahmud shuffled off to the house. Vaux thought Greaves had changed little. He was heavier than when he first met him and had grown a floppy walrus moustache. He wore a blue, very creased linen suit, English brown suede brogues, and sported the straw panama hat he had worn when the two agents used to liaise together in a sidewalk café in Tangier in the early nineties. 'You always said you planned to take early retirement,' said Vaux. 'But I see you're still in the game.'

'Something unforeseen happened, old boy. I finally got married. A secretary in the embassy. Charming girl. English to the core. Met her at the Rabat embassy where she was a lowly secretary and typist. Bought a cottage in the Cotswolds, so can't afford to retire now.'

'Well, congratulations, George. You're looking great. So married life must suit you.'

'Yes, but she's in England, and I'm here. She hates leaving Blighty since she left the diplomatic world, so there's a lot of commuting on my part.'

Mahmud brought the drinks on a brass tray and the two men remained silent as the old man, in a brown djellaba and a white *takiyah* to cover his balding pate, placed the napkins and drinks on a small glass-topped table. He left the two men alone.

'So, what's this all about, George?'

'Two days ago, I had a call from your old chief at B3, Sir Nigel Adair. They've got a special project on, and it seems he's decided that you could be a key player—if you're willing and able.'

'Oh God,' murmured Vaux. Did he want to get back in that game? He had the time, for sure. And he had to admit, his domestic life had become somewhat slow and repetitive. In his splendid isolation here in Tangier, he'd started to view a return to his old routine with some ennui, some reluctance. He had missed those dramatic episodes that the chance recruitment into MI6 had provided in his life. And the remuneration had been generous enough for him to finally buy his beloved bungalow with the fabulous country views.

Greaves sipped his fresh orange juice and casually looked around the pool area and then back at Vaux. He could see him hesitating. 'I don't have to tell you that you'd be rehired as a nonofficial- cover operative. The NOC payout, including expenses, will be highly attractive. Not to mention your presumed desire to again serve queen and country when called upon,' said Greaves with —he hoped—genuine patriotic fervor.

Vaux was not about to collapse on his knees and beg the man to hire him. 'I think you'd better tell me what this is all about, George.'

'I was hoping you'd say that.' Greaves then related the basic facts about Operation Apostate (whose title Sir Nigel increasingly admired the more he found himself using it).

'So what appeared to be a clear-cut case of defection has overnight become a disaster of mammoth proportions. Really,' said Vaux with a sigh, 'B3 does seem to be accident prone.'

Vaux was thinking in particular of the assassination of Dr. Nessim Said, a Syrian nuclear scientist who had wanted to live in the United Kingdom but had been killed while under Vaux's protection by persons unknown. (Vaux figured he had been the victim of Mossad's 'targeted killings' of Arab or Iranian nuclear scientists but the official MI6 view was that the perpetrators were more likely to have been agents of the Syrian regime.)

Greaves ignored Vaux's observation. 'Can you help, old boy? The action is switching to this very area, probably this old port town that you used to say you were so fond of...'

'Any theories about who may have done this? What groups are involved here? Why would someone want to kill this guy who was essentially a messenger boy? Not even a key player, presumably.'

Greaves said, 'Perhaps you can find the answer to that. What do you say?'

Vaux finished off his screwdriver. He looked over to the lush bougainvillea at the base of a cluster of palm trees and then to the white-capped Atlantic now ruffled by a strong wind from the west. Greaves waited patiently for his answer.

'Yes, all right. Let's get down to it.'

5

The man wore dark shades and a western gray pinstripe business suit for this important visit to a merchant who eked out a living in the small Spanish enclave of Melilla, an historic anomaly on the North African coast close enough to see Spain on a clear day, yet on the fringe of Morocco to the south. The crescent-shaped port town had few tourists and many traders—its business was in import-export, not the provision of sunny holidays on sandy beaches. To the west lay sparkling Tangier, the major market for the tiny state's sundry goods.

Mort Cohen imported and sold what his business card described as 'sundry wares'—carpets and leather poufs from Morocco, spices and scents from the Rif mountains, and other knickknacks like inlaid mother-of-pearl jewelry boxes, hashish and *shisha* pipes, and elaborate, wrought-iron wall sconces. His private inventory extended to other items that could be procured only by the good graces of shadowy men whose official position and power Cohen never questioned. Hashish and *kif* from the Rif were major money spinners, sold on to dealers whose identity Cohen wasn't much interested in.

He had been too long in Melilla; his roots ran deep, and his status was too problematic to question the authorities—whether the Spanish customs officers or the western-suited Moroccan 'businessmen' who had the power to make life very difficult for an uncooperative trader. He had learned the business from his father, an immigrant from Whitechapel in East London who had come over in the early fifties to establish a merchant enterprise in a small Spanish province that offered a balmy climate far away from those bleak and damp islands of his birth. He had felt at home as soon as he arrived; Melilla then had one of the largest Jewish communities in North Africa, historically always a thriving commercial and trading region.

But if Melilla was a political anomaly, so was the representative of Her Britannic Majesty, Queen Elizabeth II, for Cohen had been for several years the United Kingdom's unpaid honorary consul, a position casually bestowed by an amiable ambassador in Madrid who had hoped the busy trader would somehow boost Britain's flagging exports.

Now Cohen was wondering what had brought Magdi Kassim into town. He had promised the visit would be brief, which was not unusual. He had said there was good news and bad. 'Give me the bad news first,' sighed Cohen, once again resigned to sacrificing his valuable commercial time to oppressors whose demand for their pound of flesh was as inevitable as Shylock's.

They were sitting in the small, cramped office adjacent to his cluttered, one-room 'warehouse' where sacks of dried peas and lentils, argan fruits and myriad spices and raw tobacco emitted a not unpleasant exotic aroma. Kassim, a tall, slim man in his early thirties, looked out through the dusty tall windows to the busy Plaza de España. 'Something went terribly wrong. The man you sent us, the courier, was murdered on the train he took with the Englishman.

We have to make our investigation. Did you tell anyone about our little project?'

Cohen once again thanked God that at least he could communicate clearly with this man. He had been to some obscure public school in England and spoke perfect English. 'No, absolutely not. Only me, Tawil, and your people knew about this job. Good God. Poor Tawil! How on earth did this happen?'

'That, Mr. Cohen, is what we are investigating. Are you sure there were no leaks, no third parties involved with Tawil's plans?'

'Absolutely sure. Have I ever been known to let you down? I am not a loose talker—I don't think I'd be the British consul if I were. Besides, Tawil was a very dear friend of mine. We play backgammon almost every evening—or we did.'

Kassim was fully aware of the two men's friendship and their habitual evening rendezvous at the Nacionale, a kosher restaurant just off the traffic-clogged Avenida Juan Carlos. 'We will find the killers, don't worry,' said Kassim, his eyes now focused on the distant marina where the daily passenger ferry from Almeria weaved its slow way through the yachts and small fishing boats.

'And the good news?' asked Cohen, betraying a touch of impatience.

'We have another vital task for you. Perhaps its successful outcome will mitigate your sorrow over your friend.'

Cohen had never felt any antipathy toward his Arab cousins. His close friendship with Tawil was testament enough to that. But the younger generation seemed to him to show a certain coolness, an aloofness in matters of life and death. Where, he wondered, did that lack of a warm heart end and the plague of terrorism begin? For he had no doubt that Tawil's murder was somehow connected to a cruel act of nihilism. He knew Tawil had been on a highly secretive mission for Kassim and his associates. But he never knew the details of the plan. He knew nothing about any scheme to facilitate a betrayal or even who Tawil planned to talk to once he got to London.

That was all he knew: a trip by Tawil to London, a job to be done for Kassim and his 'associates'.

And now he was to be drawn in further. If he didn't cooperate, his livelihood would be threatened, even his very life. He knew he knew too much already. So he resigned himself to the cards that had been dealt. Cohen was a fatalist. As Tawil, his old friend, would have said: *It is written.* 'And the details?' asked Cohen.

'Later. Just stand by, please. It is for a just cause, Mr. Cohen. And your business will continue on—and maybe even thrive.'

With that enigmatic declaration, Kassim left the office and Cohen heard the steel door bang shut as his visitor left.

***

George Greaves, back in Rabat, called Vaux early the next morning. Momtaz, the young houseboy who helped Mahmud in the running of the Villa Mauresque, handed Vaux, still in bed, the mobile phone and placed a large cup of café au lait on his bedside table.

'Call from Rabat, the nation's capital, monsieur,' said the youth. Vaux looked up at him to see if the boy was trying to be mildly funny. But he looked very serious. 'Man says very urgent, *très pressant*, monsieur.'

Vaux had urged the boy before not to be so formal but Mahmud had scoffed at the idea and insisted that the servants treat guests of the house with respect. His one concession was that the boy could practice his French, the priority foreign language taught in Moroccan schools. Momtaz handed Vaux the phone and quickly left the room.

'Greaves here, old boy. We're talking on the scrambler, so we are free to discuss our little problem. I talked to Sir Nigel earlier this morning. He's as happy as a pig in shit. Welcomes you aboard again, and all that. He's anxious for you to get started. Channel all your requests through me. It's simpler that way.'

Yes, it was, thought Vaux. It would avoid the emotional stress of constant contact with Anne, Sir Nigel's gatekeeper. Vaux said, 'First thing is to get Micklethwait over here so I can get a feel for what really happened. I can't base my plans on secondhand reports.'

'Of course. I'll contact him immediately through our man in Madrid. I assume you think he should billet with you.'

'No, George. I want him to be conspicuous. He should stay in the Rif hotel or the Minzah—large as life. That way, our friend who wants to help us will contact him without too much trouble. That's assuming that the man Micklethwait traveled with had informed his patron of his escort's name. Even if he didn't, the Arab street's trusty grapevine will soon signal the Brit's presence here in town.'

'You think it's a good idea? Putting him out to dry like that?'

'He'll be a lure, won't he. If we want to find and contact our nameless informer, it's the only way. Meanwhile, we'd better have a code name for him.'

'Mohammed.'

'There's an awful lot of them.'

'Yes, but it's easy to remember. Are you sure there's not a better way to find Mohammed?'

'Look, if this guy is serious about trading his knowledge of terrorist plans and plots in the Maghreb for asylum and riches, and he discovers that the man who accompanied his murdered messenger boy is sitting here in town, he won't lose much time in getting in touch.'

'Yes, I think you're right. If Micklethwait stayed at the Villa Mauresque, he might feel very nervous about getting in touch. I'm sure that place is watched—by our enemies as well as by the DST.'

Vaux recalled his old contacts with the Moroccan spy agency, Direction de la Surveillance du Territoire (DST), particularly the double agent that had helped him pass on the recordings of his confidential parlays with Ahmed Kadri to Greaves, who had duly transcribed them and sent the contents to Rabat via diplomatic bag.

'Any other brilliant ideas?' asked Greaves.

'No, but maybe later, after my morning swim.'

'Ye gods! Talk about living in the lap of luxury. Just don't drown in the bloody pool, that's all.' Greaves hung up.

One hour later, Sebastian Micklethwait, enjoying a ham tortilla for breakfast and looking at BBC World Service on the oversized TV screen in his cramped hotel room, heard the bedside phone buzz. The caller told him to meet a tall man with long sideburns, wearing a brown trilby hat and carrying today's edition of *The Times* at the nearby Prado Museum. He would be standing in front of a large painting by Velazquez named *Vulcan's Forge*, in Room X1. Time: approximately 11:00 a.m.

Micklethwait was relieved. He liked Madrid's 'we never close' nightlife, the tapas bars and frenetic discos, but he wanted to get back in the game again. He felt that he was coming down from a high—the peak, of course, having been held in a dingy Spanish cell as a suspect in an assassination. He guessed that he was about to be called back to London for the inevitable inquiry into the failure of his mission.

It was a typical, early summer's day in Madrid: very hot, humid and sunny. He strode down the long, narrow and shaded Calle Santa Ana, lined by small boutiques and bars, crossed the busy Paseo del Prado, walked through the lush botanical gardens and on to the museum.

The tall man, fortyish, well over six feet tall, was sitting on a wooden bench in front of the great oil painting. On his lap, a trilby and *The Times*. He stood up as soon as he saw Micklethwait approach. Then the two men stood side by side, admiring the great master's work. 'Follow me out to my car. It's parked nearby on the Paseo del Prada,' said the man quietly.

When they got to the Aston Martin DB9, Micklethwait observed that the car bore no Corps Diplomatique plates. He sat down beside the man, looking anxious. 'Relax, old boy. My name's Bolton, one of your colleagues. I work out of Madrid, obviously. I'm officially the cultural attaché.' He passed an envelope to Micklethwait, who still looked as if something was on his mind. 'You'll find your marching orders in there. Plus an Iberia Airlines ticket to Tangier and a permit to carry the handgun. Are you OK?'

Micklethwait shook himself out of his musings. 'Yes, sorry. I just thought your tradecraft was brilliant. For all the world, you looked like a chap that picked up a young man in an art gallery.'

'What on earth are you talking about?'

'A gay encounter, that's all. Brilliant. If anyone was watching, they'd have thought little of it.'

'Never thought of that. But the museum's quite a cruisy place, I understand. So all the better.'

6

Vaux sat in the corner of the El Minzah's cocktail bar. Through the large french windows he could see late breakfasters on the terrace and a few children playing by the side of the long swimming pool. Small white-breasted sandpipers swooped down to land on the flagstones, hoping to pick up some bread crumbs from the chattering hotel guests. Pigeons pecked and strutted as though they owned this particular piece of food-producing real estate.

He had ordered a Stella Artois which, as usual, came with a bowl of olives, potato crisps and salted peanuts. He was the solitary customer—which is why he had chosen this rendezvous. Also, it was only about a mile's downhill walk from the villa.

While he waited for the young probationer, Vaux read a two-day-old *Herald Tribune*. The usual horror stories: twenty people killed in Kabul by a terrorist bomb; opponents of Syria's President Assad killed in Lebanon by a car bomb—including Samir Kassir, a prominent journalist; a suicide attack killed four US soldiers in Iraq, the biggest single toll of female casualties since the war began.

As Vaux turned the page, he was aware of someone looming over him. Vaux got up and they shook hands. Micklethwait wore jeans, a white linen shirt and suede desert boots. He had long, brown hair tinged with red, and what Vaux called 'cat's eyes'—brilliantly green, a wide mouth and aquiline nose. He was an inch or two taller and certainly slimmer than Vaux. 'Mr. Vaux, I presume,' said Micklethwait with a smile.

'Yes, indeed. And you're undoubtedly the highly recommended new man from B3.'

'Don't know about that. I'm here by an accident of fate, really.'

'Well, you'd still be here even if the man you were accompanying hadn't met his awful end, wouldn't you?'

'Oh, yes. I'm not thinking straight. Spent most of the night at a beach bar down near the Rif hotel. Couldn't get in there, by the way. All booked up with early tourists, I suppose.' The young Moroccan waiter hovered, and Vaux asked his companion what he wanted to drink. 'I'll have the same.' He nodded toward Vaux's Stella.

When the waiter was out of earshot, Vaux thought he would lob the ball into Micklethwait's court. 'Well, I presume you have thought about our assignment. What are your ideas about how we should start?'

'Start?' Micklethwait looked shocked. Here he was, face-to-face with Department B3's legendary Michael Vaux, and he was asking *him* for ideas? 'I thought you were supposed to debrief me and then I'd be sent back to London to face the music. I haven't thought about much else since the horror show in Madrid.'

'You mean being held in custody?'

'Yes. There was no reason for that sort of high-handedness from the Spanish authorities.'

'But you had to be a suspect. You were an admitted travelling companion of the victim and you slept next door to him. He was killed in the middle of the night. You could hardly expect to be given VIP treatment, old boy.' Micklethwait laughed off Vaux's attempt to see the situation from the eyes of the Spanish police. He took a large swig of beer and picked up a handful of peanuts.

Vaux said, 'Look, right now, I'm a one-man show. As usual, B3 is being reticent about what should be done—particularly how we get into contact with the guy who had promised to come across with a lot of information on AQIM's plans to cause mayhem in the Maghreb.

'So I'm beginning at the beginning, if you like. And I need all the help I can get. You're going to be with me until we find this man and send him to the UK for a proper debriefing. If we're finally successful, it'll be a great feather in your cap. So what do you say?'

'Beats going back and being quizzed by a gloating Alan Craw—who, by the way, wanted the job in the first place.'

'What job?'

'He wanted to chaperone this Tawil fellow back to Morocco. Thought it a key job with lots of praise and kudos if it came off. You know Craw, I presume.'

'Sure, I know Craw. Let's drop the subject.'

They fell silent while the barman, in baggy pantaloons and babouches, put down two more beers.

Vaux said, 'Look, I just want to lay down some parameters. This is early days. I want you to stay here in Tangier, obviously, and I apologize for not inviting you to the Mauresque. But it's not my villa in the first place. And in the second place, I don't think we should be seen with each other around town. This place is like a sieve and talk and rumors travel fast.

'My theory is that our target—code name Mohammed, by the way—will somehow discover your whereabouts by the bush telegraph…street gossip, if you like. And don't think that everyone who works in the hotel is trustworthy. None of them are. I'm sure your presence will be detected, and then our man will somehow approach you. I don't know if anyone remembers me from the old days but we can't take the risk of being seen together anymore. I'm uncomfortable right now.'

Micklethwait looked disappointed. The unpleasant feeling of isolation was coming back again. He said, 'I understand perfectly. But how do we communicate?'

'Let's put it this way: the only communication I'm interested in is if and when Mohammed makes contact. I understand you have one of those devices that looks like a regular mobile phone but can transmit coded messages back to the SIS listeners. The Spanish intelligence people presumably didn't confiscate it, did they?'

'No, no. They had no idea.'

'So you contact me through SIS in Vauxhall. They'll find a way to convey any messages to me here. Then we'll take it from there. Good luck. Is it Seb?'

'Yeah, of course. Thanks, Mike.'

Vaux got up, left a pile of dirhams on the table, and walked out to the lobby. The doorman saluted—his face was not unfamiliar—and swung the revolving doors for him. Outside, a young beggar with no legs sat on a rickety, wheeled trolley, his hands stretched out to passersby. Vaux fished a twenty-dirham note out of his pocket and put it in the cup. He walked back up the Rue de Belgique, tree-lined and shady, and up the gentle hill into the Rue de la Montagne. Last time he was in Tangier, he remembered, he used an old Hercules bicycle to get about town. He decided to look for it in the various dilapidated sheds that were scattered over the villa's grounds.

***

As a former newspaperman, it was impossible for Vaux to sit around and await developments. It was like expecting a good story to land in your lap (a journalist's dream but very rare) without some effort to speak with trusted sources or reliable contacts. Life wasn't like that.

So when he got back to the villa he asked Mahmud if the old Hercules bicycle he had used many moons ago was stacked away in one of the corrugated-iron sheds that were hidden under the stand of plane trees to the north of the property. Mahmud shrugged. He told Vaux that the three dilapidated buildings had been cleared out of all contents after the death of Madame Raafat, Ahmed Kadri's aunt. The new mistress of the house had ordered this, and he had been waiting two years for a friend and his son to come and demolish the sheds. Vaux was again reminded that in many respects, time stood still in this Arab backwater.

He told Mahmud that he'd have a light lunch at the pool. A cheese sandwich and a large Cutty Sark. (Safa had thoughtfully stocked up the villa's bar with several duty-free bottles of Vaux's favorite whisky.) He figured if he got into a mild torpor, his sluggish mind might come up with some idea that would help propel his mission on a faster track.

Then it came to him: why not try to find old Faud, the DST agent who worked at American Express as cover—but who also, if inclined, secretly cooperated with other intelligence agencies provided the offered compensation was adequate? It was Faud, the double agent, to whom Vaux had delivered the fat envelopes of miniature CDs that had secretly recorded his conversations with Kadri (B3 called them 'surreptitious debriefings').

After lunch, he asked Mahmud to drive him down to the Place de France. Mahmud, aware that Vaux had visited the Minzah that morning, was surprised. But he backed the old Mercedes 190E out of the garage while Momtaz displayed some enthusiastic efforts to clear the backseat of various magazines and wrappings. He held the back door open for Vaux who patted his shoulder as a gesture of appreciation. '*Bon voyage, monsieur,*' said Momtaz.

'Thank you, Momtaz,' said Vaux.

'Where you want I take you, Mister Vaux?' asked Mahmud as he pressed the starter. 'The Minzah, or somewhere else?' Vaux wasn't surprised at the question. The grapevine had worked again, as efficient as any encrypted electronic message system. One of Mahmud's friends worked at the hotel. A phone call—and nothing was secret.

'Just drop me off at the French consulate,' said Vaux, hoping to add to Mahmud's confusion. The large, ornate relic of the bygone days when France had helped govern what was then an international zone, looked somewhat seedy and rundown now, the lush tropical gardens overgrown. But it still functioned and was conveniently just opposite the Café de Paris, a favorite watering hole of the consular staff.

Vaux looked quickly at the bustling café whose tables spilled on to the sidewalk. He didn't see Micklethwait among the crowd and he thanked his Maker for small mercies. The Boulevard Pasteur, the main drag that led down to the center of town and the beaches, was clogged with late-afternoon traffic. Vaux dodged between cars and busses to get on the west side of the street. American Express, he remembered, was adjacent to the seedy Hotel de France. He searched for the big-windowed offices in vain. The Banque du Maroc had taken over the building and there was no sign of the Amex offices.

He walked into the bank and decided that 'boldness be my friend' was the best strategy to adopt in the current circumstances—particularly as there were very few customers and a big staff circulating behind the old-fashioned brass grills.

A slim, blue-eyed girl who wore a hijab had just finished stuffing a wad of dirhams in her counter drawer. He asked if she spoke English. She did. And then he asked if he could see the manager. The girl smiled and asked him to please wait. In less than two minutes, a well-dressed man in a gray business suit approached him. He was middle-aged, sported a Vandyke beard, and had short, iron-gray hair.

Vaux was ushered into the office. 'How can I help you?' asked the bank manager in perfect English.

'First, thanks for seeing me at such short notice.'

'Not at all. We're here to help. Do you want to open an account, perhaps? Many English are moving here, and we pride ourselves in our bank's solid reputation.'

Vaux came to the point to prevent any misunderstandings. 'Well, you never know. I have friends here, of course, and they do want me to move here. But I've come on another matter. Some years ago, I believe American Express occupied these offices—'

'Yes, that is right. A good five years ago, I think.'

'Well, where are they now?'

'Nowhere. They closed up. Amex closed many offices in Europe for some reason. I think Gibraltar would be the nearest office.'

'Well, I'm actually trying to track down a former Amex employee. He was a friend, and we've sort of lost contact. If I give you his name, perhaps you can help?'

'I somewhat doubt it. But you can try.'

'Faud—we called him Faud,' said Vaux, who instantly felt the information was too minimal.

'Old Faud el-Mullah? Yes, I do remember him, as a matter of fact.'

'That's great. Do you know how I could get in touch?'

The manager picked up his phone and muttered something in Arabic. Within a minute, a young lady in a long floral dress, her hair concealed by a head scarf, came in with a two-by-six file card. The manager took it. 'He has an account here, actually. He lives in the medina, close to the Petit Socco on the Rue des Postes. Number seven. I think it's close to the Pension Palace, a small, very cheap hotel.'

With some misgivings—Vaux knew the Petit Socco's dubious reputation—he hailed a petit taxi and asked the driver to take him there. A long, arm-waving explication in Arabic ensued and Vaux realized the man was trying to convey the impossibility of such a destination. Then he remembered: the narrow, serpentine streets that often ended in a series of steps as you approached the old casbah; the ancient, terraced houses with sagging balconies covered by intricate wooden trellises. The medieval plan of the 'small market' area had never been modernized to accommodate automobiles, even the small Renault in which he sat. But he also recalled a hectic shopping day at the nearby street market with Ahmed as guide and chief buyer for a week's provisions. He knew he could easily walk to the Petit Socco from there, so he asked the driver to take him to the marché, close to the more accessible Grand Socco. The driver nodded and smiled and with a few jolts and jerks the small car weaved into the traffic.

Faud, in a loose-hanging, gray shirt and worn jeans, opened the glossy, blue wooden door to his small terraced house. The two double windows on each side of the door were protected by elaborately patterned wrought-iron bars, also painted blue. He recognized Vaux instantly and they shook hands like former colleagues. Faud remembered Vaux as a man who always kept his promises and reliably delivered cash for services rendered. He chose not to recall that his tip-off to his old friend Abdullah al-Mawada, then the housekeeper and general factotum at the Villa Mauresque, had exposed Vaux's underhand and deceptive dealings with Kadri—which in turn led to Vaux's quick exit from Tangier. But he had learned later of the eventual reconciliation between the two old friends.

The front door opened directly onto a small, cramped room. A few small raffia mats covered a stone floor and Vaux detected the pungent aroma of hashish. Beside the small leather couch where Faud sat was a nargila pipe. Vaux sat down on a rickety folding chair with a wooden seat and broken wooden back. In the center of the small room sat a big brass filigreed tray on which was placed a bottle of mineral water and a tall glass.

Vaux noted that old Faud had aged: he was thinner now—perhaps he had shrunk over the last decade—and his short-cut hair was white and sparse. Time had chiseled deeper creases in his forehead and sunken cheeks. And when he smiled, Vaux noticed a black gap where he had lost one of his front teeth. 'I am here alone, Mr. Vaux. My wife is visiting her brother in Casablanca, and my daughter is away in Paris, studying at the Sorbonne, *al-hamdoulilah*—thanks be to God.'

'Well, that's good news. We can talk, then.' Faud's ears pricked up. He remembered Vaux's generosity in the old days. Vaux said, 'I wondered if you could help me on a delicate matter, Faud.'

'You are an old friend. Of course, I will help if I can. But can I get you a small coffee?'

'No, thank you. Some water's fine.' Vaux poured from the bottle and filled the glass. It was tepid, so he took just a couple of sips. 'Did you ever know, or have you ever heard of, a man named Mokhtar Tawil?' asked Vaux.

Faud's brown, sunken eyes looked up at the small, dusty crystal chandelier that hung from the yellowed ceiling. Whether intentionally or not, his hand came down and touched the side pocket of his threadbare jeans. He tapped the area gently. Vaux saw it as time-honored, coded shorthand.

'I will, of course, compensate you for any useful information. I always did, didn't I?'

'Oh, yes, boss. Well, you know, it's a struggle. I no longer work for the DST and the American Express closed shop. Times are tough. My daughter's education has cost much, much money. You understand.'

'Yes, Faud. I'm sure we can come to some arrangement. Now, have you heard of this man at all?'

'I'm afraid not. But tell me the whole story. Why do you want to find this man? I have my contacts…'

Vaux did not tell Faud the whole story—let alone that Tawil was dead, murdered on the *Goya* express night train. But he did say that Tawil had promised to work for him, just as Faud had done in the past. And the man had disappeared.

Vaux was convinced that finding where Tawil had come from, his home, his family, his mode of operations, would lead him to the man who had used him as a messenger or go-between to assure his asylum in Britain. It was a backup plan in case the lure of Micklethwait failed.

Faud stroked his slim toothbrush moustache. The wheels were turning fast, thought Vaux. 'Is this man from here in Tangier?'

'Yes, as far as I know. He may have contacts with some of the fringe groups—the troublemakers, those who seek violence to gain their aims. Do you understand what I'm saying?'

'Like the evildoers who killed forty of their fellow countrymen in a suicide bomb attack in Casablanca two years ago. Yes, I know what you mean. Leave it with me, Mr. Vaux. Perhaps a small deposit. This could take some time.'

Vaux fished in his pocket for the roll of dirhams he always carried with him. He put down ten hundred-dirham notes, about a hundred dollars.

Faud stood up. He suggested they meet in two days' time. 'At the Café Central in the Petit Socco—around three in the afternoon. I always spend a few hours there each day.' Vaux recalled it was an old hangout of George Greaves when he was billeted at the Minzah, busy transcribing what he liked to call the Kadri tapes.

Faud took Vaux's hand. '*As-salama laikoum.*' God be with you. He watched Vaux turn left and walk toward the Petit Socco. He had always lived by his own rules, inherited from his father, who had been an undercover agent for France's spy network during the Second World War—as well as an informer for the anti-French partisan movement that had worked for a postwar independent Morocco.

So within ten minutes of Vaux's departure, Faud decided to visit a man who conducted his business above a bustling fish restaurant on the seafront. He turned right out of his house and walked quickly down the narrow, winding streets toward the Avenue d'Espagne, a wide boulevard that ran parallel to Tangier's long sandy beach.

As always, the man he wished to see sat behind a small, leather-covered desk cluttered with small, Moroccan bric-a-brac: miniature brass elephants, stuffed leather rhinos, long Berber daggers, and brass ashtrays. An old Adler electric adding machine had been pushed to the side; and poised delicately on one corner of the desk was the man's tasseled red fez. The pro-government *Al-Alam* daily broadsheet was spread in front of him. With the wave of a pudgy hand, he invited Faud to sit opposite him on a wobbly upright chair.

'*Assalaamu alaykum.* ' Peace be upon you, said the man.

'*Wa alaykumus salaam,*' replied Faud. They exchanged pleasantries, asked each other about their respective families, enquired about their states of health.

'What brings you here, my friend?'

Faud then reported the sudden appearance in town of a former agent of Britain's secret service, the man who, according to Faud, had been instrumental in the deportation of the great Arab nationalist Ahmed Kadri, to face charges by the reactionary Syrian Alawite regime and, it was rumored, his final execution at their hands. This man, Vaux, was asking about the whereabouts of Mokhtar Tawil.

Hisham Toumert folded the newspaper slowly. He was a big, heavy man, and his friendly face carried a constant smile despite the oppressive heat in an office above a restaurant kitchen. His friends said that his inner contentment came from his deep faith. Every day, he prayed the obligatory five times from predawn to dusk. But he never let himself stray from reality. He also had an excellent memory. He knew that Faud's sweeping statement about the agent Vaux and his relationship with Ahmed Kadri, a Syrian apparatchik whose career had followed an erratic path, was wide of the mark. But he knew Faud well enough to tolerate his exaggerations and excesses. However, Faud's information was not uninteresting in the light of his committee's immediate plans.

'Thank you, Faud. As usual, your information is welcome. But I would suggest you stay quiet. There are developments about which I cannot talk. Vaux may or may not come into our plans. I will have to think about it. Meanwhile, you can put him off. Tell him you need more time. In any case, Tawil is no longer with us. He has disappeared. We are looking for him as we speak. So I want you to stay quiet and await further instructions. This adds to the mix, as I think the English say. However, at this point in time, I have one main priority. You will learn about it soon enough.'

Then Toumert, wrapped in his usual brown-and-white-striped djellaba, pushed himself out of his cushioned chair and waddled over to a large old cigar box placed on the mantel of a disused Spanish-tiled fireplace. He brought out a bunch of dirhams without counting them and placed them into Faud's outstretched hands.

'*Jasak Allahu khair.*' May Allah reward you, said a grateful Faud. He then went down the narrow staircase, spoke pleasantries to the old proprietor and the young cook, and asked for a dish of fried red mullet.

7

It was a warm, June day in London, where a continuous drizzle had kept the sun at bay since daybreak. But after a cool, blustery May, Sir Nigel Adair, head of Department B3, a sub-group of MI6, was grateful that the chill of the late spring had at last dissipated. Anne had brought him his favorite, stained 1953 Coronation mug of bitter Nescafe along with his chocolate digestive biscuits. Earlier, she had placed a pile of papers in the in-tray, and Sir Nigel now started the awkward maneuver of pulling the tray closer to him.

The first memorandum was from Alan Craw, his deputy.

TOP PRIORITY

It is ten days now since we last heard a peep out of Vaux. I have communicated with our contact Greaves (MI6 chief of station, Rabat) who says he too is awaiting news from Vaux. It is also ten days since Micklethwait arrived in Tangier. Greaves says Vaux spends most days reading mystery novels at the villa's swimming pool. Micklethwait's activities are unaccounted for.

Recommendation: I should fly to Rabat and on to Tangier to shake things up and get things rolling. The current situation is unacceptable.

CRAW

Sir Nigel knew his staff. He sighed. Craw was up to his old tricks. He picked up the internal phone and summoned Craw to his office. Craw, in a dark-blue Savile Row suit, gold-striped black tie and brown oxford shoes, came in after a few affectionate words with Anne who again marveled at some men's persistence.

'Yes, sir,' said Craw.

'I read your memo. Yes, I do think you should stir things up a bit. But these complex operations do take time, you know. I have every confidence in Vaux—I wouldn't have hired him for this mission if I didn't.'

Craw was about to say something but Sir Nigel silenced him by putting up his arm as a stop signal. 'No, let me finish, Craw.'

Sir Nigel got up and walked to the dusty sash window that overlooked the white-tiled well of the building. Small rivulets of rain mixed with soot and grime edged slowly down the window panes. He spoke with his back to Craw, who sat buffing his manicured nails while he waited for Sir Nigel's comments. 'As I see it, Vaux is practicing the well-proven art of noncommunication. We know how vital radio silence is in some of our more aggressive operations, don't we? And anyway, how can we trust that crowd of bloody Arabs over there? I don't care whether you're talking about the civil police or the intelligence people, whatever they call themselves—'

'The DST,' offered Craw.

'Well, whatever. No, I think Vaux is playing it just right. We don't know his strategy as yet but with Micklethwait there, I'm sure they're not treating this little escapade as a busman's early summer holiday—even if Vaux is taking advantage of the pool where he's staying. And don't forget, his room and board are costing us nothing.'

'Except his daily stipend, sir.'

'Oh, for God's sake, Craw, what's wrong with you? Did you have a bad night?'

Craw's face went crimson. He had to admit to himself that it had been an awful night, actually, with one of his ex-wife's old girl-friends, and it hadn't worked that well.

Sir Nigel turned to face him. 'You are right to be concerned. But let's give it more time. Greaves, by the way, is a good fellow and I have every confidence in him, too. If it makes you feel any better, I hereby appoint you Vaux's official case officer.'

For now, Craw's efforts to steal Vaux's thunder and possibly claim credit at the conclusion of an operation carried out by others had failed. So had his plans for a trip to sunny Morocco for a week or so. He passed Anne at her desk without his usual, friendly smile.

***

Vaux knew he was spinning wheels. He had just returned from meeting Faud at the Café Central on the Petit Socco. Faud had come up with nothing. But he sensed the man was playing his usual double or even triple game. He was more lubricious than usual and asked for more time. And a supplement to the initial payment he had received. Vaux gave him another thousand dirhams.

Meanwhile, he had heard nothing from Micklethwait—which, of course, was as it should be.

It was very hot and the long walk from the medina to the villa, all uphill, had exhausted him. The first thing Vaux did was plunge into the pool. He stayed there luxuriating in the cool water. Then he saw Mahmud rushing down from the house, telephone in hand. Vaux did a slow breaststroke to the edge of the pool and heaved himself up while Mahmud put a big white towel around his shoulders. He picked up the telephone.

'Greaves here, old man.'

'Hi, George.'

'Anything new to report?'

'Some progress. I'm in contact with Faud—you remember him?'

'Of course. One of our unreliable double agents.'

'Are you being sarcastic or is that what you really think of him?'

'Forget it. He's a guy that promises a lot but rarely delivers. And you never know what side he's on.'

'Anyway, I'll give him some more time and if he comes up with nothing, then perhaps we'd better have a "war council." '

'Talking of which, Craw called this morning. Agitated as hell. Says he may have to come down to get things moving.'

'That's all I need. But I guess any grand strategy talks will have to include him.'

Greaves said, 'And your boy?'

'You mean Micklethwait? He's doing what I want him to do. Sitting at the Minzah as bait. We have to give my theory a chance, George. This unnamed character who wants to give us the goods on the bad guys is bound to want to get in touch with us again. We don't know why Tawil was killed or who did it. But Micklethwait accompanied his envoy who ended up dead. The would-be whistle-blower is bound to try to find the agent who had accompanied his chosen representative.'

'Are you at the pool?'

'Yes, as a matter of fact.'

'Do you have something to write on?'

Mahmud always carried a ballpoint pen and a note pad with him. He had put them down on the glass-topped, wrought-iron table beside Vaux, who was now arranging himself on the sun lounger. 'I'm ready.'

'I recommend you contact our honorary consul in Melilla—just up the coastal road, old boy. He has an unbelievable network of informers—Moroccans, Berbers, Spanish, Brits—even Phoenicians, I shouldn't wonder. He's a wheeler-dealer, a merchant, buys and sells anything—including information. He's sometimes used as a go-between among warring factions. He's done some work for us from time to time and we've always found him loyal to the cause. But you'd have to meet him face to face. No encryption facilities or secure phone systems available, I'm afraid.'

Until now, Vaux had never given the small Spanish enclave a thought. And he was quite sure he had never met a representative of that rare diplomatic species called 'honorary consul.'

***

On this particular evening of a very hot June day, Micklethwait, after swimming a few lengths in the hotel's pool, made his way down to the Corniche. The wide boulevard runs parallel to the town's long, sandy beach, east of the main port. Excited tourists and Moroccans of all ages bustled along the noisy seafront, its small cafés and seedy bars. Micklethwait headed for Fred's Bar, one of the smaller beach bars nestled between the beach and the traffic-clogged Avenue d'Espagne. Pushing through the colored beads that hung in the doorway, he breathed in the ambient scent of *kif* and sat at a tall stool at the small bar. Fred himself was there, a short, barrel-chested, balding migrant from Liverpool, who drank little himself but enjoyed the joints of various weeds offered by the clientele—a mix of middle-aged European men and young Moroccans.

'What've you been up to today, then?' asked Fred, his forehead glistening with sweat. The bar's ventilation was reliant on the occasional sea breeze and the gentle zephyrs created by a sluggish, three-bladed ceiling fan.

'Not much. Too hot,' said Micklethwait. 'I'll have a scotch, please.'

Fred placed a large Haig's on the stained wooden bar. 'Don't be vague, ask for Haig,' said Fred as he shoveled some ice cubes into the glass. Micklethwait smiled at Fred's familiar barroom counsel and spooned out the ice cubes. 'Still don't trust the water?' asked Fred.

'Better to be on the safe side,' said Micklethwait.

He usually rationed himself to two of Fred's large whiskies before making for one of the big hotels on the front. He felt at ease in the more western ambience and sometimes met up with young, attractive girls from Germany or Holland. He hadn't made out yet, but he lived in hope. What a delightful arrangement, he thought: meet the girl of your dreams, totter upstairs to her room with a sea view, and make love all night before returning to the stuffy Minzah. He just hoped he wouldn't come across Vaux intent on the same game plan.

But on this sweltering evening, despite talking to several potential candidates, he had no luck. It was past midnight, his head was spinning, and he felt he should get back to the air-conditioned room at the hotel. He went down the escalator—the bar was on the second floor-- and a man came up to ask him if he wanted a taxi.

'A petit taxi, si'l vous plait,' said Micklethwait.

'Yes, sir. Come.'

Micklethwait followed the man in the tight western suit through the swing doors. It looked more like a limo than a petit taxi, but he was in no mood to argue. The man opened the rear door and Micklethwait muttered: 'El Minzah.' As he got in, he saw a shadowy figure in a dark suit sitting in the back. It raised no alarm in his befuddled head since Tangier taxi drivers, he guessed, like their Parisian colleagues, often drove at night with a friend as company.

But as soon as he relaxed and shifted further back into his side of the wide rear seat, he sensed that the man was leaning toward him. Before he had time to react, strong, fleshy hands gripped the back of his neck and pushed him forward so that he was forced to inhale from a damp rag. Micklethwait struggled as he tried to hold his breath, but seconds later, he had to give in and take a deep breath. The smell reminded him of almonds. Then he heard the gruff, rapid-fire orders in Arabic and the limo drove off with a screech of tires, the horn blasting as the car weaved into the heavy traffic on the Avenue d'Espagne.

8

It was Saturday morning, and Vaux sat at the villa's pool, ready to lift the white telephone as soon as it gave out the familiar, muffled purr. Anne had promised to call on Saturday mornings when she was away from the office and he was relaxing for the weekend. She would never accept Vaux's mild remonstrance: 'The spy game has no rest periods.'

Sure enough (Anne was totally reliable), the phone came to life at around 10:00 a.m. 'Hello, sweetheart,' said Vaux. He knew she would not like what he had to say.

'Darling, I've some great news. Sir Nigel's given me a long weekend leave. So I'm coming over next Thursday evening and staying 'til Tuesday.'

Vaux felt obliged to put a damper on her hopes. The way he saw things was that Operation Apostate was coming to some sort of resolution. Any day now, he was confident Micklethwait would be contacted by the mystery defector, arrangements would be made to get him quickly out of Morocco (he was toying with the idea that he could be flown out by an RAF C17 transport plane from nearby Gibraltar), and the whole deal would be wrapped up. Old Faud would have been an unhelpful diversion, easily written off. And he would get a fat paycheck, win some justified kudos and become an ex-spook again. Young Mickle, as he now decided to call him, would further his budding career.

So he had to somehow convey to Anne that her timing was not the best. Vaux said, 'Well, that's wonderful, darling. But can you put it off for another week or two? Things are coming to a head here and my full attention and dedication are needed more than ever. Please try and understand.'

Anne could never hide sadness or disappointment. 'But I won't get in your way,' she said plaintively. 'I promise. It's just that, well, we haven't seen each other for so long. I want to hold you again. I feel so empty, somehow.'

Vaux drew in a deep breath. He knew Anne's presence could provide some needed diversions. He'd been celibate for over a month. What worried him is that it hadn't bothered him too much. But he knew she was an expert at reviving his sagging libido. And he hated to hurt her. 'Well, all right, love. Call me nearer the date and I'll arrange for someone to meet you at the airport.'

'Why can't you meet me?'

'I told you. I've a feeling—call it intuition—that things are go-ing to start moving here pretty quickly. It could mean I have to travel'—he was thinking of Cohen in Melilla—'and I may not be here when you arrive. Don't worry, darling. I'll arrange everything once you give me your ETA.'

'My what?'

'When you're going to arrive, for God's sake.'

'You don't have to be short with me.'

'I'm not. But Anne, you've worked for B3 for several years now, and you should know the shorthand for "estimated time of arrival." '

'I don't do shorthand. Everyone at the office knows that—except you, because you are never there.'

'Just make sure you call me at least twenty-four hours before you leave, darling.'

Anne seemed reassured. 'Bye for now. Love you.'

***

Sebastian Micklethwait struggled to gain consciousness. His first thought was that he must at least be alive. His short-term memory still functioned: just before he had passed out, he remembered thinking that this was a rather unfriendly and violent way to make contact with him. His mind had been set to expect some sort of approach at any time. Vaux had stressed that he could be contacted by a number of methods and that he should stay alert always. The approach of the would-be defector could be very subtle. He had to be on his guard. But there was nothing subtle about what had happened to him last night—if it was last night. He wondered how long he had been unconscious.

He knew he was lying on a hard surface. It was a narrow cot with one heavy brown blanket thrown over him. He wiggled his toes and lifted his arms to check whether he had been injured in any way. He seemed to be intact. There was no sign of blood. But he felt groggy, nauseous—just as he felt when waking up after a night of barhopping. He was thirsty and he slowly turned his head to see if there was a bedside table on which he would find a glass or bottle of water. But there was nothing between the bed and the gray steel door except a stone floor, stained with smudges of spilled liquids, tea or coffee or Coke, and smothered with cigarette butts. He had a sudden, hopeful thought—and he moved his hand to his right hip pocket to check if his ersatz Nokia was still in place. It wasn't; if it had been, the MI6 monitors would have been able to trace his location within minutes, thanks to its satellite-linked two-way GPS technology.

He looked around his cell. He guessed the room measured about twelve by six feet. In the far corner, he saw something that he hadn't seen since his early childhood—an incongruous blue Willow-pattern chamber pot. The strange sight triggered an urge to urinate and he gradually raised himself. In another corner stood an upright chair over which hung his black leather bomber jacket. He was still wearing his jeans and his linen shirt was intact. But he couldn't see what they had done with the white trainers he had been wearing. As he relieved himself, he swung round to check if there was a window. All he saw high up above his cot was what looked like a small vent whose grill was covered with grime and cobwebs.

After a lengthy piss, he approached the door. He noticed an old-fashioned judas and tried to slide it open but it only worked from the other side. Then he gripped the sturdy iron door handle and he was not surprised when he couldn't move it up or down. He was locked in and under custody. He wondered what this man—code name Mohammed, he remembered—hoped to gain by treating his first British facilitator or helper in this appalling way. It made little sense. On the other hand, he told himself, who can really make head or tail of the Arab mind?

He sat on the bed and tried to collect his thoughts. He blew into the palm of his hand and bent over to breathe in his own breath. There was that slight odor of almonds he had noticed when the man forced him to inhale from the damp cloth. He recalled the Portsmouth training manual:

> *If you find yourself incarcerated, check the area for locations where eavesdropping equipment/devices could be concealed. Examples: under furniture (tables, chairs); ventilation and heating grills; under toilet cisterns; door jambs, window casements and sundry apertures...*

Where to start?

Before he answered that question, he heard a distant clang from outside the room and a shuffling that became more distinct as someone approached his door. For some reason, he looked down at his bare feet so that he didn't have to look into the eyes of anyone spying through the judas.

The judas duly slid open and then firmly shut. The jangle of keys followed, the appropriate key selected and inserted. Then the door opened slowly. Micklethwait saw a stooped, old man wearing a long, white *thobe*. He carried a small tray that he placed on the floor beside his cot. A bowl of lentil soup seemed to be on offer along with a slice of flatbread.

Micklethwait said, '*Choukran.*' The old man smiled, nodded greetings. They both heard the far-off cries of a distant muezzin as he called the faithful to prayer. The old man muttered, '*Allah Akbar.*' God is great. Then he left.

***

Soon after his unhelpful meeting above the fish restaurant with Hisham Toumert, Faud decided that he needed to know more about what seemed to be this fast-developing situation involving a known MI6 agent, Vaux, and Tawil, for whom Vaux was searching in earnest. The fact that Hisham Toumert, the known leader of an obscure nationalist group, had confirmed that he was also searching for Tawil's whereabouts only added to Faud's suspicions that something major was afoot.

So he went to work. He had not told Vaux of the ace he held that would give him a major advantage in the game to find Tawil: some years ago, he had known Tawil's father, then a manager in a large leather and brass emporium in the medina. But he also recalled that the man had died in the last month of the last century. Faud's diligent inquiries soon revealed that Tawil lived in an apartment on the Place d'Italie. He had never married, and like many young and middle-aged Moroccans, worked when he could find work.

Faud approached the old concierge, who sat on a rickety upright chair just inside the cool marble lobby of the 1930s-style art deco building. He learned that Tawil had not been seen for some weeks. The old man believed he had left Tangier to seek work but had no idea where he had gone. He often visited Melilla, he said, but he had no firm information as to his whereabouts. His small two-room apartment on the second floor would be available soon if the man didn't return to pay his rent. Faud handed the old man five dirhams. The aging concierge then asked if he wanted to put his name down for the place, and if so, the deposit would be one hundred dirhams. But Faud had already walked away.

Although Vaux hadn't revealed to him where he was staying, he knew where he could find him. In the afternoons, he often played checkers at the Café Central with Mahmud from the Villa Mauresque. They would gossip about everything and everybody— including any transient guests at the villa, which Faud knew his old friend personally managed with admirable efficiency. And he knew that Vaux would sometimes have lunch at the Minzah and have the occasional drink in the bar. So his first port of call was to the old and storied Minzah, close to the French consulate on the Place de France.

Rachid was an old friend and contact at the Hotel el-Minzah, a man who worked at the hotel's reception desk. He recognized Vaux from Faud's grainy photo (taken surreptitiously when Vaux was a frequent visitor to the American Express offices) and confirmed that Vaux had visited the hotel bar a few days ago and talked with an English guest for some time. But Vaux had never been back. Rachid wrote down the Englishman's name and room number.

Faud decided to sit in the lobby until the mystery Englishman walked in or departed. He sat on an overstuffed leather chair that gave him a wide view of the brass doors of the two narrow elevators and of the lobby. He picked up a complimentary copy of *Le Journal de Tanger* from the front desk and used the tabloid newspaper as a useful screen behind which he could conduct his observations. After about an hour—Faud had lots of time to kill—his friend Rachid nodded to Faud as Sebastian Micklethwait a.k.a. Edward Knight strode out of the elevator and walked quickly past Faud on his way to the courtyard to have his breakfast. Faud got up, folded the newspaper, and gave it to Rachid who handed him a room key as if he were a guest at the hotel.

Faud's feverish search of Micklethwait's room gave him some useful leads. He found the man's newly issued passport in a drawer of the bedside table. He memorized the photo and noted Edward Knight's year of birth: 1978. But the real telltale was the fully loaded Glock pistol he found under a pile of folded shirts. He quickly looked around the room whose french windows opened on to a large, room-sized balcony overlooking the terrace restaurant and the pool. In the bathroom, he found bottles of cologne and a big bar of highly perfumed soap labeled with the odd name of Imperial Leather. He told himself that this man's feminine taste in toiletries could be useful to know.

Faud's days were long, his evenings empty. He missed his absent wife and his adorable daughter even more. So he had nothing better to do, he told himself, than to hang around the Minzah's lobby waiting for the young man's appearance and to follow him. *An exercise in what the English call tradecraft*, he told himself, and his pulse quickened as he got back to the old game.

And so it was that Faud el-Mullah, one-time agent for the DST, Morocco's secret intelligence service, and occasional informer and facilitator for anyone who paid the price, lingered and watched for hours on that hot and noisy night, and finally witnessed the abduction of Sebastian Micklethwait outside the Metropole hotel on the busy Boulevard d'Espagne. He had been hovering in the main lobby of the hotel when he saw a dark-suited man approach Micklethwait.

He followed them to a parked limousine just in front of the revolving doors. He had peered through the open door of the car as the
young man was ushered into the rear—and in a flash he saw another passenger lurking in the gloom of the wide backseat. The speed
with which the car had taken off only confirmed his suspicion that
his Englishman was in trouble.

9

Vaux had never seen Anne look so beautiful. Her ash-blond hair hung loose and straight down to her shoulders and she wore an ivory linen silk shift dress that fitted tight around her small waist. Her strappy, high-heeled sandals were minimal.

Vaux had driven with Mahmud in the old black Mercedes 190E to the small airport, and they had waited in the arrivals hall just beyond the immigration and customs area. She ran to him, gave him a big hug and pecked him on the cheek. Long, passionate embraces could wait. Vaux put his arm around her and introduced her to Mahmud who smiled and bowed slightly as he shook her hand.

Back at the villa, Momtaz, all smiles and amiability, took Anne up to her room. Earlier, Mahmud had asked Vaux if the expected guest was his wife and when Vaux shook his head and prepared to explain the relationship, Mahmud cut him off and said he would prepare the master bedroom for the lady. She would enjoy the view of the gardens, the umbrella pines and, in the distance, the Atlantic. Vaux put up no resistance. His smaller room that looked out to the high brick walls and the villa's wrought-iron electronic gates was a few doors away on the same floor.

Vaux sat at the pool, waiting for Anne to come down after her shower and her change into less formal clothes. He heard some movement from the mosaic-tiled pathway that ran from the house to the pool area and saw Momtaz, shoeless, his white pants cut off just below his knees, running toward him. He was waving a small envelope and Vaux wondered if George Greaves had left a message while he was out at the airport.

'*Si'l vous plait, monsieur! Une lettre. Urgent!*'

'*Merci, Momtaz. Peut-être c'est très important, eh?*' Vaux figured he might as well practice his French along with Momtaz.

He opened the small envelope. It wasn't from Greaves. It read:

> Mr.Vaux:
> *I have some urgent information to*
> *extend to you. Meet me at the Café*
> *Central today please at usual time*
> > Faud

Vaux cursed under his breath. He had somehow thought this was going to happen: Anne abandoned on her first day so that he could pursue a lead. He wondered what Faud had come up with. Then he saw Anne, clad in a two-piece yellow bikini, skipping down the path in her bare feet, wrapped in a white terry cloth bathrobe. She took it off and threw it down on the sun lounger next to Vaux. Then, without a word, she dived into the water. The big splash soaked Vaux, and Faud's brief message was now as unreadable as if it had been written with invisible ink.

***

'What's so suspicious about another man in the back of the limo?' asked Vaux. 'The driver wanted company when he drove around looking for fares, that's all.'

'No, Mister Vaux. That's not so here in Tangier. If there is an exception, then the friend would be seated up front with the driver. I can assure you of that.'

'You seem certain that this man you saw get in the taxi—'

'No taxi, no, sir. We don't have such big taxis here.'

'Well, OK. But what makes you think he was English and that I knew this man?'

'That's what I think they call a leading question, Mr. Vaux. You know I have my methods, my confidential contacts. No more said. I know that man was the same man that you spoke to a few days ago at the Minzah hotel. Just leave it at that.'

Vaux knew he would have to leave it at that. 'And you say the man you presumably followed never came back to the hotel that night. Anything else you can tell me? The man who picked him up in the lobby of the Metropole, for instance—'

Faud looked thoughtful. 'Medium height, black short-cut hair, tight-fitting dark suit. Young—in his thirties. Not European but wearing European.'

'In other words, probably a Moroccan.'

'Yes, that's it. The man in the back had a heavy build and he too wore a suit. But I didn't have enough time to look closely at him.'

Vaux sipped the cloudy, yellow anise Faud had unexpectedly ordered. His mind was working on overdrive. How the hell could this have happened? *Why would our mystery defector go to such lengths to get in touch with us?* So far he had heard nothing from this man whom he had been hired to contact in the wake of Tawil's murder, the man who had promised a full dossier on Al-Qaeda in the Islamic Maghreb, AQIM—its hierarchy, chain of command, and whatever mayhem they planned. He signaled to the waiter for another anise while Faud wrote some figures down on a page in his diary. Vaux knew what was coming.

'I spent many hours, sir. You must understand. My devotion is unquestioned. I will go to work immediately and find your Englishman. Have no worries.'

'Boy, I wish it was that simple,' said Vaux. He gave Faud an uncounted wad of dirhams. But he knew he had no notes above a denomination of twenty, so it wasn't excessive. Faud counted the money carefully and looked somewhat peeved. 'That's just on account. Find my Englishman, and you'll collect your just dues,' said Vaux.

'You will have to give me his name, sir,' said Faud, even though he knew it.

'He goes under the name of Edward Knight,' said Vaux. He took Faud's ballpoint and wrote the name on the page facing Faud's expense chit. Almost as an afterthought, Vaux recalled why he had hired Faud in the first place. 'And what about this man Tawil? Any progress?'

'Yes, Sir Vaux. I now know where he lives. Just a little more time...'

Vaux thought: *You mean where he lived.* But he said nothing.

In the petit taxi on the way back to the villa, Vaux knew very well that everything had suddenly changed. The first priority was to find 'Mickle,' hopefully safe and sound. But he would have to await some sort of contact from the man or men who had taken him in the full glare of passersby—and an observant Faud. Unless, of course, Faud came up with something quickly. But the puzzling riddle was this: why would the would-be defector employ tactics that would antagonize the very people who promised him refuge and fortune once he came over?

The timing of this debacle was intolerable. Just as Anne had arrived. He could be called away any moment. He'd do anything to get 'Mickle' back. Anne had to be bottom of his list of priorities.

And, perceptive as she always was, it wouldn't take long for her to realize it.

***

Her skin was hot from the afternoon sun. Her lovemaking sated Vaux's bottled-up sexual appetite and her total surrender left no doubts about her real love for him. During the few intervals between lovemaking, Vaux found himself wondering again why the privileged girls from Roedean seemed to have a predilection for fellatio.

For her, it was to have been a mini-honeymoon: both of them enjoying each other's company in an idyllic and private corner of the world, a respite from their busy lives, and a reaffirmation of their total devotion to each other.

But it did not work out that way. Vaux was restless. No postcoital calm for him. He went down to the big kitchen, opened the door of the old, white GE refrigerator, and took out a jug of orange juice. In the morning, he would have to break the bad news to Greaves. He had bleak visions of an apoplectic Sir Nigel sending Craw over to 'sort things out.' Losing 'Mickle' meant he had lost the initiative. Had he made a major blunder by letting Micklethwait sit there in the open so that the would-be asylum seeker would make discreet contact? But what was the logic of hiding Micklethwait away (in the Villa Mauresque, for example) and making it near impossible for the man to contact them?

He could see control of his mission slipping away before it had really begun. He looked through the tall windows and toward the east he saw the first orange-and-red daubs of dawn advancing over a calm Mediterranean. It was going to be another perfect day. And it would not be long before all hell broke loose.

He had planned to tell Anne the bad news gently. Momtaz was spooning scrambled eggs onto her plate. She looked radiant in a blue-and-white-striped matelot T-shirt and white slacks. Vaux sipped his café au lait. He didn't have much appetite. 'Darling, something happened just before you got here. It's pretty serious and it could mean that I've got to leave right away,' said Vaux.

Anne looked up, her wide mouth widening in a broad smile. 'Tell me what's happened, darling. Why didn't you tell me yesterday?'

'I wanted you to relax and enjoy the place, that's why.'

'And I have—so far.' She put out a girlish giggle in praise, he presumed, of what she had considered a blissful night of love.

He waited for Momtaz to leave with a tray full of plates, cold toast, and unwanted pots of jam and marmalade. 'You know Micklethwait?'

'Of course I do. He's supposed to be over here with you, isn't he?'

'He's been here some days now. We're working together on a top-priority mission. You know I can't tell you the details.'

'I'm aware they don't trust me with their secrets.'

'It's not that. Don't let's go through this again. It's just that you haven't got full security clearance. You're too low on the totem pole.'

'Oh, thank you, Michael. What a sweet thing to say.'

'I didn't mean it like that. But you don't have top-security clear-ance and so I can't tell you what exactly is going on. But "Mickle," as I choose to call him, has disappeared. And my job, starting right now, is to find out where the hell he is.'

'Oh my God. But what do you mean, "disappeared"?' She was serious now, a frown clouding that young, flawless face.

'Just that. He never got back to his hotel after some evening excursion or whatever. I only learned about this yesterday—while you were having your siesta. So it's all hands on deck. I have to call our man in Rabat now, and the balloon's about to go up. If he doesn't reappear or we can't find him soon, then this place will become the center of operations. And you, my dear, will have to look scarce.'

Anne looked vaguely puzzled and then disappointed. She leaned across the table to touch Vaux's hand. 'I won't get in your way, darling. I'm quite happy to loll around the pool all day. It will be all right to stay until my flight leaves, won't it?'

Vaux was relieved that Anne had taken the news without the usual flare-up. Something welled up inside him—perhaps because she hadn't protested or made a scene, her usual reaction to losing his company because of other priorities. He took her hand, and they went together up the curved staircase to her room. The lovemaking seemed even better now. It would be his last plunge into carnal luxury before the old game started up.

From his end, he couldn't secure the phone line, so he rang Greaves and asked him to return the call as soon as possible. Greaves instantly grabbed the secured speech system handset and said, 'What's up?' Vaux told him the story and suggested he contact Sir Nigel immediately with a follow-up to Alan Craw, Sir Nigel's deputy at Department B3.

Greaves was nothing if not a typical Englishman. Saturdays and Sundays were sacrosanct. 'I hate to disturb your boss on a weekend. He's probably organizing some hunt on his estate or fishing in Scotland. I'd prefer to go through my people at Vauxhall and let them chase up the old man, or failing that, get Craw in on the act.'

Vaux was adamant. 'Your MI6 people have always given B3 complete autonomy, and the last thing we want them to know is that we've screwed up and want their help. Please, George, try and get Sir Nigel and/or Craw.'

Greaves, the procrastinator: 'Why not wait a couple of days? On Monday, Adair and Craw will be in the office and it will seem less panicky if we all talk then.'

'For Christ's sake, Micklethwait's in harm's way. He's gone missing. We have to do something to find the guy. We have to co-ordinate a rescue plan and we may even have to scrap this whole operation. So I want input from the powers that be. I can't freelance this thing now it's got to a crisis point.'

Greaves hesitated. He was trying to shake off his weekend sloth. 'When you put it like that, I suppose you're right.'

'It would be great if you could come here post-haste, along with your encryption handset, so we can at least discuss the whole thing with my boss. It'll be intolerably cumbersome for me to call you and then you to call them and vice versa. This place has to be where we coordinate things—at least until we find Micklethwait and finally make contact with this troublesome, defecting Moroccan.'

Vaux heard a deep sigh of resignation.

'Very well, Vaux. Queen and country and all that. I'll be there sometime in the afternoon.

'Thanks, George.'

10

What Micklethwait hated most was that there was no way to distinguish night from day. The naked bulb that gave a dim light from the ceiling enabled him to look at but not understand the Arabic newspaper, supplied, he supposed, as toilet paper more than for information. He made a resolution to take the fast track in an Arab language course as soon as he returned to civilization. Sir Nigel and Craw had badgered him about just such a course, but he was in his early probation days and had put it off.

This, he told himself, was probably his third day of confinement. He had slept a lot, dozed out of boredom, and now he wished he had bought a watch that showed the date or at least the day of the month. But he only had his grandfather's 1940s stainless-steel Cartier tank watch, a gift from his devoted ex-spook grandmother, now no doubt tending her roses in Cornwall.

The wrist watch showed eleven o'clock, and his body instincts told him it was the morning—bowel movements didn't help since he'd had severe diarrhea since his first 'meal.' The Willow-pattern chamber pot, surrounded by soaked newsprint, was brimful. But then he heard the clatter as the passage door was unlocked and the shuffling that preceded the rapid slide of the judas peephole and the slow creak as his cell's door opened.

Today they had sent a new man. He was about the same height as Micklethwait, six foot, with a full black beard and a long, hooded djellaba. He wore sandals and offered a large plate of baklava and *asaabiyya*—puff pastries stuffed with almonds and honeyed hazelnuts. Micklethwait smiled and wolfed them down. Sugary stuff, he told himself, would help keep his strength up.

The new man also looked about his own age, even though the thick beard made it difficult to tell. But the whites of his eyes were strikingly clear, and his white teeth were perfectly formed. The man shook off his hood and sat down on the bed beside him. 'My name's John, but here they call me Omar,' said the man.

Micklethwait pushed himself up on his elbow to get a better fix on the man. 'You're English,' he said.

'You can tell?' laughed the man.

'A London accent, yes,' said Micklethwait. And he remembered the Portsmouth training manual:

> *Be cautious of anyone claiming to be of the same nationality or offering friendship in your captivity. Adopt a cold, neutral posture, pending more evidence of the party's real intentions toward you—that is, will the party be helpful, or is he or she there simply to garner information and intelligence?*

'Yes, I'm a jihadist from the Edgware Road,' said John/Omar without detectable humor.

If he had set out to shock his captive, the effort fell flat. Micklethwait knew of the large Arab presence in North London, and he also knew that new immigrants from all over the Mideast and North Africa flocked to the Edgware Road, especially the

Marble Arch area. The intelligence community, not to mention the politicians, had always feared that proselytizing was rampant—especially in the turmoil of the Iraq war. The nearest mosque was in Camden Town, a constant target of surveillance by MI5, the United Kingdom's domestic intelligence agency. But this man, even with the overgrown beard and shoulder-length hair, looked English through and through. He even had blue eyes.

'Well, that's something,' said Micklethwait. He could see the funny side of the situation and he wondered whether the presumed Muslim convert had retained any remnants of classic British wit. At best, he thought, the man's visit signaled some turn of events, perhaps the first step of getting out of this hellhole.

But Omar's face stiffened. He thought his approach would have overwhelmed the prisoner, perhaps render him speechless or more defiant. Instead, he saw that the effect of his presence seemed to lighten the heavy atmosphere of the dank cell.

Micklethwait took advantage of Omar's silence. 'Perhaps you'll be good enough to tell me why I am here and what your intentions are toward me. I don't have to tell you that in Britain and most civilized countries, this would be illegal detention—kidnapping, if you like.'

Then he paused. Omar waited patiently, as if he wanted his prisoner to let off steam. Micklethwait, in an abundance of caution, was not about to ask anything about the would-be defector, the member of the AQIM splinter group, who had promised to deliver the goods on terrorist ambitions in the Maghreb. If he was being forcibly held by a gang who were allied to this prized turncoat, he knew his best tactic was to wait for their next move and say nothing more. If, on the other hand, his kidnappers were in fact members of one of the groups that the defector planned to expose, silence was still the order of the day.

Omar got up from the side of the bed. He looked at Micklethwait, now propped up on the thin, sweat-stained pillow. 'You are here for one reason, my friend. I'll tell you tomorrow. By then, we'll know more about what steps we have to make to secure our aims. So keep your chin up, old boy.'

This doesn't sound encouraging, thought Micklethwait. But he said nothing. Omar had planted a seed of uncertainty and fear that replaced an earlier optimism that all would be resolved shortly—with his release and hopefully his delivery of the man Department B3 were so anxious to meet and talk to. 'Before you go, can I ask what school you went to in North London?' asked Micklethwait. It was a mild effort to befriend the man.

'That's not relevant or important just now,' said Omar. He bowed slightly. '*Salaam alaikum,*' he said. 'Peace be with you.'

'Wait,' said Micklethwait quickly. 'Is there any chance of your finding a book I can read? Anything—a paperback thriller, biography—it doesn't matter.'

'Next time I will bring the Koran,' said Omar with a wide smile.

'And what about my mobile phone? It seems to have been taken.'

Omar laughed. 'It's on some road somewhere, no doubt crushed out of all recognition and usefulness.'

***

Mort Cohen, Britain's honorary consul in Melilla, offered Magdi Kassim a small cup of thick coffee. As usual, Kassim had come unannounced and Cohen tried to hide his irritation. 'We are very busy today, Magdi. It's the last day of the month, and I have to check my inventory,' said Cohen. 'And I'm expecting a new consignment of dried argan fruits very shortly. What can I do for you?'

'I told you I'd be back soon. And anyway, why don't you get one of your slaves to do these chores? You can afford it.' Kassim was only half joking. Cohen's tightness and frugality were legendary and the cause of much amusement among the merchants of Melilla and its environs.

But Cohen was in no mood for chit-chat. 'You have no idea what it costs to run this business. The port authority has put up our taxes again—the third increase in four years—*oy vey*!' Kassim had no comment. Cohen continued, 'So have you heard anything about Tawil? Have you caught the murderer or murderers? His girlfriend, the woman he lived with here, keeps badgering me, and I'm as anxious as she is to resolve this thing. When are they going to return the body?'

'The Spanish police take their time. The body as well as the investigation seem to be on ice just now.'

Cohen was always impressed by Kassim's mastery of English— so unusual in a street Arab. 'You know, that public school your father sent you to—they did a good job. You express yourself well, I've always said that.'

'*Al-hamdouliliah,*' muttered Kassim. Thanks to God.

The small, cramped office seemed to be getting hotter by the minute despite three portable fans going at full pelt from various parts of the room. Cohen's comment was a small effort to get on friendlier terms with this envoy of the mysterious Tangier gang who had wanted Cohen to supply a 'suitable' candidate for their secret dealings with the British government.

Kassim elaborated. 'It was a private school. My father didn't want to pay the extra fees for a good public school.'

An ingrate on top of everything else, thought Cohen. He felt he could pressure Kassim, now that they probably needed him again. 'Is that all the news you have? What about suspects? What are the Spanish investigators coming up with?'

Kassim wasn't interested in Cohen's private postmortem. He sighed as he got up. 'They think it was someone on the dining car staff. A cook, probably.'

'A cook?' asked Cohen, bewilderment in his thick voice.

'Your friend Tawil was killed with a knife from the train's kitchen—a carving knife.'

'Oh, my God,' said Cohen, quietly and more to himself than to anyone else.

Kassim got up and looked through the smudged windows to the town hall, an imposing, yellow-stucco art deco building that dominates the busy plaza. Cohen thought he looked quite dapper today—a tight-fitting navy-blue suit; white, open-necked shirt; and smart black shoes.

Still looking through the windows, Kassim said, 'This is the next job I told you about. We need you to look after someone. You know what I mean, you've done this before. It won't be for long, I promise.'

Cohen's face paled; his heartbeat quickened. He felt panic welling up inside him. This was totally unacceptable. Yes, he had provided 'facilities' twice before for these people. The men detained for a few days, perhaps a week. But it had shaken him to the core. If it ever got out, if the detainee were to escape, or if the dark secret were somehow exposed, it would mean ruination. Everything he treasured—his business, his wife, his marriage, his standing in the community—all would be smashed into oblivion. His name and his reputation in this little part of the world would be totally destroyed. And then there would be the shame: the termination by Her Majesty's government of his exalted position as honorary consul. He looked up at the official portrait of the queen as tears welled up in his yellow-tinted eyes.

But Cohen said nothing. These people could ruin him as easily as any ultimate exposure of the offense they would order him to commit.

Kassim had read his thoughts without even looking at the man. 'You have always provided such facilities in the past, Mr. Cohen. It will be just the same. A few days, and the man will be transferred out of your hands. You will be duly compensated.'

Cohen was almost speechless with internal rage. He said, 'Very well, I'll prepare for a guest. And now I must get on.'

***

Anne Armitage-Hallard bent forward over her long, slim legs to reach her manicured toenails. She was coloring them magenta while she sat by the side of the pool where she would stay for most of the afternoon, fulfilling her promise to keep out of the way. About an hour earlier, George Greaves had arrived rather grandly, she thought, in the Rabat embassy's brand-new black Rolls Phantom, the first Roller designed by Germany's BMW car group. He and Vaux were now sitting at the long rosewood table that dominated the villa's main dining room.

Greaves had driven up the palm-lined gravel driveway to the villa's porticoed front doors, hauled his small suitcase and a garment bag out of the trunk, and pressed the remote on the key fob to lock the car. Within seconds, Mahmud had run up to him, asked for the fob to reopen the doors and told him that the car would be taken to the big garage on the north side of the villa. His suitcase was quickly grabbed by Momtaz, who beckoned him to follow. Vaux greeted him in the cool marble hallway, put his hand on Greaves' big, wide shoulders and ushered him into the dining room.

'Don't they let you do anything yourself?' asked Greaves.

'Not if they can help it,' said Vaux.

They sat opposite each other at both ends of the long table. From his inside pocket, Greaves took out his encrypted telephone device. Vaux was struck by its resemblance to a conventional mobile phone. Greaves said, 'Got the phone number?' Vaux gave him the contact number Sir Nigel Adair had left with the main operators at MI6 headquarters at Vauxhall.

The phone rang only three times. 'Oakland Hall,' said a refined, English male voice.

'Good afternoon,' said Greaves. 'I wonder if I could speak with Sir Nigel Adair. It's extremely urgent.'

'May I say who's calling, sir ?'

'A business colleague,' said Greaves with a wink to Vaux. He heard the butler, or whoever it was, put the receiver down heavily. Greaves turned the device toward Vaux so that they could both hear the low voices, the shuffling, and the mild coughing of someone who approached. They both knew Sir Nigel would not like to be disturbed at whatever country estate he was spending the weekend and so the two spooks felt rather like schoolboys waiting to speak to an intimidating headmaster.

'Yes—who is this?' It was Sir Nigel's voice, peremptory and impatient.

Greaves wished Sir Nigel a good day and apologized for disturbing him on a Saturday afternoon.

'Get on with it, man.'

Greaves said that he was from the embassy in Rabat and that he was now in Tangier with Sir Nigel's colleague, Michael Vaux, who would like to speak to him on a very urgent matter. Greaves got up and handed the phone to Vaux.

Mutual greetings were exchanged between Sir Nigel and Vaux who then delivered his verbal report on what he called the current unsatisfactory status of B3's Operation Apostate.

There was a long pause after Vaux had finished. Sir Nigel was obviously shaken. 'You mean to tell me that young Micklethwait has simply disappeared, gone missing in action?'

'Yes, sir. That's why I thought it vital to get in touch with you right away. The situation has changed from a sort of passive waiting around for our Arab defector to show up to an urgent need to find Micklethwait. That's now the main priority, I think you would agree.'

It seemed to Sir Nigel that Craw had now proved his point. He made a hasty decision. 'Craw's your case officer. I'll send him down there tomorrow.'

Then Sir Nigel hung up.

II

Up to now, Vaux had managed to keep B3's Operation Apostate secure. But he doubted if it could remain so for much longer. The most vulnerable link in the chain of secrecy was Faud el-Mullah, the man who had witnessed Micklethwait's apparent abduction. But Vaux knew Tangier well enough to realize that this ancient and modern cosmopolitan suntrap teemed with agents and informers who worked for other intelligence networks and who, like Faud, often sold their information to the highest bidder.

What had not occurred to him, he thought later, perhaps because of some innate, colonial mind-set, was the possibility that Morocco's own elaborate spy apparatus would eventually cotton on to some strange happenings within the orbit of the Villa Mauresque.

And so it was that just after a leisurely lunch around the pool, Momtaz came running down from the house to announce the arrival of two unexpected visitors. Vaux looked at Greaves to share his curiosity but Greaves was forking the last remains of a big melon into his mouth while admiring Anne's slow, elegant crawl up and down the long pool.

Vaux told Momtaz to ask the visitors to wait in the European lounge, a long room furnished with bulky art deco pieces, over-stuffed armchairs and a long walnut sideboard covered in silver platters, cocktail shakers and teapots.

Still in their poolside terry cloth bathrobes, Vaux and Greaves approached the house slowly. 'I didn't tell you I brought an old army Browning from the embassy for you,' said Greaves. 'I thought the current situation called for some preparedness, old boy.'

'Don't be ridiculous, George. If anyone's after me, they're not going to come to the front door.'

'It's happened just that way in the past.'

'In the Mafia, maybe. Relax. I can't think what it's about. Perhaps some friends of Safa's.'

The two men were standing at the big window that overlooked the flagged terrace and the Atlantic in the distance. They turned around as they heard Vaux and Greaves enter the room. Momtaz, who had followed Vaux, asked whether he should bring some re-freshment and they all opted for a large bottle of mineral water.

'How can I help you gentlemen?' asked Vaux. Greaves sat down heavily in one of the armchairs. The two visitors remained standing. They were wearing casual western clothes and were of medium height, both clearly Moroccan. The older one was balding and had a pocked face. His younger partner had shaved his head. But his blazingly blue eyes betrayed Berber ancestry. Greaves checked their tight-fitting jackets and could see, as if by X-ray, the bulk of their handguns.

'Good morning, messieurs,' said the older man. 'I'm Major Driss Ghali of the Sûreté Nationale. This is my colleague, Lieutenant Didi Hassan.' He waved a small ID card with a photo.

Vaux gestured toward the big couch. He knew the Sûreté Nationale, Morocco's police force, had been modeled on the French institution, so he wasn't surprised that the major chose to address them in a sort of 'Franglais'—English dotted with French words. '*Non, merci*, we rest *debout*—standing. '

'I am Michael Vaux, and this is my friend, George Greaves.'

'Ah, *you* are Monsieur Vaux,' said the major, as if he'd been looking for him for some time.

Greaves now wished he'd brought along the false passport bearing the name of his alias, Bernard Harris. But it was too late, anyway. Vaux, in his innocence, had introduced them both by their real names. This, he thought, could get messy and the lawmen's suspicions would only intensify when they learned that he worked for the British embassy—even as a commercial attaché.

Vaux left it to the major to continue.

'Monsieur Vaux, you are a former visitor to Tangier, non? '

'I like it here. Just a short vacation with friends.'

'You have some business here?'

'No, I'm on a vacation. Invited here by Safa Robinson, who's currently in the UK with her husband. She owns the place.'

The two men looked at each other as if they were relishing the situation. Maj. Ghali said, 'But that is not the whole story, *je pense*. Just so that you know, we are from the local Sûreté Nationale, immigration branch. It's our job to keep a check on all foreigners who appear to have nondeclared interests in our country—besides tourism. To put it briefly, we believe you are using this place as a front for, shall we say, clandestine activities which may or may not be legal but are nevertheless undeclared to the authorities.'

Lt. Hassan produced a packet of Camels and offered them all round. Greaves shook his head but Vaux accepted. They were his favorite brand before he quit smoking. The lieutenant flipped a silver Zippo and Vaux inhaled in full knowledge that Anne would accuse him of committing a cardinal sin. 'Well, Major, I don't know where you are getting your information from, but you are wide of the mark...'

'*Comment?* How you say?' asked the major.

'Sorry. Let's just say your information or intelligence is faulty. I'm here for the sole purpose of winding down—you know, relaxing. I'm due to go back as soon as my friend Safa, who owns this place, gets back from England. I'm sort of house sitting, you see.'

The major looked skeptical. The lieutenant had a smug grin on his face as he smoked and enjoyed the view from the window. 'I see. This is your claim. Then may I ask why you asked one of our, let's say, "contacts," to trail a fellow Englishman, a man who had been staying at the Minzah hotel on the Rue de la Liberté and has now apparently gone missing? His hotel bill unpaid. His clothes still in his room?'

Before Vaux could come up with an answer, Lt. Hassan turned from the window to look directly at Vaux. 'Did you know this disappeared Englishman? Yes or no?'

So he's the bad cop in the good cop-bad cop routine, thought Vaux. He said, 'Yes, I knew him. I was worried about him. I know his mother, you see. And she told me that he had come here suddenly and she feared his main interest was the drugs that, as you well know Major, are cheap and freely available on the street here. He has a love of *kif*, apparently, and his mother feared he could easily fall prey to more serious substances like heroin.

'So, after she called me, I asked an old acquaintance who had worked for years at the old American Express offices on the Rue Pasteur to keep an eye on the young man. I didn't dream he would find anything sinister in my request.'

'Um.' Maj. Ghali was skeptical. Lt. Hassan exhaled a big cloud of blue-gray tobacco smoke. Then Maj. Ghali turned to Greaves. 'And what is your connection to Mr. Vaux? A fellow ex-journalist, perhaps?'

The question was enough to tell Vaux that the police had probably opened a file on him back in the days when he had stayed here with Ahmed Kadri, former economist for the Syrian central bank and later the chief arms buyer for the Syrian armed forces. They no doubt had shared their information with the DST, who would have known about his past efforts on behalf of MI6. But he doubted that they knew much about Operation Apostate.

Greaves hauled himself up from the soft armchair as if to show some impatience. He doubted if they knew he worked for the embassy, but hell, that's why he had a good cover. 'I'm the commercial attaché at the embassy in Rabat, Major. I've known Mr. Vaux over the years when our paths crossed on various foreign assignments. I think I met you in Singapore, didn't I, Michael?'

Vaux nodded.

'Ah, yes, I see. Two globe-trotters like you are bound to come across each other quite often, I should imagine,' said the major, still skeptical. Maj. Ghali, just perceptibly, nodded to his colleague. Time to leave. Lt. Hassan stubbed out his cigarette in a large mosaic ashtray. 'Monsieur Vaux. Please keep us informed of your whereabouts while staying here in Morocco. It's just routine. You should have come to us about this missing young man in the first place, not some private operator like Faud. Meanwhile, our colleagues are already on the job of trying to trace this young man. He's probably stoned out of 'is mind in some drug house in the medina. Thank you, gentlemen.'

After the men had left in their unmarked blue Citroen C3, Greaves climbed the stairs and asked Vaux to wait in the dining room for him. Momtaz hovered, picking up glasses and the empty bottle of Evian. He asked Vaux if he could bring him something.

'No, I'm fine, Momtaz. But where's Mahmud? I haven't seen him all morning.'

'He at market, sir. *A la marché.* Back later,' said Momtaz.

Greaves came back with a small notebook. 'I have a quiver in my bow that you don't know about, my friend. In this little black book of mine, I have the phone numbers of our staff at the UK consulate in this great port city. Have you ever had occasion to deal with them? They hang out on the Rue d'Amerique du Sud, not far from the French consulate.'

'No,' said Vaux. 'I decided to give them a wide berth. I don't imagine any dealings with them would remain secure for long—a lot of Moroccan staff, for one thing.'

'My man there is tried and tested. Don't worry.' Greaves then sat down behind the long rosewood table and picked up the phone. He dialed a number. 'Hello, Duncan. George Greaves.'

Greetings were exchanged.

'I have a little job for you. Very urgent. Can I come to see you?'

Three hours later, Greaves approached Vaux at the pool. Anne was lying on her stomach, finishing off her tan. She was to leave the next morning.

'My suspicions were justified,' said Greaves. He sat down on a striped, yellow-and-white deck chair. He wore his crumpled white linen suit and pulled off his panama. Vaux saw sweat stains around the black hatband.

Vaux was just finishing chapter fifteen of Donna Leon's *Doctored Evidence*. He put the book down on the mosaic tiles. 'What are you talking about?' he asked Greaves.

'My man—he's a lowly No. 5 at the consulate here—got the duty officer in Rabat to fax over some files and pictures. Very interesting. Our visitors were DST, Vaux. Not your ordinary policemen.'

Anne turned over and shaded her eyes as she looked up to the looming hulk of George Greaves. He was taking his jacket off and wiped his brow with a starched white handkerchief. 'What's DST?' she asked.

'Direction de la Surveillance du Territoire, Morocco's secret intelligence service,' said Greaves like a man who had solved a riddle.

'Why are you so certain?' asked Vaux.

'Don't ask silly questions, Vaux. We've got files and photos of everyone who works for DST in their Tangier offices—of every man or woman who works for them throughout this great kingdom, for that matter. Rabat sent pictures of the DST team that works out of Tangier, and Bob's your uncle. Both their handsome faces stood out a mile.'

'That means they're on our case,' said Vaux.

'Well and truly. Now we have to decide whether to use their good offices or treat them as unfriendly players. Come to think of it, in this quest for the mysterious contact, our very own Mohammed, why wouldn't we seek the help of the Moroccan spooks? The guy's not betraying the state, he's betraying a terrorist cell—or cells.'

Vaux shook his head and nodded toward Anne who had turned back on her stomach and appeared to be sleeping. Greaves nodded. The subject was closed. 'Craw can decide on such a weighty matter as that,' said Vaux who picked up Donna Leon's latest thriller as Greaves got up and walked back to the villa for a delayed siesta.

Omar Sala, a.k.a. John Keen, brought Sebastian Micklethwait, a.k.a. Ed Knight, a bottle of mineral water and three dry croissants. Micklethwait was ravenous. It seemed like his last meager meal had been about twelve hours ago. But he didn't know for sure. Usually on these occasions, his English captor sat briefly on the side of his bed, watched him consume whatever was offered and then left. There had been little conversation since their first meeting. The old man, who also served the occasional snack, had been relegated to chief disposer of the stinking Willow-pattern chamber pot.

'Today, we talk, Mr. Knight,' said Omar. He handed Micklethwait's passport back to him. He had been carrying it on the night they took him.

This sounded encouraging, and Micklethwait put on a brave smile. 'That would be a nice change,' he said. 'You have some good news?'

Omar's rather stilted English seemed to relapse into a more natural Londoner's accent. 'I've been ordered to be very frank with you, mate. We are going to move you very shortly. About a two hours' journey, something like London to Brighton, know what I mean?'

Micklethwait's hopes collapsed. He had dared to hope that they were about to release him. 'Go on,' he said.

Omar got up and started to pace the room like a lawyer in a Hollywood movie. 'We know you work for the British government, so there's no point in you trying to hide that fact.'

'I wasn't going to,' said Micklethwait.

'So you are a valuable commodity, you understand. We are holding you because we believe—in fact, we *know*—that your people, with the help of the Americans, are responsible for the abduction and disappearance of one of our own: Abdul Juhayman. Your own Special Forces with their American colleagues in tow, took this valued leader from his house in the middle of the night. His wife pleaded with them—there were six raiders—but to no avail. This was three months ago and there is no trace of him. We believe this totally illegal action—what your American friends call "extraordinary rendition"—has resulted in Abdul's total disappearance. He is either dead or being held at one of your so-called black sites, in a godforsaken hole somewhere in Morocco or in some other country whose regime favors the imperialistic aims of the United States and Britain.' Omar paused. He seemed to be waiting for some response.

Micklethwait appealed to reason and logic: 'But this has nothing to do with me or the people I work for. I appall this "rendition" stuff. It's against international law, I believe. You have to understand that I am a diplomat. I work for the Foreign Office. I have no knowledge of these special maneuvers or whatever they are by Special Forces. You can't think I have any influence in this area, surely?'

'Come on, mate,' said Omar. 'Who's kidding who?'

Micklethwait appreciated the lightness of this very English remark. He felt that if he could somehow affirm their mutual English bonds, he might find that John Keen, former resident of the Edgware Road in North London's teeming Maida Vale district, had a vulnerable chink in his armor. He had, after all, English genes, an English education and probably liked pubs (before he converted to Islam), and maybe even followed soccer, the national obsession. 'OK. But why pick on me? All I want just now is to get back to Blighty and enjoy the test match. We're playing the Australians next month and we might get back the Ashes this time. Do you follow cricket, John?'

'Omar. John is another man, a man who for all intents and purposes is dead. You have no idea how fulfilled I feel as a Muslim. And no, I never did follow cricket.' Omar sat down again on the side of the bed. He put his hand on Micklethwait's exposed shoulder and pressed gently. 'You are a good-looking young man and I hate to think what could happen to you in one of our detention camps. They are in the middle of the desert and there is no escape. There are also no women. You know the Arabs.'

'Don't try and intimidate me, Omar. I'm bloody innocent of all these charges. It's got nothing to do with me.'

'But we are all fighting in the same war. You are on the other side. You and your American friends support King Mohammed the Sixth, an absolute monarch, five years on the throne since he succeeded his ruthless father, Hassan. Just like you people support the Saudis—they're very democratic!—and the Gulf States. Then there's Hosni Mubarak in Egypt, whose family wealth is probably only exceeded by Morocco's king. They call Mohammed "the predator king." He's richer than your own queen. Did you know that?'

Micklethwait said, 'All I know is that, yes, you may have a case, but why grab me off the bloody street and incarcerate *me*? What's Morocco's king got to do with me?'

Omar got up. 'The bottom line is this: once your people release Abdul Juhayman, you will be freed. Simple as that.'

'And have you communicated your demands to those you call "my people"?'

'Now we come to the bloody gist of all this, mate.' Omar's re-version to the English idiom helped to calm Micklethwait, who was beginning to see the hopelessness of the whole situation.

'We know why you are here in Morocco. We sent Mokhtar Tawil to your people and we know that you accompanied him back through Spain.'

'But who killed the poor sod?'

'That we don't really know—but we have our suspicions. The whole thing was a ruse—to get someone like you over here so we could abduct you and use you as a bargaining chip to get Abdul back. We never dreamed Tawil would be assassinated. It's still a mystery. Now you understand?'

'I think I'm beginning to. In other words, there *was* no defector from some AQIM cell. It was a trick to get someone—his UK diplomat chaperone if you like—to come here and wait to be kidnapped.'

'You've got it, mate.'

Micklethwait realized that Department B3 had fallen for the clever ruse—hook, line and sinker. 'What now, then?'

'Tell us the quickest way we can get our message to your people without endangering our security. In other words, whether it's by messenger pigeon or one of our helpers, just tell us how we contact your immediate bosses, who would then sound the alarm and get things moving. If and when we get Abdul back, you'll be free as a bird.' Omar again gently squeezed Micklethwait's bare shoulder. Then he got up and headed toward the door. 'Think about it. Give us a contact, preferably here in Morocco, so that we can get the fucking ball rolling.'

'I want to ask you one more question—'

'Go ahead, mate.'

'What made you choose Morocco? Why not join the jihad in Afghanistan?'

'Smaller pond, bigger fish. Besides, I'm not ready to be a martyr. Too much to do for the cause.'

Micklethwait thought he'd learned something that could come in useful.

***

There was a gap of only one hour between Anne's departure time on Air Maroc's Flight 141 to London and Alan Craw's arrival by British Airways. Vaux, with a heavy heart, hugged her closely and knew he was in for a black period after she left. He would miss her terribly—despite the relief of her leaving in the midst of a growing crisis. She looked dazzlingly glamorous—silver-blue chinos tucked up above her bare ankles, white sneakers and blue-striped, silk crepe de chine blouse. 'I'll miss you, darling.'

'No, you won't. You're too busy. You won't give me a second's thought.'

'Rubbish and you know it.' He held her in his arms again and they kissed each other as if she were embarking on a long journey to Asia and months would pass before they could see each other again. Mahmud, who had brought them to the airport in the old black Mercedes, stood at a distance. He had got into a lively conversation with one of the many security guards who patrolled the crowded concourse.

Her flight was announced in Arabic and French and then in English over the speaker system and Vaux walked with her to the check-in. They kissed again and, boarding pass and UK passport in hand, she joined the stream of passengers who were heading for security checks and the departure lounge. She turned to wave a final good-bye. Vaux waved back and then looked around the crowded hall for Mahmud. He caught up with him at the perfumes boutique. Mahmud embraced the young security guard and joined Vaux as they walked quickly to the area beyond the customs hall where they expected Alan Craw to soon emerge.

He came through wide, sliding automatic doors and was surrounded by several porters. They carried his four Louis Vuitton suitcases of various sizes as well as three garment bags. Vaux noted his elegant traveling clothes: a Savile Row blue lightweight suit, an incongruous khaki baseball hat with a wide visor, and the usual black Gucci loafers. To shade his eyes from the stark North African sun, Craw wore an elegant pair of Bvlgari aviator sunglasses.

Mahmud had rushed up with a trolley and loaded the bags as Craw examined his paper money closely and then paid off the porters. Vaux introduced Craw to Mahmud and they shook hands. 'How do you do?' said Craw in the classic Oxford accent he reserved for minions.

'Yes, sir,' said Mahmud quietly. He packed the suitcases into the trunk, held the rear door open for Craw while Vaux piled in behind him.

'Good trip?' asked Vaux.

'Not bad, old boy. B. A. always treats me well, you know. Can't go wrong, really.'

'Not if you travel first class,' suggested Vaux.

'Right on,' said Craw as he looked at the sparse, arid landscape that flitted past his window.

Vaux said, 'You'll like it at the villa. A beautiful place and great views.'

'What?' exclaimed Craw. 'Didn't you get my message? I only stay at one place in Tangier and that's the storied Minzah, once the haunt of our dear, departed colleagues Burgess and Maclean. Besides, it offers a bit of luxury in this bloody, flea-bitten town.' He looked into the rearview mirror to see if his derogatory description of the old port city had penetrated the mind of one of the natives.

But Mahmud concentrated on the busy road and the heavy traffic. It was Vaux who was shocked. He hadn't received any message about Craw's accommodation preferences. And to drag up the ancient history of the two most despised MI6 traitors Burgess and Maclean, seemed strange. Fifty years on, and the old hands at MI6 were still smarting from never suspecting those two brilliant double agents who had exposed the incompetence and complacency of Britain's Secret Intelligence Service.

'Well, first off, I got no messages about where you preferred to stay. There's plenty of room at the villa and I assumed you'd want to stay there. It's the center of operations at the moment—'

'One reason you failed to get my message is perhaps the fact that our secretary and Girl Friday suddenly disappeared for a long weekend—in Tangier, I gather,' said Craw testily.

So that was it. Poor, frustrated Craw was in a bad mood because of fresh evidence that he and Anne were still having it on. He remained silent for a while.

'And besides,' said Craw, 'aren't you staying at the villa that used to belong to that Syrian fellow, Kadri? I really don't think I want to be associated with that man or his sumptuous lifestyle.'

'It was his aunt's place. He got to use it when he was kicked out of Syria for being a Sunni when the Alawite purges were going on. I visited him there while we were running Operation Couscous, if you remember.'

'Oh yes, Vaux. I remember, all right. Actually, to be fair, it was a feather in your cap. The end result, I mean.'

This is a first, thought Vaux: a compliment from Alan Craw.

'Of course, your success was rather spoiled by your taking off for Cairo instead of coming back to report to us,' said Craw.

Vaux thought the old sod must have looked up the Registry archives before coming over to Morocco. 'Ancient history,' said Vaux, refusing to get drawn into explaining his actions or motivations in the early nineties. 'Mahmud, take our guest to the Minzah, please. I hope there's a room available.'

'Room? My dear Vaux, you know I always take a suite. I need the extra space for this sort of operation. Your center of operations will now be at my hotel. I hope to hell they have a vacancy.'

13

Mort Cohen was a fastidious man; his sense of decorum and general fussiness were the bane of his patient wife's existence. But Rachel loved and respected him for his commercial success and above all for his civic respectability as the UK's honorary consul, the representative of Her Majesty, Queen Elizabeth II, in the Spanish province of Melilla. Rachel had been born in Shoreditch, East London, and she and Mort were the same age. She had met him during a shiva for her departed mother. Mort had worked for her father, also now deceased.

As Cohen swept the dusty floor of what he called his bolt-hole, he thought that things would be a lot easier if Rachel could help out on this latest project—if she knew *everything* and he didn't have to hide the unpleasant facts from her. She knew all the good things, but none of the dubious things he had to do from time to time. She didn't know what 'contraband' meant, and she was blissfully ignorant of his clandestine dealings with shadowy groups of men whose agenda he was never able to grasp, anyway. These were the facts of his life. He shrugged and resigned himself to some of the immutable facets of a businessman's existence. God knew he meant well.

He would ask Magdi Kassim no questions: he would simply comply with requests, look after the prisoner. Or was he a captive, or even a hostage? He didn't know. It wasn't his business. They would pay handsomely for his services, and Kassim had promised that the project would be over within a few days.

The bolt-hole was a small room off the basement of the narrow building that for years had served as a warehouse for a variety of merchants and their wares. The building's main entrance on the Avenida Juan Carlos, just as it opens onto the grand Plaza de España, boasted a shiny brass plate informing visitors that within the drab warehouse, they could find the UK consulate there to help perplexed British travelers, tourists in trouble or in need of new passports or to fill up forms to replace a stolen one. The chances of any hapless visitor actually meeting the honorary consul were very slim, and that is where his only part-time employee, Rachel Cohen, earned her keep as far as Mort was concerned. She was unforeseeably efficient, polite and even too sociable at times (he had told her that she was not a servant to these hapless people, but the employee of an eminent member of Melilla's diplomatic corps).

He stacked two long shelves with canned food: Fray Bentos corned beef, Heinz baked beans, Canadian canned salmon and tuna, small jars of fruit salad, assorted biscuits—but no soup. There was no way to heat anything in the small room, so the 'guest' would have to make do. There were spoons and forks and one blunt table knife. He bent down to check the narrow bed: three blankets (hardly necessary this time of year and given the stuffiness of the basement) and a flattish, uncovered pillow. An upright wooden chair in the corner would serve as a table. These people couldn't expect luxuries, and in any case, he couldn't afford them.

A spy hole in the heavy, steel door would let him see the captive, and if ever the man got curious and looked through from the other side, Cohen's face would be distorted beyond recognition.

There was no moon that night. The still air was hot and heavy. They had come on schedule at 10:00 p.m., and Cohen had left the garage doors open so that they could drive the car up to the loading platform. Kassim had done this before and he knew where to press a big rubber button that lowered the garage door once they had entered. Kassim and two men helped the captive out of the car; he was handcuffed and his head was covered with a black hood. Cohen watched from his second-floor office, the door just open enough for him to see Kassim turn the heavy key in the steel door, pull it open and push the prisoner in. The two men went inside. The dim light bulb went on and the two other men stood by the car, a shiny black Audi A6 saloon. Then he saw Kassim exit the cell, close the door and turn the key. As arranged, he left the key under a wooden pallet that supported a big crate labeled TANGERINES, PRODUCT OF MOROCCO just beside the steel door. They backed the car out of the garage. The operation had taken less than ten minutes.

Cohen closed his office door and went over to his desk. He picked up the phone. 'Rachel, dear. I'm going to be late. Don't wait up.'

Rachel never argued with her husband. She laid out a cold plate of gefilte fish—his favorite late-night snack—and went to bed.

Cohen sat down at his big cluttered desk but couldn't concentrate on the invoices he had planned to prepare. He thought of the human being down there in his small bolt- hole, small as a cell but probably less comfortable. At least the captive had a small shower and toilet and plenty of food. Kassim had promised that they would move him out within three days. But what was this man's ultimate fate? Would he be killed? What had he done to deserve the wrath of his captors? He lit a cigarillo with the old Ronson lighter he had

picked up from a secondhand store on the harbor front. And he put
such existential questions aside.

Then he heard it: three loud thumps, then a short interval, and
three more bangs. It was the steel door and the captive was signal-
ing that there was something wrong. He stubbed out his cigarillo
in the old, cracked ceramic ashtray and moved quietly to his door.
He opened it and listened. Three more bangs, then a gap, and three
more.

There was no alternative. Even at this hour, someone on
the street might hear the noise and decide to find out where
the banging came from. He went down the iron staircase to the
garage, approached the door and looked in through the spy hole.
He saw a young man with longish light-brown hair just in front
of the door. He saw a fist raised and the man banged another
three times.

He had to quiet the man. But this would mean speaking, something he had avoided with all the previous prisoners. He swallowed
and tried to lower his already husky voice a few more octaves. A
Spanish nuance, perhaps, would further disguise his real voice. '*Si,
senor*. I hear you. You 'ave a problem?'

'Do you speak English?' asked Micklethwait.

'*Si senor, un poco.*'

'I need a tin opener. I'm starving, but I can't get to any food.'

'*Pronto, senor, pronto.*'

Cohen ran up the staircase and went into his office. He went
through every drawer in his desk, looked around the shelves, but
knew that there was little hope of finding a tin opener. It was too
late to expect a restaurant or a bar to be open. So he ran to his
small apartment building close by on the Calle Cervantes, took the
narrow, shaky antique elevator to the fifth floor and let himself in.
All was quiet, his wife fast asleep. He flew into the kitchen, opened
several drawers and failed to find a good old-fashioned tin opener.

He remembered his wife used something affixed to the wall by the side of the dresser. He looked at the contraption: immovable, and no use anyway without electricity.

There was no alternative. He couldn't have the man bang on the door all night. People, or—God forbid—the police, would get curious and annoyed, and he faced disaster if a man was found locked away in a cell. So he rang the doorbell of his neighbor. After about three minutes, a tall, gaunt, disheveled man in his pajamas opened the door slightly. When he saw Cohen, he lifted the chain latch and let him in. Cohen said he needed a can opener to make a tuna sandwich and he didn't want to disturb his wife at this hour. The tall man shrugged, smiled resignedly, and went through a long passage to his kitchen. Without a word, he gave the handy universal gadget to Cohen. '*Gracias, gracias!*' shouted Cohen as he ran down the internal fire escape for a quick exit.

When he got back to the warehouse basement, his heart pounding, he put his ear to the steel door and heard nothing. But how could he give the tin opener to the man without opening the door? Maybe it was a trick. He could be overpowered—the man looked young and strong. He had to make a quick decision. It would be expected of an honorary consul. He went over to the pallet, picked up the key and quickly unlocked the door. He opened it an inch and threw in the tin opener. He heard its clattering progress toward the cell's far wall as he quickly slammed the door and turned the key again. He heard nothing more. Micklethwait was fast asleep on his hard narrow bed.

But Cohen's worries were not over. He got home and undressed. His wife was dead to the world. He got into the bed as quietly and carefully as he could. As he began to drop off himself, it suddenly hit him. He sprang up as if thwacked by an electric shock. 'The man spoke English!' he shouted.

'What man?' muttered his wife.

***

Alan Craw thanked Vaux for dealing with the people on the front desk and securing a suite on the third floor. His bags still unpacked, Craw stood at the long windows and checked the view. He saw a rather shabby, winding street that went down to the Grand Socco and further into the medina. 'No sea view but it will do,' said Craw.

'The problem is that this place is as unsecure as any house telephone,' said Vaux. He had visions of Craw coming up to the villa on a daily basis to supervise the operation despite his reluctance to go near Ahmed's old place.

'You're not telling me that your phone lines at the villa are secure,' said Craw.

'No. I've been using Greaves's portable encryption device.'

'Micklethwait was issued one of those gadgets. I wonder where it is now?'

'If we knew that we might have a clue as to *his* whereabouts,' said Vaux.

Craw approached the mini-bar. 'Care for something, Vaux?'

'I could use a beer.'

Craw presented him with a can of Flag Spéciale, a hoppy, brown local ale. 'Message from Sir Nigel: "Keep up the good work." Now I'm here, we must all redouble our efforts. First, what about this MI6 fellow from the Rabat embassy—Greaves?'

'He's been very helpful.'

'Yes, but we don't need him to be reporting back to Vauxhall on all our moves. We're semiautonomous at Department B3. I don't have to tell you that. So get rid of him. Send him back to Rabat and thank him for all his help.'

'Talking of which, he helped to confirm that the two gendarmes that came up to visit us were DST officers.'

'Um. Well, I've no doubt he has excellent contacts in this part of the world. So we'll use him as and when we see fit. But do send him back to his lair. We'll use his talents when we feel they are needed,' said Craw. He had given himself a large vodka and was about to mix it with dark-red tomato juice from a small can he'd found in the recesses of the minibar.

Vaux had remained standing as he finished off the beer. He knew Craw would be noncommittal, but he had to ask the obvious question. 'So what is our strategy, Alan?'

'First, I want to see your own plans. We have to get Micklethwait back, that's bloody obvious. That's the number-one priority. Forget about this defector who'd promised to give us the goods on AQIM's terrorist strategies in the Maghreb. If he shows up, well and good, but he may never show up. This man Tawil was supposed to be the go-between to help us contact him—Mohammed, to use his code name.

'But his murder on the Madrid night express put the kibosh on all of that. The cold-blooded killing of his envoy in the compartment next to Micklethwait's could have scared him away from doing anything for us. In short, Vaux, I think you've been wasting your time—putting Micklethwait out there as bait to haul in this character. I don't have to remind you that your strategy has ended in disaster.'

Vaux said, 'Look, kidnapping is an old terrorist tactic. Al-Qaeda and its affiliates have extorted millions in recent years. And the West has generally given in to their demands to get their people back and avoid bloodshed. How many missionaries have been taken as pawns, how many charity and health workers, how many journalists?

'What we have to do, it seems to me, is make contact. We have to wait. They had a reason for taking Micklethwait, and we can't do too much unless they start communicating and tell us what they want in return for our man.'

'You are right. I'm just getting orientated, old boy. I didn't mean to criticize you. You did your best. But it was obviously the wrong tactic. Instead of luring the defector, you lured the terrorists. Nothing more to be said. What do we do now?'

'I think we need some help—in manpower, I mean. Not brainpower but brawn. We'll need Special Forces—just a few, in case it comes to some sort of confrontation. Our opponents are violent and ruthless people, so we need some physical backup—some firepower, if you like.'

Craw looked stunned. 'This is a bit unlike you, Vaux. I thought you were one of those cerebral types who had faith in brainpower rather than military muscle.' Craw went back to look at the bustling crowds walking down to the souk and the small shops in the medina. He had his hands behind his back. 'Of course, we don't know yet who is holding our probationer. It may have nothing to do with terrorism. Could be just a straight kidnapping for ransom.'

'That I very much doubt,' said Vaux.

They agreed to meet later. But Craw had one last comment. 'Get this chap Greaves to leave you with the encryption device. We'll be needing it to talk to London.'

***

It was not a common occurrence, but when it did happen, it was not interpreted as a social or even friendly call. Sir John Livermore, the current head of MI6, known simply and sometimes affectionately as 'C', invited Sir Nigel Adair, head of his B3 subgroup, to lunch. Sir John's favorite location for such confidential assignations was a corner table in the gilded sumptuousness of the River Room at the storied Savoy Hotel, hostelry of the rich and famous. Across the room, he would often observe the lively antics of film stars, stage and TV actors, playwrights, celebrity authors and theatrical impresarios. These performances often provided agreeable distractions from the business at hand.

The two men could have been brothers: both had thick steel-gray hair that curved over the ears in leonine luxuriance. Both habitually wore dark-gray suits and both often boasted their Oxford college ties—Sir John had gone to Balliol, Sir Nigel to slightly less prestigious New College. They were both in their late fifties and had spent their lives as sedentary, behind-the-desk spymasters who trudged home to the suburbs every evening where neighbors thought they were 'something in the City.'

They met at noon, and Sir John, after ordering two large vodka martinis without checking Sir Nigel's preferences, came quickly to the point. 'My CIA liaison chap's been in a flap about your Moroccan venture. To put it as succinctly as I can, Langley wants us to cease and desist. They're handling it—and, as you know, they have the manpower in that area of the world.'

Sir Nigel winced as his first sip of vodka trickled down his parched throat. It was late June and the temperature hovered around thirty degrees. The meteorologists had forecast a long, hot summer. Through the tall windows they could see the heat haze rise from the Thames whose busy river traffic, for some reason, always reminded Sir Nigel of Britain's long and illustrious history. 'I had lunch a few days ago with Murray Sinclair. He never mentioned anything about this. And I certainly didn't brief him on the Moroccan deal. Can I ask how the CIA knew anything about our current operations there?'

'Come on, Nige, that's a silly question.'

Sir Nigel said, 'I'm not going to pull our men out of there, if that's what you want. We're making good progress, and this little job's cut out for the sort of work we're supposed to be good at. Craw's over there now and we have other assets whom I have every confidence in.'

'I don't know—because you haven't chosen to tell me—all the details. But I gather you're dealing with some terrorist outfit for whatever reason.'

'It's more complicated than that. You remember the Arab you sent us because your people didn't want to deal with him—namely one Mokhtar Tawil?' To get Tawil's name right, Sir Nigel had flipped through a small black diary that he kept in the inside pocket of his jacket.

'Vaguely, yes. The Mid-East desk thought he was full of baloney. They checked out his story and there was no there there. Bottom line: they thought him a bit of a nutcase, an asylum seeker who could bring us no useful intelligence despite his so-called contacts among Morocco's terrorist fringe groups. Bottom line: there was a credibility problem.'

Sir Nigel thought that his chief must have nominated today as the 'day of bottom lines.' He said, 'With all due respect, John. This is my fault, I suppose. I haven't kept your people informed. First off, Tawil was just the messenger boy—the front for the high-value defector we'd hoped to bring in. But you know there's an attitude at Vauxhall Cross. The old hands there have always scoffed at B3's special assignments and freelance ventures, but what counts is the *bottom line*: we've had results—a few fiascos, yes, but many triumphs.'

Sir Nigel had given Sir John another bottom line to ponder. Sir John tried hard to recall the triumphs, but he gave his colleague the benefit of the doubt.

The sole meunière arrived, and Sir John helped himself to a few dollops of sauce béarnaise. He passed the silver sauce boat to Sir Nigel. 'Well, for God's sake, Nigel, stop being so secretive. Tell me what you know.'

'Secrecy is our profession,' said Sir Nigel. He smiled to reinforce his attempt at some lightheartedness. He sensed that 'C' was in no mood to reconsider his promise to the cousins. It seemed to be the order of the day—especially since Britain had got entangled in the Iraq war—to suck up to Washington, no matter what. Tony Blair, the prime minister, had a lot to answer for, thought Sir Nigel, and subservience to Langley was one more facet of the pushy man's dubious record.

With his silver fish knife, Sir John slid the fillet off the bone as smoothly as a veteran maître d'. 'Come on, Nige, spill the bloody beans. Stop playing cat and mouse. Fill me in, so I know what I'm talking about when that bloody Kingsley man calls.'

Sir John, who had a penchant for mixing metaphors, referred to Brad Kingsley, chief liaison officer for the Central Intelligence Agency in London. Kingsley had told him that CIA agents assigned to the Maghreb and based mainly in Algeria had detected a significant increase in communications traffic in recent days and their signals intelligence (SIGINT) sources had confirmed coded messages related to some big event—probably a massive suicide bomb attack in a major town like Casablanca, or more high-profile kidnappings to raise funds.

Sir Nigel decided that prevarication was probably counterproductive at this point. He told Sir John the whole story. Sir John's face looked flushed. 'But this is preposterous,' said Sir John. 'You mean to tell me that one of our own men has been shanghaied—you haven't yet found him and you haven't a clue where he is! What's more, this Tawil character was murdered on the Spanish night train while he was under the watchful eye of your man Micklethwait— the operative that's gone missing?

'And now you tell me you've co-opted this man Vaux to help over there. I never did understand that man—didn't he defect at one point?'

'No. After his Operation Couscous assignment—which, if you recall, turned out to be highly successful—he simply decided to give up on B3. He went to Cairo and then on to Syria to join his friend, Ahmed Kadri.'

'But weren't those two lover boys? Much like that unlamented traitorous couple, Burgess and Maclean?' Sir John now downed the last drop of his second large martini.

Sir Nigel was at a loss to see the relevance of Sir John's assertions, and as the man who had called Vaux in from the cold, he went to his defense. 'They were old university friends. Bristol, I think. Hardly lovers. In fact, John, my current, very attractive secretary has had a steady affair with Vaux for some years. Besides, the Burgess and Maclean business happened when we were toddlers. Why can we never file that regrettable case away in your dusty archives at Registry and forget the whole damn fiasco?'

'Our files don't get dusty these days—they're all on discs or tapes or whatever, so far as I know.'

The two men came to a very British compromise. Sir John would hold off any CIA meddling for two weeks, during which Department B3 would have to find young Micklethwait. If the mystery defector, the man who had sent the late Tawil over to work out a deal with the SIS, showed up, then it would be a happy bonus.

14

Mort Cohen had a sleepless night. The situation was totally unacceptable. They had never told him he would be engaged in a coconspiracy to incarcerate an English prisoner—a citizen of the nation he officially represented in this small Spanish enclave, a geographical chunk of North Africa that Morocco claimed was theirs.

It was no exaggeration to say that he was in a total state of panic. Cooperating with these Moroccan adventurers was one thing, so long as it boosted his total revenues. But to be a party to a presumed abduction of a subject of Her Britannic Majesty was beyond the pale. Exposure of his treachery could mean a messy end to the life he had built over the last decade or so—a shameful dismissal from his official appointment as honorary consul and the collapse of his business enterprise.

He riffled through a cluttered drawer at the top of his antique, kneehole desk. Here it was: his passport's first page. His duty was written in quaint English, but the message was clear to all and sundry: Her Majesty requested *to all those whom it may concern to allow*

*the bearer to pass freely without let or hindrance…and to afford the bearer
such protection as may be necessary.*

If this man in the basement wasn't English and a bearer of
a British passport, *he* wasn't a Jew. What if all this went terribly
wrong? Who was this man? A hitchhiker taken off the highway? A
political agent, a spy?

He had heard no noise from the bolt-hole. The garage remained
empty. There had been no consulate car since the Foreign and
Commonwealth Office (FCO) had carried out the sweeping budget
cuts forced through by that frugal Scotsman Gordon Brown, then
and to this day Prime Minister Blair's chancellor of the exchequer.
Today, he expected no deliveries of any sort, so at least he would
not have to deal with anyone who might detect his panic. He got
up from the desk and looked through the long windows to the busy,
sun baked Plaza de España. Across from his building he noticed a
stocky figure in a panama hat and white linen suit. The man walked
briskly in the direction of the port. Probably another Englishman,
he thought.

But the vision had triggered his memory. The man from the
Rabat embassy who some time ago had decided to make a social call
on his country's honorary consul in Melilla had said he was always at
his service should the need arise. Well, it bloody well had. He didn't
know what he was going to do. But this situation was intolerable,
and he couldn't live with himself if he went on doing business with
these brigands to the detriment of the very people whose safety and
security he had sworn to protect.

The man had left a business card. Where was it? Again, he
riffled through all the desk drawers. It was nowhere to be found.
When had the English diplomat come on that surprise visit? Maybe
eighteen months ago. He went over to a long wooden shelf where a
collection of job-related books had gathered dust as they sat there,
never consulted. He dragged his forefinger along the spines of several big tomes—*Who's Who* (1990 edition), an even fatter *Debrett's*

Peerage and Baronetage in red-and-gold binding, a battered 1979 edition of Fodor's *Morocco,* a pocket-sized *Atlas of the World,* and a small, dog-eared English-Spanish *Minidiccionario*. But books of reference, no matter how prestigious, were no help to him now.

His mind was wandering. He told himself it must be a defensive mechanism. His heart pounded—a panic attack or, God forbid, a coronary? He hadn't heard from Magdi Kassim. How long was he expected to put up with this situation? Then he remembered. Deep in the recesses of an official Diplomatic Corps attaché case he hardly ever used, he was pretty sure he would find a red, leather-covered book that listed all the British embassies and consulates around the world. It had been a gift from the FCO a few years back—a Christmas gift in lieu of a bonus, he had told his wife. The attaché case was stashed in the bottom drawer of the E–H steel filing cabinet.

***

Like Mort Cohen, Faud el-Mullah was in the midst of a severe emotional crisis. But unlike Cohen, the cause for his concerns was not a question of personal survival. At the root of his restlessness was the urge to get back to that world of secrecy and confidential exchanges, of anticipating treachery from your closest allies or shared intelligence from those who used ambiguity to camouflage their true loyalties—in short, a desire to get back into action. He was poised on the verge of becoming useful again. He knew the players and his seasoned intuition told him that gathering forces were about to embark on a conflict whose resolution no one could foretell.

The man he knew as Ed Knight, whose abduction he had witnessed and duly reported to Michael Vaux, that old hand in British intelligence, was still presumably being held. But by whom—and where? What was the Englishman doing in Tangier and what was his connection to Vaux? In all his conversations with Vaux, the man had never explained his concern for the Englishman. So was he a colleague? A fellow agent, perhaps, working on some operation that he, Faud, knew nothing about?

He'd got the brush-off when he visited Hisham Toumert above the fish restaurant. Toumert, he knew, was close to a group of agitators who had played a part in the Casablanca bombings two years earlier. The Moroccan government had blamed AQIM for the outrage, particularly the so-called Free Salafist (FSG) subgroup that operates out of Algeria but is now spreading its tentacles to Morocco, its neighbor.

Faud had heard that FSG's specialty was kidnapping Western aid workers and sometimes diplomats and journalists. The ransom money—reportedly more than $50 million over the past few years—provided the funds they needed to pay bills and finance their great cause: final liberation from the West and its puppet regimes.

So here he was. There were ominous developments in his old bailiwick. He knew from past experience that persistent digging would yield information that would be useful to all the players in this game. And information always commanded a price.

He decided to revisit Toumert. The old man had paid him cash to stall his efforts to find out more about Vaux's mission. And he had told him that there were 'developments about which I cannot talk.' Those were his words—and he had told him to wait for instructions.

Well, he had waited long enough. He headed for the fish restaurant on the Avenue d'Espagne, just over from the beach.

To his surprise, Hisham Toumert welcomed him warmly. '*Salaam. Allahu Akbar!*' Greetings. God is great! He motioned Faud to sit on the low, scuffed leather couch under the slow-moving ceiling fan. 'Faud, dear friend, you have come at just the right moment.

Things are starting to move. I want you to take a message to this man Vaux at the Villa Mauresque, on the mountain. You know the place, I think.'

Faud thought that this could compromise his position as Vaux's confidential agent—the man he had hired to help find the missing Englishman.

Toumert, whose large forehead was beaded with sweat, noticed Faud's hesitancy. 'What's the problem, dear friend? You'd just be the messenger. You would not be implicated in any way.'

'I am trying to build on his trust, Hisham. He would ask where the message came from and what did I know about the sender.'

Toumert's habitual smile changed to sudden concern. 'But what are your dealings with this Englishman? Please explain why his "trust" is so important to you at this moment. At our last meeting, you told me about this man Vaux's arrival and his background with British intelligence. I asked you to hold off any investigations until further developments in our current plans.'

'I promised Vaux I would find the missing Englishman, Edward Knight. They are friends, or perhaps colleagues. Knight, who stayed at El Minzah, was taken suddenly by persons unknown. So I have the burden of finding where this man is and reporting back to Vaux.'

His elbow resting on his desk, Toumert put his hand up to his hot forehead to rest his heavy head. This, he told himself, was getting complicated. And he liked to keep things simple so that there was only a very narrow margin for error. 'Faud, my friend. In our previous discussion, you told me you were looking for a man called Tawil, Mokhtar Tawil. Now I learn you are searching for some Englishman. Are you trying to open a "missing persons" bureau?'

Faud's face betrayed a reluctance to treat current matters with any levity. The two men were silent. Toumert raised his head and shuffled some papers on his desk. He had made a decision.

'I can tell you now that Tawil is dead. He was murdered on the train that he had taken in Paris to return here. He was on a mission to bring over a representative of the British government. He was working for us. And we still don't know why he was killed or who perpetrated the foul deed. But we needed a hostage to further our plans generally; but in particular, to persuade the British bastards to free our beloved Abdul Juhayman from one of their black sites, or wherever they are holding him. So our expected hostage duly arrived—but without our loyal Tawil. Simple as that, Faud. Now, will you cooperate with my people or not?'

Faud felt that he was being sucked into a whirlpool of the darkest intrigue. He had never expected Toumert to reveal such confidences. So this vanished Englishman was the captive of Toumert's associates. But who were they? There was now no turning back. 'I will do as you say, Hisham.'

'*Tamam, al-hamdoulilah!*' said Toumert. Well, thanks to God.

He rummaged through a pile of papers and produced two envelopes. On one was written: *To whom it may concern.* The other, simply: *Faud.* Later, Faud found twenty one hundred-dirham notes in his envelope—about $195.

When he got back to his home on the Rue des Postes, Faud went quickly into the kitchen and lit the small butane-gas stove. He poured water into a stained saucepan. The steam and a sharp Berber dagger helped him prize open the flap. He read the message:

> *The price of Mr. Knight's freedom is the*
> *release of our friend and ally Abdul*
> *Juhayman, taken from his home in*
> *April, 2005.*
> *Leave official response at synagogue in*
> *Rue des Synagogues, under loose stone*
> *at base of first pillar of right-hand nave.*

Faud pressed down on the envelope to reseal the flap. He would arrange delivery of the ransom note tomorrow.

***

Brad Kingsley, chief of the Central Intelligence Agency's UK liaison committee, was a stalwart patriot, a CIA career man who, as he shaved every morning, proudly but quietly cited his employer's august motto: 'The Truth Shall Set You Free.'

'Yessiree,' he would mutter as he wiped away what was left of the shaving cream. In the shower on this particular morning, as his wife made coffee and scrambled some eggs, he had thought about his meeting with Sir John Livermore and the follow-up phone conversation when he had promised to 'press the pause button' on any planned action to step up the CIA's ongoing anti-terrorist drive in the Maghreb. Frankly, he was skeptical that the Brits could, within the fourteen-day deadline, come up with anything substantial to explain the SIGINT data on the sudden increase in telecommunications 'chatter' among suspected terrorist cells in the region.

Kingsley, a tall man in his forties with a short crew cut, wore rimless spectacles and conservative Brooks Brothers gray suits. Some of his younger colleagues said he looked like the son of former President Lyndon Johnson's controversial defense secretary, Robert McNamara. But he wasn't. His father had been a New York plumber whose main aim in life was to see his son through college. It was a version of the American dream—and worth fighting for. And Kingsley told himself he was in the front line.

After talking with Sir John, his first move had been to pick up the red secure phone and punch in the code for the US embassy on the Avenue de Mohamed El Fassi in Rabat.

'Yes,' said Bill Harvey, officially, the embassy's deputy cultural attaché.

'Bill—Brad here.'

'Yes, sir, what can I do for you?'

'Just to follow up on our talk last week. There's a Mossad agent who could be useful. Look him up in the directory. He's a member of the royal court—you know, the king's entourage. He has his fingers on many pulses, and he's our link man with the *sayanim*, who could be key in this particular operation.'

Harvey scribbled this new word on his writing pad. 'What makes you say that?' he asked.

'No names, no pack drill, OK? But our Moroccan friends tell us that somehow, a Spanish Jew is involved in this latest hornet's nest. You know how the Jews stick together—especially in that part of the world. The *sayanim* would be the obvious "go-to" outfit on this one.'

'I'll look into it.'

Bill Harvey was new to the job. He had been posted from the backwaters of the Caribbean to fill the shoes of Murray Sinclair, his predecessor in Rabat, who had dropped dead at an extravagant embassy reception six weeks earlier. The autopsy gave the cause of death as a heart attack. No one was suspicious. Sinclair had had a history of cardiovascular troubles.

Harvey got up from his desk, stretched his arms, and to kill a sudden urge to smoke, peeled off a strip of Wrigley's Spearmint gum. He began to chew while he pondered his next move. He wasn't about to expose his ignorance of the Mideast milieu, even if he hadn't been in the saddle more than a month or so. So he sauntered into the outer office where two Moroccan girls clad in traditional hijab were busy typing. He walked through to the small records room. There were some twenty steel filing cabinets and he knew which one would contain the information he wanted. The affixed label read: ANTI-TERRORISM.

He took out the file and went back to his desk. He ran his finger up and down the amateurish stapled index—compiled, he figured, by someone who meant well but whose reliability was doubtful. But he did find what he had hoped to. He ran his finger over the word his London-based senior had used: *sayanim*. He riffled through the file pages and found the relevant entry.

According to our sources, the sayanim are diaspora Jews who for 'patriotic' reasons collaborate with the Mossad or other Zionist agencies and provide them with assistance as required...The sayanim organization is a worldwide network of non-Israeli Jewish operatives.

Harvey sighed. Somehow the gum had lost its zest and he ejected the gooey ball into an old and tarnished tin ashtray.

15

Vaux was preparing to leave with Mahmud for a breakfast meeting with Alan Craw. Craw had phoned the previous evening to say that he had studied Vaux's update on the situation and was now ready to take action—his words. Vaux was looking forward to what Craw had to say. Mahmud had driven the Mercedes round to the white double-front doors and stood waiting. As Vaux came out of the ivory marble hallway, he saw a boy in his early teens running up to the house. He wore a long cotton shirt that just covered his knees. Vaux noted that the boy's Roman caligae sandals were in a good state of repair. 'Mister, mister. This for you, please!' shouted the boy as he waved the envelope at both men.

Mahmud took the envelope, examined it quickly and handed it to Vaux. Vaux said, '*Choukran, choukran,*' and fished a five-dirham note out of his pocket and gave it to the young messenger. The boy smiled, turned and ran back to the gates.

Vaux read the ransom note. Mahmud watched as he saw Vaux's eyebrows rise and fall several times—a sign of surprise and astonishment, he would tell his café friends later.

Vaux knew that this changed everything. Craw's 'action plan' would be thrown out the window before anyone bothered to read it. He sat back in the soft backseat of the car and admired the beautiful pink-and-white villas and their lush, tropical gardens as they rushed by on their way down the sun-dappled mountain road to the Place de France.

He found Craw in the internal courtyard where breakfast was served. He wore a white-and-blue striped seersucker, the sort of lightweight summer suit favored by New Yorkers. A blue shirt and the usual broad-striped blue-and-black Worcester College silk tie. He was carving into a huge slice of ham accompanied by two poached eggs.

Vaux, in his usual khaki chinos, navy-blue blazer and brown oxfords, approached the table. Craw stood up to welcome him, his chair scraping on the flagstone floor. They had met only yesterday. Vaux wondered if such a formal gesture had any significance. Perhaps Craw's arrival meant that Vaux's usefulness to Department B3 was over. But Vaux had news for him. After he ordered a café crème, Vaux handed over the opened envelope.

Craw looked at it as if he knew it contained only bad news. Perhaps he had had a premonition about notes handed to him out of the blue and just as his planned operations were about to get underway. He propped the envelope against a silver coffee pot and went on eating. 'This ham is to die for,' said Craw. 'Amazing, really, considering it's a Muslim country, eh?'

'It's an international hotel, Alan. With only a handful of Muslim guests, I would imagine.'

'Yes, I suppose you're right. After all, you know this territory better than anyone. You keep coming back, too.'

'Mainly an accident—or accidents—of history,' said Vaux. He waited for the question he knew Craw was dying to ask. While

Craw finished off his ham and eggs, Vaux tore apart a big croissant and chewed on it until the arrival of his coffee.

Finally, Craw wiped his big plate with the crust of his toasted bread. 'All right, Vaux. What's this all about?'

'The envelope?' asked Vaux. He was always reluctant to make it easy for Craw, so he chose not to give him the gist of the short message.

'Damn it, yes. The envelope, Vaux.'

'You'd better read what's inside,' suggested Vaux.

Craw delved into the envelope and pulled out the hand-written note. As he read it, his face betrayed no emotion. He laid out the note on the table and smoothed the curling edges. He said nothing for at least three minutes while his eyes never moved from the text of the message. Vaux remained silent. He guessed Craw needed time to get his mental processes to kick into action. 'I've never heard of this man they want released.'

'But at least it means we can get Micklethwait back,' said Vaux.

'Perhaps.' The old, familiar, cautious Craw.

'Alan, we'll have to act within a couple of days. At least we're now in touch with his kidnappers.'

'Yes, by way of a synagogue, of all things. These bloody terrorists at least have a sense of humor—or perhaps irony.'

'It's the only synagogue left in Tangier. Kadri took me there when he was showing me around town—some years ago now,' said Vaux.

***

Faud had watched the boy run up the road to the wrought-iron gates of the Villa Mauresque and waited in the shade of a tall plane tree for the return of his messenger. When the boy ran back, Faud demanded to know if he had been tipped for his trouble. '*Baksheesh!*

Show me,' he demanded. The boy opened his fist; Faud took the tattered note and gave him two dirham coins in return.

'*Imshee, imshee!*' Go away! The boy bowed slightly and ran down the road toward the medina.

His main task achieved with absolute anonymity, Faud turned left down a narrow lane lined with makeshift ateliers with corrugated iron roofs and breeze-block walls, used by iron workers, car mechanics and electricians. There were fixer-uppers of used furniture, the occasional stall of Arabic bric-a-brac and secondhand cooking stoves and clapped-out iceboxes. Bargain hunters flocked around old clothes stalls, and sometimes from among the crowd a man would rush up to greet Faud, shake his hand, or hold his arm. But on this day, Faud had no time for idle talk or gossip. He had made up his mind. He was about to embark on a simple plan that he was certain would not only solve the riddle of the missing Englishman but yield great personal rewards.

The small Hotel Marco Polo stands at the corner of the narrow Rue Marco Polo as it turns onto the Avenue d'Espagne, Tangier's busy, traffic-clogged Corniche. The guest rooms are sometimes rented by the hour and even if the tourist wished to stay the night, the room rate never exceeded two hundred dirhams, about twenty-five dollars. For the locals, the rate was even lower. Faud handed over sixty dirhams for three nights to the old white-haired man behind the reception counter. They had known each other for nearly half a century, so Faud knew he could figure on an ample discount. Besides, the old proprietor liked to have the occasional long-term resident—it added a little class to the old, rundown hotel. The proprietor handed Faud the key and two threadbare towels. Faud walked up the narrow stairs to the third floor.

He had chosen this particular room because he knew its sash windows looked directly onto the fish restaurant below Hisham Toumert's office. The room was small, with a double bed that sagged into a hollow in the center and with pillows stained by hair oil and sweat. But this was to be Faud's center of operations. From this handy lookout post, he would observe the comings and goings of everyone who did business with Toumert. He had checked that the office on the first floor had no other exit than through the ground-floor entrance of the fish restaurant.

***

Micklethwait lay on the hard narrow bed listening for sounds—any sound that might give a hint of his location. Once he thought he heard the low, vibrating blast of a ship's siren and he guessed he must still be in Tangier. But he had noticed also that the labels on the food cans were in English or Spanish. In Tangier, he remembered from his walks around the town, the labeling was mainly in Arabic. He opened another large bottle of Mondariz mineral water, another Spanish brand. There were still some twenty bottles left. And then what? Food was plentiful but monotonous, and sometimes he craved for some bread or fresh vegetables to go with the canned protein.

But he was grateful for small mercies: he could tell the difference between night and day, thanks to the gap at the bottom of the steel door. He could also hear the clatter and rattle of a roll-up metal door as if his cell were inside a large garage. Occasionally, he had heard the roar of a truck engine and men shouting as they unloaded their goods. Exhaust fumes confirmed his suspicions that he was hidden away in a big garage attached to a warehouse—better, perhaps, than being alone in some desert hole far from any other human being. He had tried to get attention by banging on the door, but the garage was noisy and his efforts unheeded.

He heard the rattle of keys. The steel door opened and he saw a man he never dreamed he'd be happy to see again: John Keen, a.k.a. Omar Sala. He spoke his kind of English and now perhaps he would get some answers. And for some reason, his hopes were raised by the western garb Keen wore: a black T-shirt and blue jeans. But barefooted in leather sandals and still the long hair of hippiedom.

Micklethwait got up and put out his hand to greet the jihadist from the Edgware Road. After all, he told himself, he was still a bloody Englishman. But Keen/Sala didn't take his hand. He merely nodded in acknowledgment of the gesture. He sat down on the high-backed chair Micklethwait used as a table to eat on. His tin opener was tossed onto the bed and a few bits of corned beef were brushed onto the floor. Micklethwait sat down on the side of the bed and waited.

'You will soon be transferred out of here, my friend,' said Omar. 'It hasn't been too bad, I hope.' He produced a pocket-sized tape-recorder. He punched the RECORD button and placed it on the floor. Micklethwait thought he probably had to report back to his militant bosses to give them the flavor of his conversations with the infidel.

But at least he's playing Mr. Nice Guy. 'Could be worse, I suppose.' Micklethwait was not yet ready to play nice. He was affronted by this nonsense, and the longer it went on the harder it was to like or respect this interlocutor or whatever he was.

'Look, why don't you see my point of view? It might make things easier for you—at least in the long run.'

'What's that supposed to mean? I'm not interested in the long run, John—or is it Omar today? You have to release me. The Brits know I'm missing and it won't be long before all the security forces in this part of the world will be searching for me. And when they find me, what will happen to you and your cohorts?'

John Keen dismissed Micklethwait's question with a derisive laugh. 'I want you to understand what motivates me. Then perhaps we have a chance to see eye to eye. Maybe then you will join our struggle. Not like me, of course. I have embraced Islam. We don't expect you to do that at this juncture of your life. But there are ways

you can help us—when and if we let you return to your old life. We
know you work for British intelligence, Edward. There's no point
in denying it. You came here with our man Tawil in order to ensure
the defection of a traitor to our cause. You were to arrange for this
mysterious Judas to get back to London and to spill the beans—as
we say in jolly old England—about our plans in the Maghreb and
our contribution to AQIM's overall strategies. No?'

Micklethwait said, 'My name is Edward Knight, and I work
for the Foreign and Commonwealth Office in London. I came to
Tangier on holiday.' That statement, thought Micklethwait, approxi-
mated to the old military order to personnel captured by the enemy: *Only reveal name, rank and number.*

John Keen smiled again. 'Why do you and the Americans continue to prop up King Mohammed, whose greed and corruption
even exceeds those of Saudi Arabia and the ruling families of the
Gulf States?'

'I'm not responsible for the British government's policies in
this matter,' said Micklethwait.

'Do you have any moral hesitation, let's say, in supporting this
tyrant—who, like his father, has acquiesced in the torture and
murder of thousands of Muslims who have fought for liberty and
justice?'

'How can I comment? I don't know the facts...'

'But you know that your government and the Americans continue to support this man? Even the Moroccan government's own
Truth Commission, set up last year, found that during Hassan's long
reign at least ten thousand Moroccans died in the prisons or were
killed by the police forces. Hassan's son also has the blood of many
Moroccan patriots on his hands, my friend. Many students have
been killed in recent years as well as many ordinary citizens—just
because they held demonstrations for more democracy or against
soaring bread prices. These are facts, Edward. I want you to be
aware of why we are fighting this battle. It is not just to spread the

word of Islam, it's a struggle for justice and democracy—the same as you have in the West.'

'Ah, so you admit we are democratic and have a viable justice system!' said Micklethwait.

'But what's good for the West is not offered by you people to the three hundred and fifty million or so inhabitants of the Arab world! How about some justice for the Palestinians? Occupied by the Israelis for forty years, and never any real Western pressure on the Israelis to get out and give some dignified freedom to the Palestinians.

'The Palestinians have been handed the bill for the holocaust— and they had nothing to do with that unspeakable evil. They are the Semitic cousins of the Jews. Yet they lost their homes and their land—and continue to do so with the building of more and more settlements all over Palestine's West Bank.' John Keen got up from the chair. 'Think about it, Edward. Join our cause, work for us. Right is on our side, my friend. And the sooner you see the light, the sooner you will gain your freedom.'

'And what if I agree to work for you and as soon as I am free I change my mind?'

'I think even you must know we have long tentacles. Just like the Mossad, my friend, no one is safe or secure if we feel they work against us and betray our cause. Perhaps you can start to help us by naming your man in Morocco who would be close to this situa- tion—perhaps the man you came to join.'

Micklethwait said, 'I came to join no one. As I told you, I came here for a few days' holiday. I suggest you contact the British gov- ernment through the embassy in Rabat.'

'I thought there could be a more direct route to a negotiator who understands our position. We need someone to talk to,' said Keen, almost sadly.

Communications between the various factions of the militants was erratic, at best. Keen had not been told of Hisham Toumert's recent, successful efforts to establish contact with their adversaries. So he pressed on.

'Once we can start a parley with your people, the sooner we can get Juhayman released and the sooner you'll be a free man. That's all I'm saying. Then you can take your time and decide whether you want to join our just cause.' Keen now stood at the door. 'Be ready to move out tomorrow. Perhaps by then, you will be more cooperative.'

'Does that mean you're going to let me go?'

'No. We are taking you back to our country.' Keen slammed the door, and Micklethwait heard the key turn. His mind raced over an imaginary map of North Africa. He was probably in Algeria, then.

Earlier, Mort Cohen had expected Magdi Kassim, not this hippie with an English accent. Even so, he had been polite. He offered John Keen a coffee (every morning Rachel gave him a thermos flask of hot black coffee), but Keen shook his head. He wanted to see the man they were holding. He wasn't there on a social call. When Keen climbed back up the wrought-iron stairs to Cohen's office, he told him that the man would be taken away the next day. He thanked him for his services. Cohen breathed a sigh of relief. The man had been driving a Jeep TJ and when he went to the window to see Keen drive away, he noted the Moroccan license plates. He knew that the last number would indicate where the Jeep was registered in Morocco. He wrote all the numbers down before he forgot them.

16

Alan Craw was shaken by the ransom note. He changed his mind about operating out of the Villa Mauresque. It was probably more secure than the hotel, he told Vaux, who had commented that the Minzah was infested with secret agents and corrupt staff with malleable loyalties. And the old-fashioned phone system could only be used for the most innocent conversations. 'Have you checked this place for bugs?' asked Craw as if to justify his earlier reluctance to use the villa as the center of operations.

They were sitting at the long rosewood table in the dining room. The encrypted mobile phone reluctantly bequeathed by Greaves sat in front of the two men. 'Why would anyone bug this place? Anything to do with espionage and its agents disappeared along with Ahmed Kadri and me several years ago. Besides, Ahmed's servants were all very loyal to him and his aunt who owned the place.'

Craw, now nervous about the way things were shaping up and worried about what to do in the face of Micklethwait's abduction, grunted as if to suggest some skepticism. 'What about the current staff? Mahmud—you trust him?'

'I have no reason not to,' said Vaux. 'Anyway, this phone's super secure.'

'Yes, but an eavesdropper can hear you speaking into it,' warned Craw.

'So we'll speak softly and muffle our words. The fact that none of the staff here speaks good English is another plus.'

'I suppose you're right.'

Vaux wanted to stop wasting time with Craw's hypercautious approach. 'So, are we going to call Sir Nigel now?'

'Yes, go ahead. You tell him I am here, and then hand me the phone.'

Anne answered the phone at Department B3's offices and was delighted to hear Vaux's voice.

'Darling, I can't talk. I'll call you as soon as I can—tonight, perhaps. Meanwhile, we urgently need to speak to the boss.'

'Which one?' asked Anne.

'Don't be silly—Sir Nigel, of course.'

'Because my other boss, Mr. Craw, is away at the moment,' said Anne.

'Yes, I know. He's sitting right beside me.'

Without another word, she put him through.

'Who did you say?'

'They call him Abdul Juhayman,' said Craw, who had taken the phone from Vaux as soon as he heard his chief's voice.

'Never heard of him—but then I wouldn't, would I? He's not exactly a household name here in the UK.'

'No, sir. The thing is, we must find out where this man is being held. Then negotiations can get underway and we'll get Micklethwait back.'

'So where should I go? Special Forces, I suppose.'

'I would check with your contacts at the CIA, sir. They operate these black sites, I understand. They surely must have a list of suspected terrorists they are holding.'

'I'll have to discuss this first with Sir John.'

Craw hoped his name would come up when Sir Nigel discussed the crisis with MI6's top man.

***

From the sea-salt encrusted sash windows of his shabby room, Faud peered through a pair of battered old French army-issue Jules Huet et Cie. binoculars. He focused on the entrance to the fish restaurant on the Avenue d'Espagne. It was about midday and the dead-calm sea glittered like silver from the high sun. He saw a Jeep TJ drive up and a man in jeans and black shirt jump out and enter the busy lunchtime restaurant. It was the same man he had seen a few days earlier. He had gone into the restaurant and the man had disappeared—presumably up the stairs to Toumert's office. The man stayed in the building about half an hour and then took off, heading east to Cap Malabata.

Faud went downstairs to the small front desk. No one was there. He picked up the old rotary phone and dialed. He arranged a car to be at his disposal from early the next morning.

***

Bill Harvey lost no time in communicating with Elias Mansour, a veteran politician in his seventies whose friendship with King Hassan, the present king's late father, dated back to their childhoods. He had been a member of Hassan's royal court, a sort of kitchen cabinet that in medieval fashion had ruled over Morocco for decades. Mansour was the chief architect of a rapprochement with Israel that led to cooperation between the two countries in intelligence matters and in the acceleration in the emigration of Moroccan Jews to Israel. The besieged Israelis always thought of Mansour as their friend and ally and subsequent Israeli cash payments in offshore tax havens ensured his loyalty to their cause and, not incidentally, King Hassan's blessing to the North African version of the entente cordiale.

Contact between Harvey and Riad Zandberg, a senior operative of the *sayanim*, was arranged via a dead-letter drop whose location Harvey had learned over lunch with Mansour at the plush brasserie at the Hôtel la Tour Hassan. Harvey's note simply asked for an early meeting on an urgent matter.

Zandberg replied within twenty-four hours via a secure phone line to the US embassy. 'Of course, I will help if I can. Please meet me tomorrow at the Café Maure. It's in the Casbah beside the Andalusian Gardens. Say, three in the afternoon. They have wonderful pastries.'

'Sounds good,' said Harvey. It would be his first visit to the renowned Kasbah des Oudaias. He hoped it wouldn't be too touristy.

After lunch the next day, he got Joan, his middle-aged American secretary, to help wire him for the meeting with Zandberg. He didn't want any misunderstandings—his conversation with this man who apparently worked for Mossad, yet seemed to be cheek-by-jowl with high-ranking Moroccan officials, would be recorded to prevent any second-guessing by his superiors. He was told Zandberg would be reading *Time* over a glass of mint tea. He boasted a heavy beard and would be wearing a black suit, white open-necked shirt and sandals.

Harvey saw him at a corner table, an open *Time* in his hands over a plate of half-eaten pastries and crumbs.

They shook hands but didn't use any names.

'You must be the new man,' said Zandberg, whose heavy salt-and-pepper beard was speckled with pastry crumbs.

'Yes, I've been here just a few weeks.'

Zandberg looked around the café for possible CIA watchers or DST agents who, despite his contacts with the palace, often shadowed him. He recognized a Mossad security guard and he decided that he would have to make known his disapproval of this overzealous urge to protect him.

Harvey said, 'The Brits have a hostage situation on their hands. They have told us that an AQIM terrorist outfit took one of their own men who had been sent here on some mission. So far, they haven't said what that mission is all about.'

Zandberg asked how much money they were demanding.

'Not money. They want us to release a party that we are holding here just south of Essaouira. We moved him recently from Temara, which is getting overcrowded. We haven't admitted we are holding this man but the Brits are going bananas. They want their man back, and they haven't a clue who this Al-Qaeda guy is or where he's being held.'

Zandberg noted the tidbit of intelligence. Temara, a notorious but tolerated CIA black site just south of Rabat, was apparently full to the brim. 'Understandable. So why do you tell me this? What has it got to do with me or my organization?' asked Zandberg.

Harvey picked up a baklava cookie and fell silent as he savored the delicious combination of filo pastry, almonds and honey. 'It's a sort of side issue. May I call you Riad?'

'Of course, Mr. Harvey.'

'We understand from our sources that a Spanish Jew is involved with these people. That's all we know. But he somehow fits into the equation…'

'The what?'

'Somehow, he's involved. It seems that he's working with, or at least aiding and abetting, AQIM—and for obvious reasons, with the OK from our friends in Spain's CNI—'

'CNI? Where do they come into this?'

'Well, it seems to me that Spain's intelligence service, the Centro Nationale de Inteligencia, would presumably keep tabs on any troublesome Spanish nationals operating here in Morocco. You presumably liaise with them.'

'Of course we have contacts within the CNI. But I have very little to do with the Spanish situation.'

Harvey brushed this dubious claim aside. 'Anyway, we want to get this guy because we think he could be key to discovering this terrorist cell before it does any more harm.'

'And you think because I am Jewish, I should know this Spanish Jew who you claim is helping Moroccan terrorists to perpetrate their crimes here in Morocco?'

'We thought you could be of help, yeah.'

'Let me tell you this, Mr. Harvey. Your problem, as I see it, is to find and release this hapless English spy. If you cannot find the English gentleman and you are holding this terrorist at one of your sites, then you have the power to help the British get back their man. It's a dilemma, yes. But I cannot see any other solution.' Zandberg drank the last of his mint tea.

Harvey looked nonplussed. He wasn't getting anywhere. 'So you don't keep a check on Spanish residents here?'

'Of course, Moroccan intelligence tries to keep tabs on all sorts of immigrants. But I don't work for them. My organization, the *sayanim,* fulfills other functions. But unless you can give me a name for this Spanish Jew who's presumably also a jihadist—something, to be frank that I find highly unlikely—where do I start to look? There are thousands of Jews who are still here despite the pressure over the years to get them to move to Israel...'

'Pressure? Who from?'

'You want a brief history lesson? Look, in the eighties, there was a big push by Israel to get more Moroccan Jews to emigrate to their homeland. Any population boost is welcome in Israel. King Hassan went along with the Israelis because he thought he had little to lose—and probably something to gain in terms of getting money from the Israelis for his tacit approval of their program. But many of us remain here. I'm one of the holdouts. That's all.' Zandberg shrugged.

'OK. I'm learning something every day here,' said Harvey. Zandberg looked at his watch. The meeting was over and he rose from the table. But Harvey had one more question. 'Perhaps you could fill me in on another matter. As you know, in this Iraq war, we're facing this sectarian divide between the Sunni and the Shia. It's complicating any progress toward pacification there, according to my colleagues. What's the situation here—in Morocco? Do these people have the same problem?'

Zandberg sat down again. He was shocked that this senior emissary from the United States hadn't done his basic homework. 'Relax, Mr. Harvey. The Muslim community here is ninety-nine percent Sunni. We have no such problems as in Iraq. Our chief troublemakers are the radical fundamentalists—jihadists, if you like. But we're confident we can control the situation—with the help of the Stars and Stripes, of course.'

Both men stood up, shook hands, and Harvey promised to keep in touch.

***

In a croaking and rattly old 1970 Renault Clio, Faud tried hard to keep up with the Jeep that sped eastward toward Tetouan and Nador. He guessed his quarry was headed toward Oujda, the next sizable town but the Jeep turned a sharp left to go north toward Melilla. Faud cursed because he hadn't brought along any identification, let alone a driving license to show the Spanish border guards. When he arrived at the checkpoint, he pulled up behind a long slow-moving lineup of cars, pick-up trucks and tourist coaches. Some drivers got out and talked through open windows to other drivers; some families sauntered away from their minivans to urinate or open flasks of coffee.

The Jeep was ahead of Faud's car by about six vehicles and he decided to get out and walk toward the Jeep as if he was taking some casual exercise. As he approached the Jeep, he made sure his head and eyes turned as if he were looking at the traffic situation or toward the border checkpoint. As he passed the vehicle, he quickly looked under the canvas roof: the man, probably in his thirties, had short, dark hair and wore a navy-blue European suit. He had seen the same man often visit Toumert's office above the fish restaurant.

The Moroccan border guards waved him forward. No checks, no passports necessary. They knew their own. Why make life difficult for an old man? But when Faud got to the Spanish barrier, friendly cooperation changed to suspicious hostility.

Not surprising, thought Faud. Riots had broken out recently as the Spanish border police turned back hundreds of would-be immigrants who lacked official papers and even passports. Some came from distant, economically depressed countries like Senegal and Mali to claim refugee status; others just wanted to find a job in Spain or pass through on their way north to France and the UK. He had heard that the Spanish planned a high, razor-wire border fence to put an end to the embarrassment.

Ever hopeful, Faud told the Spanish police that his easy passage through the Moroccan checkpoint was sufficient evidence of his bona fides. But he was told to go back and collect some documentation and try again. As he turned into the parking area on the Moroccan side of the border, he saw the Jeep speeding toward the hot, dusty outpost of metropolitan Spain.

17

They collected the man very early the next morning. Cohen quickly put things in order: he removed the blankets and the empty tins and the plastic water bottles. Unopened cans were repacked into a cardboard box and left in a corner of the cell. He never knew when the next 'guest' might arrive and he always locked the door to prevent the entry of curious visitors. They had given him a fat envelope for his troubles and when he counted the money, it came to $5,000.

But he remained anxious and more nervous than he felt he should now that the visitor had left. Having climbed back up the iron staircase to his office, he sat down at the cluttered kneehole desk and wondered about his options. He thought that the tension created by the last 'guest' had sprung from the fellow's Englishness. When they spoke to each other that first night, he knew the man had to be an Englishman. And he, Mort Cohen, the British honorary consul, had sworn to protect the rights of Her Majesty's subjects, wherever they may be.

He lit a cigarillo and sipped the hot coffee from his thermos.

His telephone rang sharply. He noticed that his hand was shaking as he picked up the receiver. Because the same phone number served for his import-export business as for the consulate, he never declared his identity. 'Hello. 68 78 56.'

'Mr. Cohen?'

'Yes,' he replied cautiously.

'Good morning. My name's Westropp. I'm on a business trip to Morocco, British exports promotion, that sort of thing. But I'm due to be in Melilla tomorrow. I have to make a side trip to Malaga and I have a small passport problem that I think you could resolve quickly for me,' said the caller.

Cohen was hesitant. 'Where are you staying, Mr. Westropp?'

'Well, I'm in Tangier at the moment.'

'I think the British consulate there could help you—and probably faster than I can. I have very limited staff at the moment and—'

Vaux had expected that one. 'No, I've already been there. They say because my next destination is Malaga—by ferry from Melilla—I should call in on you.'

Faud had contacted Vaux as soon as he got back to Tangier in the battered old Renault. Earlier, a thick envelope had arrived at the villa via the diplomatic pouch from the British embassy in Rabat to the consulate on the Avenue d'Amerique du Sud.

Vaux emptied the white envelope's contents on the rosewood dining table. Greaves had written a small message:

Michael:
Herewith your old Westropp working
passport.
Always useful to have a spare—and
frankly, I prefer your old nom de
guerre!
Plus some moulah for your avaricious

contacts.

Don't hesitate to call if you need me.

George Greaves

Vaux flipped through the old passport—the same battered document they had resurrected for him in Cairo when he had had to make his getaway under cover. It had been updated so it was still valid. His photo assured him that he hadn't changed much in five years; only his brown hair a little more salt-and-pepper and certainly shorter. But he wondered if he would really need it. This operation was fairly straightforward and he felt it was coming to some sort of conclusion. His hopes had been raised by Faud's request to meet him 'soonest.' He stuffed a wad of George's dirhams in his blazer pocket in anticipation of some good news.

***

Brad Kingsley was not happy with Bill Harvey's report from Rabat. He wondered if his man in Morocco's capital city had an attitude problem. He had always got on with the *sayanim* guys and cooperation with that select group of pro-Israel Moroccans had usually paid big dividends. He decided to tackle the problem obliquely—by tapping into his sources at Morocco's intelligence outfit, the DST.

His main contact there was the man who had led the negotiating team that established the black detention site at Temara. The Moroccans had agreed to let the CIA interrogation teams do their thing, as if the bleak, isolated location south of Rabat were US sovereign territory.

This was where suspected jihadists were sent under the 'extraordinary renditions' program, now commonplace in the war against terror. The man's name, if memory served, was Driss Ghali. Kingsley's secretary located his whereabouts: he was apparently on temporary assignment in Tangier. Kingsley decided to fly down and see if he couldn't trade some useful information that would help thwart what he believed was an imminent Al-Qaeda-inspired outrage.

***

'You are quite sure that you saw this same man enter the building off the big Plaza?' asked Vaux.

He sat with Faud in the back of the old glinting Mercedes while Mahmud drove carefully and well within the 120-kilometer-an-hour speed limit. Faud wore an open, flower-patterned shirt that made him look like a tourist from the Caribbean. His red fez had been thrown in the front passenger seat. Vaux kept his blue blazer on to help conceal the Browning 9 mm in the holster. The old car's ineffective AC did little to make the journey more comfortable and Vaux felt his shirt sticking firmly to his back.

'Absolutely, sir. I will guide Mahmud to the very door where I saw him enter. You understand. I don't make up fairy tales.'

'No, of course not,' said Vaux. He hoped not. He had paid Faud seven thousand dirhams toward expenses—mainly the car rental—and for services rendered. The Moroccan border guards waved them through without examining any documents. Mahmud shouted something through the open window; the guards looked at Vaux and Faud and then waved them on. The Spanish police examined Vaux's Westropp passport and then Faud's ID—some sort of identity card plus driving license. And then they drove into the town.

Earlier, as they left the suburbs of Tangier, Vaux had asked him how the DST's Ghali knew that he, Vaux, had asked him to help find the Englishman. Faud replied: 'They are spies—what do you expect?' Vaux left it at that.

They pulled up in front of Cohen's warehouse. Vaux noted the distinct flag hanging limply from a pole that stuck out at a 45-degree angle from the second storey. It was a union jack with the unmistakable UK consular service crown logo imprinted on the intersection of the three red, white and blue crosses of the patron saints. 'But this is the British consulate,' exclaimed Vaux, now somewhat skeptical of the quality of Faud's information.

'Mister Vaux, yes. Please look there.' Faud pointed to the glistening brass plate that also declared that within the old, gray warehouse visitors would find the reassuring presence of Britain's consulate in Melilla.

They sat in the car. A pickup truck entered the garage and the roll-up doors cranked and rattled as they descended again.

'Well, OK. This is a hell of a coincidence. I planned to come here today, anyway. I'll go in and look around. Mahmud—would you park the car somewhere and come back in exactly thirty minutes?' Mahmud nodded and Faud pointed down the road, presumably to a likely parking space.

Vaux recalled Greaves telling him that one of his early priorities should be to contact the consul in Melilla. Greaves had said the man was well connected and knew everything about everyone and his dog.

And Faud had told him that he had followed the mystery man from Tangier twice—once to the border and the second time all the way to this building. Faud had never said why he followed this particular target but assured Vaux that there was some connection with the disappearance of Vaux's English friend. But what could be the nexus that linked the British honorary consul with Faud's suspect in the abduction of Micklethwait?

The highly polished brass plate was placed at the side of a single door that opened on to a wrought-iron staircase leading up to a number of small offices. Frosted glass adorned the upper half of the old varnished doors. Various names and titles were stenciled on the glass—among them: UK CONSULATE.

Vaux knocked gently on the glass. He saw a vague figure moving slowly toward the door and he wondered why a consulate would appear to be so dauntingly inaccessible to desperate tourists and other citizens in need of some help.

Mort Cohen stooped before him, holding the door as if he might shut it again very quickly, his eyebrows raised as if surprised to receive a visitor.

'Mr. Cohen? I called you yesterday. Westropp.'

'Ah, yes, yes. Please come in.'

Cohen pointed to a straight-backed chair and sat down opposite Vaux in the high-backed, ergonomic desk chair his wife had insisted on buying when she thought he was developing a stoop. 'About a passport problem, I recall,' said Cohen.

'I'll be frank, Mr. Cohen. You are the British government's official representative here and so I think I can be candid with you. I am not a businessman. I'm working for one of our intelligence units and my job at the moment is to find a missing Englishman.'

'Police?' asked Cohen. He felt his heart begin to pound. This was the beginning of the end. They had cottoned on to his clandestine activities. He would deny everything.

'No, I told you—intelligence.'

'But what can I do? I know nothing about any missing Englishman,' said Cohen. The small office was stifling. Sweat ran like mercury beads down his forehead.

'We understand that our man is being held by a terrorist cell— not here but in Morocco. However, there seems to be some link with Melilla and we think they could be using the territory as a safe hiding place for their hostage.'

'Terrorists? Hostage?' asked Cohen. He heard his own voice. Its pitch was getting higher. He must get control of himself. He wiped his forehead and face with a Kleenex grabbed from a big box on a small table by the side of his desk.

'I was told to get in touch with you by people at our Rabat embassy. They said you had many fingers in many pies, and there was little going on around these parts that you didn't know about,' said Vaux.

'Well, I don't know about that. It's very kind of them to think so highly of my contacts, and so on. But really, how could I possibly know about terrorist antics and that sort of thing. Those people would stay out of my way if they wanted to keep their activities secret. That's obvious, isn't it?' Cohen calmed himself a little: he thought he had made a convincing point.

Vaux felt uneasy. Cohen was not the usual calm and collected diplomat. 'You're an honorary consul. So you obviously engage in other activities beyond your diplomatic duties. I guess you run a business of some sort.'

Cohen relaxed a little. 'Import-export, Mr. Westropp. We buy a lot of foodstuffs—spices, tangerines, other citrus fruits and so on—from Morocco and export them on to Spain and the common market. That sort of thing. Oh, and we import car parts to distribute to the Moroccan auto repair shops. I make a living.'

Vaux took a calculated gamble. 'May I look around? I see you have a warehouse and garage downstairs. It'll give me some idea of what your business is all about.'

Cohen thought the request unusual. 'Are you from Inland Revenue?' he asked. He knew it would be a great relief if Westropp was, indeed, just a tax inspector.

Vaux ignored the question. He got up and waited for Cohen to rise from the desk and conduct a tour of the premises. Most proprietors would be proud to show a visiting fireman around. But in that old phrase Vaux now recalled, he could see that Cohen wasn't 'best pleased' at the prospect of a tour.

The Mercedes waited at the curbside. Mahmud opened the rear door but Faud was nowhere to be seen. Cohen had conducted a quick tour and Vaux had noticed the gray steel door of the cell. He wondered why what Cohen described as 'just a small storage room' had a spy hole in its door.

When he emerged from the dull-gray warehouse, Vaux observed what was essentially the hub of the small port town: the wide roundabout that formed the core of the plaza, its center marked by an ornate, gushing fountain and its perimeter dominated by large, faded-yellow art deco civic buildings—the Defense Ministry's *Casino Militar*, the local headquarters of the central Bank of Spain and the ornate, balconied city government center. Beyond the plaza was the lush green, palm-dotted Parque Hernandez whose entrance boasted a tall war memorial dedicated to the fallen in the three Rif wars of the nineteenth century (against the Muslim Berbers) and the Spanish civil war—which had ignited in this small part of Spanish Morocco in 1936.

They picked up Faud at La Pergola, a busy bar that overlooked the bustling waterfront—about a mile north-east from the plaza. On the terrace, weathered men sat and talked and drank red wine and beer. Vaux looked out to the crowded port's skiffs and trawlers—all of which, including the small power boats, offered a quick and easy way for any miscreants to get out of this safe-haven Spanish territory and to the world beyond.

18

When Vaux got back in the late afternoon, Craw was lounging by the pool on a canvas chaise longue with a red drink in a tall glass. Ice cubes tinkled and a slice of lemon floated on top. 'A very weak bloody mary, old boy,' said Craw sheepishly.

Vaux gave him a summary of the day's events. But he said nothing about Faud or his pursuit of the mysterious figure who paid regular visits to the fish restaurant and whose car he had tailed to the offices of the honorary consul. He let Craw infer that he had gone to Melilla on the advice of George Greaves.

'So you're saying you found the man needlessly jittery, a bit nervous. Funny—considering the buildup old Greaves gave him. You said yourself, Greaves told you to go see him and find out what he had to say. He's supposed to have his ears to the ground, that honorary consul of ours.'

'What else is going on?' asked Vaux.

'Had a call from the guy Greaves discovered is a DST operative—you know, this Arab, Ghali, and his sidekick who posed as
your everyday gendarmes when they came to pay a social call on
you and Greaves.'

'What did he have to say? Probably that I should liaise with him
more, report my whereabouts.'

'More to the point, old boy, he says they have still found no
trace of our missing colleague. They searched all the drug dens in
the medina and the slums out in Dradeb. So your alleged theory that
the Englishman was bent on a drug holiday and never returned to
the hotel because he was tripping on heroin or whatever has been
thrown out the window, of course.'

Vaux said, 'That was a cover story—as you know. I told them
I knew his mother and she was very worried about the drug scene
here and her son's addictive propensities.'

'Yes, well, that was an elaborate whopper of the first order.
Anyway—get yourself a drink. Momtaz!' The loud summons
reverberated around the walled grounds and the pool. Momtaz
came running across the lawn, tray in hand. 'Bring this gentleman a drink, my boy,' ordered Craw. *How quickly the upper-class
Englishman abroad slips back to the old colonialist mode*, mused
Vaux.

'*Merci, messieurs*,' said Momtaz as he ran back to get the
drinks.

'I thought you might need a drink when you hear what I have
to tell you.'

The drinks arrived and Vaux watched Momtaz as he poured the
beer carefully. 'So, what do you have to tell me?'

Craw waited until Momtaz was out of earshot. 'This chap Ghali
is coming to see us later this afternoon.'

Vaux relaxed. 'I can handle him better, now I know who he's
really working for.'

'Yes, Vaux, I'm sure you can. But he's bringing with him what he calls an "associate" from Washington who has expressed a desire to meet you—us, perhaps I should say now.'

'And what's this associate's nationality?'

'Ah, there's the rub. I would bet a pound to a penny it'll be one of our friends from Langley.'

***

Mort Cohen had been mortified by Vaux's visit and the man's obvious suspicions about his business dealings. What did some bureaucrat from Whitehall know about life here in this obscure Spanish enclave in North Africa? He couldn't know what pressures had been brought to bear on him, what quid pro quos were extracted to gain import permits from the slow-moving, corrupt and incestuous bureaucracies of Morocco and Algeria. And then there was the burden of his semiofficial position as the honorary consul. The man's probing questions had been directly related to his part-time diplomatic duties. If he had not been Her Britannic Majesty's representative in Melilla, he wouldn't have to face any hassle from visiting and curious officials. He thought he might resign his British post and get on with making a living.

But what was he thinking? He had finished a cold lunch of boiled carp and sliced beets at the Nacionale, the restaurant that he and his old, departed friend Tawil had frequented on many weekday evenings. He had picked up a two-day-old London tabloid that someone had left on a banquette and searched the paper for news from London.

Defying the skills and aims of news editors the world over, Cohen read newspapers by starting at the back and working methodically forward to the front page. He sipped the last of his espresso. And then the *Daily Mirror*'s front-page headline hit him:

ISLAMIC SUICIDE BOMBERS KILL 57
TUBE STATIONS TARGETED

He was stunned. He was overwhelmed by a sense of guilt. Old Faisal, who had been the maître d' for forty years, told the small clique of regular customers that Cohen had turned white as a ghost and had stormed out without paying his bill.

***

Micklethwait's head was swimming; he felt drowsy and his thoughts were jumbled. He knew he had been woken during the night, his few things gathered together, and with his hands cuffed and a hood over his head, taken to a vehicle—from the sliding side doors, he guessed a minivan—that had bounced and swayed for about twenty minutes. Then he was led quickly to a creaking, steep gangway and pushed onto the deck of a boat: the floor beneath him swayed gently and the smell of diesel fuel and salt water left him in no doubt that he was to embark on a maritime trip. The engine had revved and men shouted orders and instructions in guttural Arabic.

Now he found himself on a bunk in a small rear cabin. The door was locked and he had been left alone.

He was glad he couldn't sleep. At least they hadn't drugged him. He went over to a small port-side porthole and saw dim lights dotted up and down the coast like a distant necklace of glittering diamonds. He wondered if this was his last journey: they could be taking him out to sea to dump him—a convenient way of getting rid of incriminating evidence. On the other hand, his people could have agreed to hand over this man who John Keen had said was a valuable AQIM operative and then, God willing, he would be freed.

He resolved not to get excited at the prospect of getting out of the clutches of the terrorists, just as he refused to panic at the thought of an imminent burial at sea.

The up-and-down rock of the boat and the steady, throbbing rhythm of the engines finally induced sleep. He woke as somebody shook him and told him in Arabic to get ready to disembark.

***

'I am just a facilitator, Faud. A go-between. I sit here directing traffic. So don't try and weasel information out of me, because I shall tell you nothing of any consequence,' said Hisham Toumert.

Faud had walked over from the Marco Polo to pay a social call on the old bookkeeper whom he now knew was involved in the disappearance of the Englishman, Edward Knight.

The sealed note Toumert had asked him to deliver to Michael Vaux at the Villa Mauresque proved he was working for the people who took away the Englishman that night outside the Metropole. He did not know who this Abdul Juhayman was, but he guessed it all had something to do with the activities of the nationalists, antimonarchists and trouble-makers who were at the root of the Casablanca bombings and other outrages. His trip to Melilla with Vaux had paid off in money terms, but he didn't know whether Vaux had learned anything more about his missing English friend.

'No, no Hisham. I am not prying into your affairs. You misunderstand me. I am simply offering my services if you require anything to be done at all in the coming days,' said Faud.

'You could keep a watch on that villa. I hear the man Vaux has been joined by some other Englishman who is staying at the Minzah but who spends most days up there with Vaux. Perhaps you could find out who he is and what's his business through your contacts at the hotel?'

Faud got up, bowed slightly and waited.

'I'll pay you for your information when I get it.'

'*Choukran, machi.*' Thanks, it's a deal.

Meanwhile, Faud el-Mullah's friends and board-game rivals at the Café Central began to wonder if old Faud had finally undergone a sinister conversion. For the talk on the café's terrace suggested, sometimes darkly and with foreboding, that the old man's frequent visits to the ancient synagogue on the narrow Rue des Synagogues in the Petit Socco suggested a late-life awakening to the dark rituals of the Jewish faith. Or, perhaps, as the inevitability of death approached, he had decided to hedge his bets—just as he did too often when he played his favorite card game—the *ronda.*

But Faud kept his own counsel. If Abdul or Said, his frequent opponents in backgammon, asked obliquely if he were going to the mosque for morning prayers, his answer would be evasive and he would claim that these days he was busier than he had ever been in his 'traditional profession.' Everyone knew what that meant—his father, many years ago at the time of the French occupation, had launched Faud into that secret world of informers and semiofficial journeymen for the entrenched powers that be. But his old friends were not convinced: Abdul had asserted with worldly wisdom that his excuses were just a cover—the usual subterfuge and deception in which spies of all calibers indulged.

Ever since Faud had steamed open the envelope with which Toumert had entrusted him, he knew he had struck the mother lode. Why, it could be his Ali Baba moment—the chance discovery of rich dividends. The location of the dead drop had been written in plain black and white; communications between the two parties could now be intercepted. Pre-knowledge of the messages these antagonists sent each other would surely command a premium. He even had the power to wreck any mutual efforts to resolve their problems. But Faud knew the gist of the matter: Hisham Toumert, the wily, old bookkeeper, had demanded the release of one Abdul

Juhayman. In return, the English were offered the release of this man Edward Knight, the Englishman whose abduction he had personally witnessed.

What third party, he had asked himself, could be interested in clandestine communications between the two antagonists? The answer flashed so fast to his brain that he now knew he was a long way from being too old or too decrepit for his former trade: the Direction de la Surveillance du Territoire, the DST, his former part-time employers, would surely place a value on his ability to tap into messages between two clandestine entities that were operating in an area that could well affect the immediate national interests of the Moroccan state.

Ghali accepted Faud's invitation to meet him at the Café Central in the Petit Socco. There, he could talk to old Faud alone and assess Faud's offered information in calm isolation. They both ordered glasses of mint tea.

Within ten minutes, Ghali knew he had struck gold. He wondered whether he should pass on Faud's invaluable intelligence to the Americans. It would reflect on him well: Moroccan-US relations had never been better; it was the flavor of the times, the *plat du jour*. Operation African Leopard, joint US-Moroccan war games in the Western Sahara, were scheduled for later that summer.

Faud's long, elaborate and colorful story about the 'dead drop' (he chose not to reveal its location) and the demands of the terrorist kidnappers, was concluded by a pledge to provide the DST with all further information about the demands and the responses of the two adversaries. If necessary, Faud said, he would put himself on a twenty-four-hour surveillance of the dead drop 'area' and await events. But there would be a price for further cooperation.

The men walked together down the winding, narrow streets toward the Sûreté Nationale building on the Avenue de Mohammed V.

Ghali threw himself down in his soft high-backed leather chair. He rearranged a few items on his desk. At his end of the two joined desks, Didi Hassan kept his head down and continued to write notes. 'Faud, *mon ami*! Why can't you help us as a patriot? What is all this talk about price, money, rewards?' asked Ghali.

'Mister Ghali, sir. I worked for your people for nearly forty years—off and on. My blessed father before me worked for the French Deuxième Bureau—he was a senior officer here in this very building during the French occupation—'

'Yes, your father worked for the French secret service. We know all that, Faud. But again, why can't you help us without bargaining with us? It makes me very uncomfortable.'

Faud knew he had to go through this haggling just as if he was buying a chicken at the souk. So he remained tight-lipped and said nothing.

Ghali sighed and looked over at Hassan. He was still busy writing. 'Very well. One thousand, five hundred dirhams as a retainer. More if it all works out successfully,' said Ghali. At the Café Central, Faud had suggested a retainer of two thousand dirhams.

'One thousand, seven hundred and fifty,' said Faud.

'Done,' said Ghali.

Faud waited in Ghali's office while Hassan fetched the cash.

After counting the crisp new notes, Faud left.

'The Brits are living up to their reputation, Didi,' said Ghali.

'What do you mean?'

'Albion is being perfidious again. They have chosen not to disclose some vital and relevant facts in this kidnapping situation. What do you think their motives are?'

'They're playing their own game—keeping their cards close to the chest. What else is new?'

Ghali nodded and casually lit up a French Caporal.

19

Maj. Driss Ghali called the villa and asked to speak to Vaux. He wished to postpone the meeting until tomorrow morning. It would now be held at 9:30 a.m. at the Old American Legation building, formerly the US consulate but now used mainly for conferences and official meetings of one sort or another. The ancient palace, a sultan's gift to Washington back in the late 1700s, is located within the labyrinth of narrow passageways at the edge of the medina near the beach. An entire wing is devoted to the books, paintings, and music of Paul Bowles, an American writer and composer who lived in Tangier most of his life.

But within the complex medieval building's interior maze of conference and exhibition rooms, there is also a cheaply furnished, small chamber with a long, white Formica-topped table surrounded by eight steel folding chairs. The bare room is used for *ad hoc* meetings suddenly called by community agencies and, less frequently, by obscure pro-Western political groups that liked to keep a low profile.

The four men assembled around the table. Nobody chose to preside at the head seat. Craw and Vaux sat together opposite what Craw would describe in later debriefings as 'the interlopers.'

Crew-cut Brad Kingsley laid his rimless spectacles on the hard white surface of the table, looked intensely at Vaux and then at Craw as if he were a sergeant major examining the characteristic features of two new recruits. Craw shifted his legs and looked uncomfortable under the intense scrutiny. Vaux craved for a forbidden Camel.

'Shall I start, gentlemen?'

'Please do,' said Craw. He sighed quietly as if bored already.

'This is what we understand so far. My information from Major Ghali here and from our own intelligence sources in Morocco is that the situation is relatively uncomplicated: we, that is, the Central Intelligence Agency, are holding a Moroccan terrorist named Abdul Juhayman. He is a prominent leader of the Al-Qaeda in the Islamic Maghreb gang, or AQIM for short. Like its sister organization, AQAP, Al-Qaeda in the Arabian Peninsula, AQIM's aim is to spread havoc and despair among the populace so that eventually they will opt for the Muslim paradise they all seek...'

Maj. Ghali smiled as he slowly massaged his moustache: only he knew that the 'intelligence sources' cited by Kingsley could be attributed to just one man—old Faud, Ghali's newly recruited and now highly valued informer.

'That's a very good "appreciation of the situation,"' said Craw who decided he wasn't going to sit there with Vaux and listen to a lecture from a self-important CIA man who had just parachuted into Tangier and apparently decided to tell them nothing they didn't already know. He continued: 'But let's cut to the quick: we want our man back, and he's now in the hands of this group of terrorists. You have the means of getting him released and back into friendly hands. What's your decision on this?'

Vaux's frequently skeptical view of Craw's talents and abilities was somewhat modified.

'You're jumping the gun a little there—Alan, is it?' said Kingsley.

'Yes, it's Alan,' said Craw with an impatient sidelong look at Vaux for some support.

'Let me tell you both some facts about this character Juhayman,' said Kingsley. 'He has quite a long rap sheet—'

'Rap sheet?' asked Craw.

'Yup. You don't watch too many American movies, do you? A rap sheet is a record of offenses and crimes and subsequent charges, built up over someone's lifetime, if you like. Now may I continue?'

Craw nodded. Vaux busied himself with crazy doodles on a notepad that had been placed earlier in front of each man by a smartly dressed middle-aged and carefully coiffed lady who had darted into the room as the men were deciding where to sit.

'A couple of years ago, twelve suicide bombers blew themselves up in a Spanish restaurant in Casablanca. All twelve of them died— but they took thirty-three innocent civilians along with them. A few months later, again in Casablanca, two bombers blew themselves up in an Internet café, injuring scores of young students who frequented the place. That incident was followed by two bombers who blew themselves up in front of the US consulate, again in Casablanca. The bomb maker and organizer of all three incidents was this man Juhayman.

'Again last year, a Casablanca court sentenced three Saudi members of Al-Qaeda to ten years in prison. They were accused of planning attacks on US and British warships in the Strait of Gibraltar. We know that Juhayman, then still on the run, played a key part in that conspiracy.

'Finally, gentlemen, just recently, two men were sentenced to long jail terms for participating in the Madrid train bombings last year. These two men finally squealed on their leader—our friend, Juhayman.

'In a predawn, black-ops deal, we chased him down to a slum outside Casablanca called Sidi Moumen. That's where most of the Moroccan terrorists come from. Needless to say, we held him for lengthy interrogations at our facility in Temara, and just a few weeks ago we had to transfer him to Essaouira where they have medical facilities. The man is showing the worse for wear.'

Vaux looked up from his doodling. 'You mean you've tortured him to the brink and now you're trying to save him.'

'Something like that—between these four walls,' said Kingsley. Craw now surveyed the room for possible eavesdropping devices and looked suspiciously at the small potted palm by the side of the door. Kingsley continued: ' "Enhanced interrogation" is the new euphemism for such techniques—and I can assure you, Mr. Vaux, they are highly effective.

'To summarize,' said Kingsley, 'Juhayman is a high-value detainee, and as things stand now, I can tell you we are very reluctant to give in to any pressure to release the son of a bitch. I think you will find that Major Ghali here agrees with us.'

Vaux and Craw looked at Ghali who had been quiet so far. Vaux observed a newly grown Clark Gable moustache and his salt-and-pepper hair had been cut very short. He wore a tight-fitting western suit, a white shirt and no tie. Ghali spoke: 'We at the Directorate agree that it would be a great mistake to let this man back onto the streets of Casablanca or wherever. But in order to meet our British friends halfway, we think we have come up with a strategy that could be worth the risk...'

'That sounds ominous,' said Craw.

Kingsley jumped in. 'What the major means is that the DST will seize the opportunity to tail the guy if and when we release him. Every technical and human means known to tradecraft will be used to follow and monitor Juhayman once he regains his freedom and your man is sprung from the terrorists' clutches. In other words, as a result of our deal, we'll have laid the groundwork for an unprecedented assault on terrorist cells throughout the Maghreb.

'This major operation will be spearheaded by the CIA's counterinsurgency group here in Morocco, combined, of course, with the DST'S finest anti-terrorist detachments. We are sure that our killer Juhayman will inevitably gravitate toward his fellow bomb throwers and comrades-in-arms once he is free again.'

Vaux said, 'The exchange of prisoners will have to be worked out carefully. We can't put our man at risk. Our main aim is to free him, and we don't want some sort of O. K. Corral breaking out in the middle of the desert.'

Kingsley put a stick of chewing gum in his mouth. His head was shaking as a signal to his next declaration. 'The way we organize things, nothing like that is going to happen. Your man, gentlemen, will get home safe and sound. All we have to do now is work out the timing and logistical details. Sirs—thank you kindly.'

Craw looked at Vaux and wished they had discussed earlier what he was about to say. 'Before we all leave, I think you'll be interested in a major breakthrough in this situation. Vaux, please tell our colleagues the latest in the communications area.'

The contact with the kidnappers through the dead drop was something Vaux wanted to keep as an ace up his sleeve. The CIA had arbitrarily assumed command of the situation, and he felt B3's leverage could only be strengthened by keeping the ongoing contacts undisclosed. But Craw had now stumbled into revealing their one advantage in this sorry situation and had forced Vaux's hand. He decided to be enigmatic. 'Yes, well, it confirms what you say: the man called Juhayman is the prisoner they want released. Our antagonists have in fact now found a way to contact us, and we can say that lines of communication have been established with the captors—'

'What?' exclaimed Kingsley. Ghali registered no surprise.

Vaux said, 'I received a note indicating how we could communicate with these people—'

'But why didn't you tell me? Are you saying that they have already opened lines of communication?'

'Yes, I am.'

Kingsley assumed the attitude of a patient father after hearing that his wayward son had misbehaved. 'OK, could you please tell me, if it's not too much trouble, the mechanism by which you are in communication with these terrorists?'

'They sent me a note and gave me a means to reply via a dead drop.'

'A dead drop?' Kingsley looked at Ghali with a questioning expression. 'Did you know about this, Major?'

Ghali recalled Faud's recent debriefing. But he quickly decided he would not reveal that he possessed any such exclusive intelligence. The DST had some rights to confidential information despite what he saw as the CIA's arrogant desire to take over every aspect of the operation. 'No,' said Ghali. 'I had not been informed. Perhaps Monsieur Vaux could tell us more.'

'We haven't yet replied to the note,' said Vaux. 'When we do, I think we will have to ask them for more time while we work on the logistics of the exchange.' He noticed that Craw, head down, was now busy drawing exotic but unfathomable patterns on his notepad.

'*You* think we should ask *them* for time?' Kingsley was now beside himself with outrage—feigned or real.

'What, then, would you recommend we do in the circumstances?' asked Vaux.

'Here's what we would have done, OK? We'd have surrounded the area where the dead drop is with a small black-ops squad, and when the guy showed to pick up your reply note, why, we'd have taken him out.' Nobody spoke for a perhaps sixty seconds. But then Kingsley realized the problem with his suggested course of action. 'Well, of course, I don't mean that literally. But we would certainly have taken him in and put him through the necessary interrogations. And finally, no doubt extracted from him the whereabouts of our quest—this Micklethwait character. Then we'd have saved us a hell of a lot of trouble and still kept our high-value detainee, Juhayman.'

Vaux said, 'On the other hand, learning that their messenger had been taken in a double-cross just as they were showing their willingness to negotiate in good faith, they could simply have written off the whole episode and killed Micklethwait because they figured we had no intention of dealing with them honestly.'

Kingsley could see the logic of Vaux's argument. But the missed opportunity of grabbing one of the conspirators gnawed at him. 'So I presume you will be in touch with these banditos shortly. What will we say?'

Craw felt he had been quiet for too long. 'May I suggest we give them an outline of how we plan to proceed—a sort of interim report? Then, when we have prepared the whole operation, we will tell them where and when the exchange will take place.'

Kingsley hated the thought of any communication with these terrorist criminals. He would have preferred a search-and-destroy operation. But he had to recognize that the Brits were concerned about the life of one of their own. 'All right, gentlemen. Let's call it a day.'

They all stood up, the metal chairs scratching against the blond pinewood floor.

'Oh, just one thing, Vaux. Can you give me the location of the dead letter drop?'

Vaux looked at Craw who shook his head. 'At MI6, we do everything on a need-to-know basis, Mr. Kingsley. I'm sure you understand,' said Vaux.

Kingsley gave no response, and Craw and Vaux left the room as the American and his Moroccan ally got up and stood silently at the Formica table—whether out of respect or outrage, Vaux was never to learn.

Craw considered the one advantage of meeting at the Legation was that it was only about ten minutes' walk from his hotel. He invited Vaux for a drink. As they walked up through the narrow twisting alleys of the medina, they kept their own silence. They turned right on to the Rue de Portugal, a wider street, clogged with slow-moving vans and small cars that pushed and honked their way through a crowded and hectic street market. Sidewalk stalls sold an array of goods from used wrist watches and scuffed leather jackets to fresh silvery sardines, live chickens and slaughtered goats. Vaux noticed that Craw held a silk paisley handkerchief to his nose as he passed the purveyors of fish and raw meat.

As soon as they entered the lobby of the Minzah, Craw gave his verdict on the meeting: 'That was some bloody conference. The Yank did most of the talking. Still, we had the trump card. I think he was a bit lost after you told him we were already in touch with the other side.'

***

Vaux left Craw at the hotel. He had said he was tired and would have a siesta. They had decided to have a light lunch that turned out to be a longer and heavier meal than they had really wanted. Vaux had goat tagine and Craw opted for fried whiting. Craw had asked Vaux, who had the secure phone at the villa, to call Sir Nigel and update him on where they were in the negotiations to gain the release of their colleague.

'We haven't even begun to negotiate, Alan.'

'No, my boy. You don't understand. I'm now giving you the OK to drop the terrorists a *billet doux*. Tell them that we will give them instructions within, say, forty-eight hours as to our plans to release their hero from the Americans. Stall them. Say the Americans are being stubborn and we still have to iron out details of the exchange—its location and the logistics, all that stuff.'

'Don't we have to wait for the Americans? We haven't a clue how and when or even where we are going to do this exchange,' said Vaux.

'Yes, well, these Arabs still hold all the aces and they still hold young Micklethwait. So drop them a note anyway—just to let them know we're on the ball.

'Meanwhile, our endeavors should, if anything, be intensified by this tragedy in London, don't you think?' said Craw. They had discussed the London tube bombings on their way over to the hotel.

'Of course. These deluded people seem to be getting close to home,' said Vaux.

'And Anne—safe and sound, I hope.'

'She's staying with her father at the moment and takes a commuter train to Euston. From there, she picks up a cab for the office.'

'Splendid, splendid. Just wanted to check, old boy.'

In the study where he had spent so much time with Ahmed Kadri on his first successful mission for Department B3, Vaux recalled the deliberate betrayal of a friend's trust his employers had demanded as the price of forgiveness for what they asserted were his earlier misdeeds. And then, again, his subsequent abandonment of their precious principles in order to repair the damage he had inflicted on his unique relationship with Ahmed. It was all a long time ago, and the anguish only intensified when he recalled his love for Ahmed' s political ally, Alena, a Palestinian refugee with whom he had shared his life for several years in Cairo.

Now they were both dead: Ahmed murdered by old political enemies within the new Bashar al-Assad regime; and Alena, the talented and beautiful double agent, shot to pieces by the home team as she was trying to come back in from the cold—to him and to their side.

He sat down at Ahmed's old oak desk. He sensed someone at the study's door. It was Momtaz, unusually in blue jeans and a red

T-shirt and no shoes. 'Good timing, Momtaz. Bring me a large whisky, please. Cutty Sark, if there's any left.' With a glint of pearl-white teeth, Momtaz ran to the kitchen where drinks were dispensed under the watchful eye of Mahmud.

Vaux took a moment to look at the print he had bought Ahmed on his first visit to the villa. It was a copy of Matisse's *Window at Tangier,* a view of the casbah and medina, in hazy blues and yellows and soft greens, loved and treasured by Ahmed who had supervised the elaborate operation to hang the painting over the big brick fireplace. Then he pulled over the ancient, upright Imperial typewriter, carefully removed the mottled leather cover and inserted a page from a nearby tray of foolscap.

He typed:

We will be in touch within 48 hours.
Optimistic that an exchange can be arranged. There may be some
conditions. Please be patient.

Later that evening, he would take the note to the synagogue dead-letter drop in the Petit Socco.

20

Cohen wearily climbed the narrow black wrought-iron stairs to his office. He sat in the high-back ergonomic chair, his elbow on the desk, his head resting in the palm of his hand. *That I have come to this? A helper and associate of people who blow up innocents as they go about their daily lives?*

The man who claimed he was from a British intelligence unit had been looking for an Englishman who, he said, had been abducted by terrorists. He had never thought of Magdi Kassim and his associates as terrorists. He thought they were fast-living gangsters, petty criminals. He had been forced to deal with them to keep his business intact—the old extortion racket, as common in the East End of London as anywhere else. But there could be little doubt now that the man he had locked up in his own private bolt-hole was the vanished Englishman.

So, in that classic phrase of the British justice system, he had aided and abetted terrorists who were engaged in kidnapping and murder—the horrific London bombings he had read about that evening were blamed on militant Islamists. And he was dealing with these people, the sworn enemies of Israel, his natural homeland where one day he had hoped to retire.

Yet he had never wished any harm toward the Muslims. He had always got on with them—they were racial cousins, after all.

It would all come out. He had no doubt the British and the Moroccan security services would pull out all the stops to rescue their Englishman. By sending this man Westropp, it was clear that they were already closing in. The shame of having participated in this crime was too much. He was not just some ordinary English trader washed up in the backwaters of North Africa. He was the honorary consul, the man who had been trusted for many years to protect the United Kingdom's interests here and to act as guardian to Britain's citizens who found themselves in difficulties or in danger within this small area of his jurisdiction. True, his duties had never taken up much of his own time—he had Rachel to thank for that.

But he had never had any complaints from the Foreign and Commonwealth Office. They had always been happy with his performance. He had heard that in a few years, he'd be in line for a CBE, a stepping stone perhaps to a knighthood. Sir Mort Cohen, he thought, would have had a nice ring to it.

But he had failed.

In the locked side drawer of his desk, Cohen had always kept a Webley .455 revolver, once owned by his father who had been a captain in the Observer Corps in the Second World War. The key ring was on his desk. He unlocked the drawer.

He took out the gun, spun the cylinder and counted the six rounds in the chambers. He took out one of the bullets. He spun the cylinder again. He would play Russian roulette in reverse. Instead of one bullet in one chamber and five empty chambers, just one bullet would be missing from the six chambers. If he was still alive after he pressed the trigger, then God did not wish him to die.

He took a piece of paper from his out tray and chose his old school Waterman's fountain pen from the cracked Toby jug crammed with ballpoint pens and pencils accumulated over the years.

He wrote: *I did my best. I leave to my beloved wife, Rachel, all my worldly goods.*

Then he picked up the revolver, pointed the barrel at his temple and pulled the trigger.

***

Vaux opened his eyes slowly. The early morning sun had filtered through the slats of the white venetian blinds and projected bright parallel lines on the parquet floor. At the break of dawn, he had heard the distant call of the muezzin from the loudspeakers atop the minaret of the grand mosque at the peak of the 'mountain'—the first of the five calls to prayer the faithful would heed during the daylight hours.

He heard a gentle knock on the door and Momtaz in a long, blue striped nightshirt entered with a small tray. His usual café au lait with croissant. 'Monsieur Vaux, telephone *pour vous*. Monsieur Craw. *Très urgent*, very urgent.' From which, Vaux gathered, Craw wanted him to call him back now. He looked at his old Accurist wristwatch and saw it was only 6:30 a.m.

Craw was in his hotel room and answered Vaux's call after the first ring. 'I'm speaking from my room, Vaux. And on the unsecured land line, I presume. Got a late-night call from Sir Nigel. He wants me to fly back today and give him the rundown. He's furious about the interlopers—says we should stall the Yankees as long as possible. So he wants a complete debriefing, and then I suppose he'll give us his armchair advice on how to proceed.'

Vaux had never heard Craw sound so bolshie. 'It's more or less out of our hands. You know that. They're holding the man whose freedom will trigger Micklethwait's release. The cousins have to come up with a date and a time and a place to make the exchange. Until I hear from them, there's little we or Sir Nigel can do,' said Vaux.

'Yes, yes, dear chap. But we have to *look* as if we are still in charge—if only for Sir Nigel's sake.'

'I took a stalling note to the dead drop late last night. So we've bought a little time. I'll get on to Kingsley this morning and tell him time is of the essence. That's all I can do,' said Vaux.

'You've said quite enough, old chap. We're talking on an ordinary land line. I'll call you from London.'

Vaux put the old rotary phone down on the table in the large hallway. He figured he saw the fleeting figure of Mahmud as he dashed from the dining room to the European lounge. He followed him into the lounge. Mahmud was waving a feather duster over the chunky, 1930s furniture. In a far corner of the room, Vaux noticed the old radiogram that Ahmed had loved to play in the evenings. He opened the small doors to the record racks and selected his and Ahmed's favorite—a 33 rpm recording of Duke Ellington and his orchestra at Carnegie Hall in 1952.

He sat on the long buttoned-leather sofa in his pajamas and immersed himself for a few minutes in the nostalgia conjured by the Duke's rendition of 'Lullaby of Birdland.' When the tone arm lifted and clicked its return to base, he came back to the present. And he wondered how much patience Micklethwait's captors had—more, he hoped, than Sir Nigel Adair.

***

Vaux had decided nothing was to be lost by a friendly visit to Driss Ghali at the Sûreté Nationale offices on the Avenue de Mohammed V, south of the medina and a short walk to the Avenue d'Espagne and the beach.

A lengthy conference took place among four police guards at the reception desk in the main marbled lobby. Vaux had shown his real passport (Ghali had addressed him as 'Vaux' at the villa and knew him as Vaux, so there was no point in using his alias) and asked if he could see Maj. Ghali, whom he had talked with only yesterday about a problem Ghali would be well aware of. But, no, he had not made an appointment. Another lengthy debate broke out between the guards. Vaux countered the negative shrugs and body language with assertions in French that the need to see the major was urgent and of national importance. He mentioned the full name of Ghali's intelligence outfit and the police guards fell quiet while they flipped through various books and directories as if to find the location of this Major Ghali.

At last, he was taken to the third floor. Ghali greeted Vaux with a firm handshake and showed him into a small office with two desks placed opposite each other. At the far desk, with his back to a grimy sash window, sat Lt. Didi Hassan. He looked up and smiled and Vaux returned the compliment.

Ghali indicated a high-backed wicker chair and Vaux sat down. 'What brings you here, Monsieur Vaux? We saw each other *hier*— only yesterday.'

'I thought perhaps a follow-up discussion with you might help things along.'

'*Mais oui*. If I can help I will.' He looked at Didi Hassan who guessed his job was to be official witness to the conversation.

'First of all—have you any idea how long it's going to take our American friends to organize this exchange?'

'No more than you, monsieur. Didi, have you heard anything from our friend, Mr. Kingsley?'

'Nothing,' said Hassan. Vaux thought back to their visit to the villa under the guise of being regular policemen. Didi hadn't been much help then, either.

'But time is of the essence,' said Vaux, wishing he could throw out that old cliché and come up with something else. 'Our man's rotting in some stinking jail. God knows how his health must have deteriorated in the past few weeks, and our side is ready to go.'

'Yes, we understand that. But it's out of the DST's control. The Americans are in the driver's seat—one of their expressions, I believe. And there's nothing I can do to speed things up until they decide to act, *non?*'

'But you could perhaps keep reminding them that a quick decision on their part could save our man's life. We fear for his well-being, you see.' Vaux knew his persuasive powers were waning. It was perhaps a wasted journey. But to his surprise, he saw Ghali pick up the telephone and dial. Vaux heard the ringing tone.

Ghali put his hand over the mouthpiece. 'This is Kingsley's 'ot-line,' said Ghali, as he waited for someone to pick up the handset. Vaux wondered why he or Craw hadn't been given the hot line number. It would have made this journey unnecessary. 'Hello, Mr. Kingsley? *Bonjour.* Any news yet on the timing of our little exercise?'

Kingsley gave a long, excited reply but Vaux couldn't decipher what was being said—except that it sounded as if the Americans had moved forward since yesterday.

Ghali put the phone down. 'He says he's about to contact you at the villa. They have fixed a date for the exchange but he didn't give me it. He's calling for a meeting tomorrow—all of us, to discuss how we're going to get down to a place called El Jadida.'

Hassan moved over to look at the yellowed, fly-specked map that hung on the wall. His finger ran down the west coast of Morocco from Tangier to Casablanca and then south to El Jadida (in minute print), a small coastal village about two hundred miles north of Essaouira where the Americans were holding their highly prized prisoner.

Vaux rose from his hard chair but just as he turned the brass handle of the door to exit, Ghali called him back. 'One thing I forgot to mention—forgive me. We had confirmation just this morning that your friend Tawil, Mokhtar Tawil, was murdered by the *sous chef* in that Spanish night train. He confessed finally to the Spanish CNI and admitted he did it for a small fortune.'

'Any indication who his paymasters were?'

'Very confidentially, they suspect it was a state-sponsored, targeted assassination. Tawil was working for some Salafist terrorist outfit connected to AQIM, and we've little doubt that some Western spy agency wanted him dead. Sounds to me like a Mossad job.'

'Um. But why wouldn't they have checked who his companion was? If they saw he was accompanied by a British agent, perhaps they would have had second thoughts,' said Vaux.

'Per'aps they knew all about the ruse these terrorists were playing on you. Per'aps Mossad knew it was all a sham and that nobody in the Salafist cell was about to defect to Britain,' said Ghali.

'What the hell is that supposed to mean? Do you people know something that we don't?'

Ghali gave a Gallic shrug. 'Just a theory—'

Vaux struggled to stay cool. 'Want to share this theory with me?'

'Too early, Monsieur Vaux.'

'In any case, whatever hypothesis motivated Mossad, it was their duty to inform us,' said Vaux.

'The Mossad keep themselves to themselves. They are born loners, *non*? And perhaps they knew this Tawil was pulling, 'ow you say?—a fast one on the Brits, *non*?'

Vaux didn't reply, skipped down the three flights of worn, marble stairs and left the building.

He thought he would walk down to the beach and perhaps take a beer at one of the bars. As he turned right on the Rue de Portugal, he saw Faud, in a fez and flowing robe, walk swiftly by. Neither man acknowledged the other and Vaux turned to watch Faud enter the police building. Vaux dismissed any dark thoughts: perhaps old Faud was applying for a new driving license or visiting old colleagues.

21

When, some eighteen months later, the official inquiry finally got underway to assess the outcome of Operation Apostate and its offshoot, Operation Rescue, one of the few unanimous verdicts of the three-man board of inquiry was that Michael Vaux's failure to follow up on the significance of Faud el-Mullah's visit to the offices of the Direction de la Surveillance du Territoire (DST) proved to be a major turning point.

The nitpickers argued that old Faud's divided loyalties were at the core of Vaux's lack of success in finding Micklethwait in the early days of Operations Apostate and Rescue. But Vaux claimed that whether Faud had two or even three paymasters was irrelevant. The AQIM cell was always two steps ahead of him.

Faud now paid almost daily visits to the DST offices. He considered it a duty to show his face in the wake of his new association with his old employers. His resolve to work for his former spymasters was fortified by his conviction that his leverage with Vaux had ended with his failure to find the Englishman, Edward Knight, in

Melilla. He had seen Toumert's man visit the British consular offices but the excursion with Vaux had failed to produce anything significant, let alone the discovery of Vaux's colleague.

Meanwhile, Vaux had decided to repair some neglected fences. He called Safa Robinson, his one-time lover and now owner of the Villa Mauresque. She had left a number for him to contact her if and when he needed.

'Michael! How are you?'

'Well, it hasn't exactly been the holiday I planned.'

'Why ever not? Is something the matter? You're not sick, are you?'

'No, my dear.' Vaux didn't quite know what to call her anymore. He felt that 'Safa' was a bit too informal in view of their short, hot affair, way back. And he could hardly call another man's wife 'darling.' So he stuck to the banalities of convention. 'It's just that my former employers have sucked me into another morass and it's not been easy to extricate myself—not yet, anyway.'

'Oh, no! Don't tell me they've got you to work on some hugger-mugger job in Tangier, the notorious nest of spies!' She was laughing now.

'I can't talk about it, Safa. But I hope you don't mind my staying in your place for at least another few weeks.'

'Of course not, darling. We're not going to be back for some time. Try and get a real vacation once you've finished whatever job they've got you to do.'

'That's very kind. I wish we all could have spent more time together.'

'Yes, of course. But Paul's doing two jobs now—since his partner in the practice died so unexpectedly. He still hasn't found a replacement, so it doesn't look as if we'll be able to get away for some time.'

They said their good-byes and then Vaux dialed a number in Hatch End, a leafy middle-class neighborhood about twenty-five miles northwest of London.

Anne's father, about the same age as Vaux, answered in his usual formal style: 'Six one six seven five.' The last five digits of his twelve-digit number.

'Oh, is Anne in, by any chance? It's Michael Vaux, Harry.'

On a disastrous visit last Christmas, Harry Armitage-Hallard, Anne's stockbroker father, had invited Vaux to call him Harry. The Armitage-Hallard bit, he admitted, was rather a mouthful. But Vaux knew he would never be acceptable. The age difference with Anne was a bridge too far for Harry and most of his generation.

'Yes. Wait a jiffy, would you?' Cold but polite.

'Michael.' Anne sounded out of breath.

'Are you busy? I can call back.'

'No, no. I've just walked in the door. The train was late again.'

'Thank God you don't have to take a tube. That was a terrible business.'

'Yes, it was. You must feel your work is all the more important now.'

'I'm stuck here for the foreseeable future, Anne. I just wanted to say hello—and, of course, I love you.'

'There's no chance of my coming down, I suppose.'

'Everything's in a state of flux right now. I may see some more space opening up in a week or two. As soon as I think it's OK for you to spend a few days, I'll call.'

They had no more to discuss. It wasn't a secure line and Anne knew she was forbidden to say anything about goings-on at the office, let alone any gossip about the staff. She was dying to tell Vaux of Craw's shouting match with Sir Nigel, but it would have to wait.

No sooner had Vaux put down the phone than it rang its low-volume tinkle. 'Hello?'

'Greaves here, old boy. Some bad news, I'm afraid. Old Cohen just shot himself. You know, our honorary consul in Melilla. Did you ever go and see him?'

'Good God,' said Vaux, shaken. 'Yes, I did, as a matter of fact. Only a few days ago.'

'Get anything out of him re the overall situation with these bloody terrorists?'

'Not really.' Vaux wasn't about to discuss his abortive attempt, prompted by Faud, to find Micklethwait somewhere in Melilla. 'But why? Any reason?'

'Just a note leaving everything to his wife. You know suicides. No rhyme or reason. Something seems to possess them. My own brother committed hari-kari four years ago.'

'Not literally, I hope.'

'Good God, no. He decided the Romans did it best: he slit his wrists and died in a hot bath. He was a classics professor at Oxford.'

'I'm sorry,' said Vaux. And he wondered whether his visit and his questions had had something to do with Cohen's decision to end it all.

He went into the kitchen where Hamidah, Safa's cook, was busy with a pastry roller. Her hands and arms and her long black abaya robe were covered with white flour. She smiled broadly as Vaux nodded to her and went to the temporary bar Mahmoud had set up for his European guests. 'Please, I do for you,' said Hamidah.

'No, please. I can get a drink myself.' It was nearly midday, so he opened a cold bottle of Flag lager.

Back in the study, a sense of helplessness began to overwhelm him. Why would Cohen suddenly take his own life? He had seemed nervous during Vaux's short visit but there must have been more to it—could such an act of desperation have had anything to do with old Faud's suspicions that there was some connection between him and the terrorist cell who were holding Micklethwait?

But still, the operation was now going as fast as he could have hoped. Young Mickle was now presumably on his way to this obscure little place south of Casablanca. Vaux now felt a little happier— the signs were auspicious. He would soon see Micklethwait, the young, bright and hopefully resilient probationer, alive and well again, and the sad episode would finally be resolved.

Old Faud had said that if ever he needed to contact him, he could always find him at the Café Central in the Petit Socco from 3:00 p.m. until 5:00 p.m.

Vaux looked at his old Accurist and decided to see Faud. At least he'd be doing something positive, and who knew what tidbits of information Faud had gathered in recent days?

He found Mahmud polishing the Mercedes in the driveway. He asked if he would take him into town. 'Any place, sir? The hotel, perhaps?'

'No, just drop me at the market.' Vaux would walk from there to the Petit Socco where he hoped to find his confidant.

Faud was sitting by himself, red fez at a jaunty angle, smoking a nargila pipe, a small black coffee on the old, cracked marble-topped table. 'I was going to send you a note,' said Faud. 'Something happened this morning. They arrested a youth who worked for this man Toumert. He was just a runner, a messenger, but they nabbed him.'

Vaux tried to decipher Faud's ambiguous report. 'Hold on. What are you talking about? Where was this guy nabbed, and who by?'

'Don't know, sir. You have to check.'

'I will. But what's it got to do with me?'

'There was much commotion at the synagogue. Nobody knows why the young man was there. But the police took him away.'

'The synagogue?' Vaux began to suspect what this could be about. 'Faud, please. Why does this concern me?'

'I thought you would be interested in the information, sir. You pay me a retainer, so I'm always looking for information that can help you.'

There was no answer to that. But Vaux suspected Faud was playing a sly game: what did *he* know about the dead drop? Were the terrorists trying to leave a message? Of course, that's what it was. But how the hell did the local police come into it? 'Do you mean the regular police or your old friends at the DST?'

'I wasn't there, sir. Witnesses, old Jews, come to me and give report. That's all.'

Vaux declined a coffee, got up and walked quickly to the DST offices. It was early afternoon, and presumably Ghali would still be there. This time, he was waved upstairs without a word from the chattering phalanx of uniformed reception officers in the grand lobby.

Vaux knew that the only two parties who knew about the location of the dead-letter box were himself and the terrorist cell that held Micklethwait. The only weakness in that supposition was the boy who delivered the message. Vaux dismissed the possibility of the young boy playing some ignominious role—he was too young and almost certainly couldn't read English. And the synagogue had been selected by the alleged Salafist terrorists presumably only to rub in the irony. So how would he broach the subject with Ghali?

'Yes, Monsieur Vaux, how can we help you?' Didi Hassan looked up from his blotter in anticipation of Vaux's reply.

'I understand that some youth has been arrested near the Petit Socco, and my sources tell me he was a known messenger of the Salafist cell that we are all assuming are holding our man—'

Ghali looked surprised. 'Didi, do you know anything about this?'

'No. But I can check with the locals downstairs. They'll have a list of who they've taken into custody today.' He picked up his phone and talked with someone for five minutes about their respective families. Then Vaux noticed a more serious tone and guessed the relevant questions were being asked. Didi nodded several times and wrote something down on his blotter. He looked at Ghali as if to ask permission to pass on the information. Ghali gave him the go-ahead. 'Seems a youth of fifteen was arrested this morning at the Temple Nahon on the Rue des Synagogues. Says he was interested in the interior of the old building. He aims to study architecture, he says.'

'So are they going to let him go?' asked Ghali.

'No, they're holding him for further questioning.'

'So, Mr. Vaux. What is your interest in this matter and why on earth do you suspect this young man of being a messenger of a Salafist cell?'

Vaux knew he had been outfoxed. So he changed the subject. 'There's a man called Toumert, Hisham Toumert. My sources tell me that in some way, he's tangled up in this conspiracy. Nobody can prove anything but one of my reliable contacts says he's sometimes used as a go-between for these various terrorist outfits. I understand he's a bookkeeper or an accountant, and he operates out of an office on the corner of Marco Polo and the Avenue d'Espagne. He might be worth a visit.'

'Where did you get this information?' asked Ghali. 'These are serious allegations.'

Vaux got up. 'All I can tell you is that they are reliable sources. Good day, Major, Lieutenant.'

Ghali smiled at Didi. Vaux had confirmed one of old Faud's reports that Toumert had some association with the group that was holding the English diplomat. Before long, they would have to pay the old, overweight accountant a visit. But first, they would join the two men who had been summoned to Tangier by the CIA's Brad Kingsley from their base in Rabat. They were now talking to the boy in an interview room in the subbasement of the building.

22

Sebastian Micklethwait, a hood over his head, arms tightly gripped by strong hands, legs loosely manacled around his ankles, crossed a short gangplank and shuffled toward a waiting vehicle. He heard the side door slide open and then he was pushed into the vehicle. He groped for a seat, sat down and felt two men squeeze past him to find their own seats.

He was relieved to be on terra firma. At least they hadn't pushed him overboard. It looked like some deal might have been worked out by his people and the gang who had abducted him. He had lost count of the days he'd been in captivity and felt he was in some dreamy world where time meant nothing. He had never been given a newspaper and had only a vague idea of what day or month it was.

The engine revved up and the van bounced along what seemed like a potholed farm track. Then they climbed on to a smooth tar-macked road and the Peugeot 807 minivan picked up speed. He felt a hand on his shoulder. 'You can take off the hood now. Enjoy the countryside, mate,' said the unmistakable English voice of John

Keen a.k.a. Omar Sala, the self-described Edgware Road jihadist, who now sat behind him.

Micklethwait took off his hood, turned round and said: 'Hello.' Through the windows, he saw the early orange and red streaks in the sky of a new dawn. Ahead of them, keeping a steady distance, an aged and dusty Land Rover Defender, presumably the vanguard of the little convoy. He felt relieved to see Keen again. He understood now what they meant by that strange empathy that sometimes grew up between a hostage and his captors: in his Portsmouth training manual, they had called it the Stockholm syndrome. 'You again,' he said.

Keen/Omar smiled. His luxuriant dark-brown beard now seemed even longer and he wore the familiar long, brown woolen djellaba. On his head, a tightly fitting traditional knitted white *takiyah*.

The heavily built, dark-skinned Arab who sat beside Keen now moved to the seat behind him. He had tightly curled black hair and wore western clothes—jeans and a loose-fitting dress shirt. An exposed handgun holster hung at his side. Micklethwait guessed he would provide the muscle should their prisoner become rebellious on the open road. The driver, the third man, looked younger than Keen and kept his eyes on the road. Micklethwait noted the AK-47 that lay on the front seat next to the driver. 'I suppose I can't ask where we are and where you're taking me,' said Micklethwait.

Again, Keen squeezed his shoulder, a gesture of reassurance, perhaps. 'Be patient, chum. It's a long ride, but in a couple of days or so your ordeal should be over.'

'Thank God for that,' said Micklethwait.

'Thanks be to Allah, *tamam, al-hamdoulilah*,' said John Keen. 'We shouldn't talk, mate. I'm just going to give you some basic facts that will help you endure the journey. Then you can have some water and bread—we have plenty in the back. The boat docked along the coast from Melilla at a place called Al Hoceima. Now we're heading to the west coast and then a long drive south.'

The muscleman in the rear seat snored gently, lulled to sleep by the heat and the drone of the engine.

***

At this moment in time, fifteen hundred miles west of the road to Tetouan and points south, the cramped, anonymous Gower Street offices of MI6's Department B3 were empty (it was 8:30 a.m.) except for dutiful, attractive Anne Armitage-Hallard, who, as usual, got the early train up to London and had taken a cab from Euston. By the time she'd arrived, she had read two morning newspapers: *The Times* because she thought that august publication a must-read for anyone working within the corridors of power, and the *Sun*, a racy tabloid full of royal-family gossip and celebrity stories that one read to keep abreast of the social whirl of swinging London.

Anne was in the small storage room where she made bitter cups of Nescafé and dispensed an assortment of biscuits from old, round tins whose faded lids depicted a more elegant London: the vanity fair of top hats, crinoline dresses and horse-drawn hansom cabs. She heard the shuffling of the first arrival and to judge from the gasps and grunts that accompanied the shedding of a trench coat and the clatter of an abandoned briefcase, she guessed it was Sir Nigel Adair, her boss. It was unusual for him to arrive first, though it could be that the staff car had had to take Lady Adair, an enthusiastic West End shopper, on to somewhere else.

Anne strode into the small foyer and greeted Sir Nigel. He grunted his reply, picked up his leather briefcase, and opened the brown, varnished door to his office. He turned as she took his trench coat off the ancient coat tree and began to maneuver the traditional taupe accoutrement of his trade onto a plastic hanger, which was then hung from a large brass peg attached to the wall behind the coat tree.

Sir Nigel waited for the maneuver to be completed. As soon as he thought Anne was satisfied with her work, he asked her to call Alan Craw, his deputy. 'Tell him it's very urgent. I want him here now. I don't want any more of this ten-thirty-in-the-morning-arrival nonsense—not while we have a major crisis on our hands. We've a man missing in action, for heaven's sake.'

Anne braced herself for a stormy day. She called Craw but there was no answer. Then she called the hospital. She wanted to find out whether Chris Greene's condition was unchanged or improving. He'd had a strange kind of pneumonia for several weeks now. She was fond of Chris and she knew Vaux would want the latest news about him when he called again.

She was told by a curt nurse that Mr. Greene remained on the critical list. Then she flipped through her Rolodex to retrieve the fall-back number Craw had given her if she couldn't reach him at his Kensington apartment.

'Hello.' A low, actressy voice. For a moment, Anne thought she could be speaking to Joan Collins. She asked if Mr. Alan Craw was there. 'Just a minute, please.' It sounded to Anne as if they were still in bed. Sheets rustled, a voluble sigh and dulcet whispers.

'Yes?' It was Craw, all right.

'You'd better get over here fast. Sir Nigel's on the warpath.'

***

The Arab street boy sat opposite Lieutenant Tony Mann and Staff Sergeant Mike Huntley, both officers skilled in the arts of interrogation that in the post-9/11 era took in the gamut from polite interviews to the more 'enhanced' methods of extracting key intelligence from detainees they suspected of aiding the enemies of the United States and the free world. Both men had learned Arabic at the American University in Beirut but they were having difficulty communicating with the boy because he had lived in Tangier all his short life and he spoke Maghrebi Arabic, the local dialect, not the Levantine Arabic they had learned in their classrooms in Beirut.

The boy said his name was Hamid. In a statement he had made to the police sergeant on the first floor, he claimed he didn't think it was a crime to visit a synagogue. He wanted to be an architect but he admitted that he had left school two years earlier.

Lt. Mann decided they needed help. He rang Driss Ghali, head of the DST's small unit in Tangier. Kingsley had told them he was in the same building. Hamid looked sullen. The sergeant offered him a strip of chewing gum. He grabbed it, his eyes still focused on the floor.

Ghali entered with a manila folder. Still standing, he flipped through the file and retrieved a piece of paper. 'Hamid Nackla,' said Ghali, reading from the rap sheet. At last, the boy now heard his own language spoken. 'In trouble with the local police for possession and the sale of *kif*. Warned and let go. Last year: charged with selling yourself—prostitution. But no witnesses found to back up the charge. One break-and-enter into a bakery in Dradeb—let off because your mother claimed you hadn't eaten for three days.

'And now I understand you broke into the sacred synagogue in the medina. What do you have to say?'

Hamid sighed. He was relieved that at least he could now understand what was being said to him. Anyway, what were these two American stiffs doing here? What had they got to do with anything? He looked up at Ghali. 'I didn't break into no synagogue. The door was open already. It's sometimes locked up, but this was very early on their sabbath. And I didn't steal anything, honest.'

'Then what were you doing there?' asked Ghali.

'I told these two men: I was admiring the old temple or whatever it's called. The chandeliers are beautiful and the marble columns—'

'Never mind the marble columns. Who sent you there?'

'Nobody, honest. Why can't you people believe me?'

Ghali looked at Lt. Mann and Mann looked at Huntley. They were not getting anywhere.

'Let the boy go,' said Ghali. 'He'll only create trouble. Now he's going to tell everyone in town that the Americans grilled him for all sorts of information and he'll be a hero on the street.'

Hamid didn't understand Ghali's English any more than he had understood the Americans'. He took the gum out of his mouth and stuck it under the trestle table where the Americans sat. Ghali told the boy to get lost.

Lt. Mann quickly asked Ghali if they had the manpower to tail the boy. 'If he was sent there for any reason, I think he'd be heading for the people who had sent him and got him into all this trouble. He'd give a colorful report, no doubt.'

Ghali shrugged. 'It's Saturday. There's nobody around.' Then he left.

The two American interrogators looked at each other. 'We'd better go see Kingsley and ask him what this is all about,' said SSgt. Huntley.

23

Something kept nagging him. Vaux felt that some piece of this jigsaw was missing. Old habits die hard. So he did what he usually did when he had a problem: he reached for a page of foolscap and started to type out what he knew—and tried to connect the dots.

He remembered now that Anne had brought over one of those laptops he'd seen around, a smallish portable computer that Anne had claimed was fast replacing the big and cumbersome desktop computers. He went through to Ahmed's old study where he had left it, so far untouched. Momtaz, who had been tidying up the room, watched as Vaux carefully opened the Dell laptop and studied the keyboard. More or less same as any typewriter. He pressed the power button and the screen came to life. But a few seconds later, the screen went blank and he pressed the button above the keyboard again. Nothing happened.

'*Non, non*, monsieur. Please, *laissez-moi*, let me.' Momtaz unwound a thick, black cable and pushed a two-pronged plug into a nearby wall socket. The screen came to life again.

Vaux thanked Momtaz. He sat down and began to type.

Operation Apostate

June 29 2005

What we know so far:

1 / A high-ranking officer / member of a sub-unit [Salafist?] of the Al-Qaeda in the Islamic Maghreb [AQIM], *an affiliate of the wider Al-Qaeda terrorist network, sought asylum in Britain and in return promised a heavy dossier on the leaders and members of the group plus details of their terrorist plans such as car bombings, possible train bombs [see Madrid] and kidnappings—their main source of funds to finance these activities.*

2 / Wary of a British double-cross, the defector sent a messenger, Mokhtar Tawil, to prepare for his postdefection arrival and to obtain reassurances plus a substantial cash deposit from the UK government. He stipulated that Tawil, on his return, be accompanied by an intelligence officer. [On his recent arrival in Tangier, Craw told me a subvention of $100,000 had been paid by the SIS as an earnest or gesture of good intentions.]

3 / On the train journey back to Morocco, Tawil was accompanied by an MI6 agent seconded to Dept. B3, Sebastian Micklethwait [Mickle]. Mickle's task was to reassure the defector on our pledge to guarantee him security [and possibly career prospects in counter-intelligence] and to accompany him on his journey to London [by train / air / boat?].

4 / The name of the defector was never given. Tawil had promised his patron this confidence and it was presumably an insurance should anything go wrong with the defection plans.

5 / Tawil was murdered on the Paris-Madrid overnight Express. He was alone in his sleeping compartment. Mickle was asleep in the next compartment. Morocco's DST has learned from Spanish intelligence that they suspect a 'targeted assassination.'

Tawil was apparently on Mossad's 'priority elimination' list as a high-profile target due to his senior position with the Salafist group—known by the acronym GSP. But there could be other intelligence outfits that wanted Tawil dead: the DST, the CIA, perhaps Spain's own Centro Nacional de Inteligencia [CNI]. In any case, MI6 clearly did not have him on any terrorist watch-list. We were reaching out to him at his request. This, then, is a classic case of 'crossed wires' among the various national intelligence agencies.

6 / So who killed Tawil and why?

7 / On the theory that our would-be defector still wanted to defect, we used Micklethwait as a lure to ferret him out. My idea was that the hapless defector would find out that Mickle had accompanied his aide-de-camp— whoever Tawil was—on that fatal train trip and would contact him as to his best way forward. Mickle was put up in the high-profile El Minza hotel and the theory was that in a relatively small port city like Tangier the bush telegraph would soon inform the defector as to the location of his potential helper.

8 / But now Micklethwait has been abducted and the would-be defector never materialized.

9 / Faud el-Mullah, an ex-spook in these parts, volunteered to help me chase down what few leads we had. He followed one of the men he suspected had something to do with a terrorist outfit to Melilla. According to Faud, the 'suspect' visited the British consulate there.

10 / Mort Cohen, the UK's honorary consul in Melilla, carried on an import-export trading business. I paid him a visit: it was a fishing expedition and yielded no results. But some ten days after my short visit, Cohen shot himself. Did he have business problems or was his despair related somehow to his dealings with Arab terrorists?

11 / The CIA got involved two weeks ago when intelligence sources informed them that 'a Spanish Jew' was involved in the kidnap plot. Their agents in the Mossad volunteered to help but so far they have come up with nothing.

12 / The Salafist group [GSP] have opened communication. They want the release of one Abdul Juhayman, now held by the CIA at a Moroccan black site, for the safe return of Micklethwait.

Conclusions:

A / The CIA are pulling the strings: they have promised to release Juhayman but as yet no timetable has been set. Official US policy is 'never to negotiate with terrorists.' But my impression is that they have very reluctantly agreed to this deal because they're between a rock and a hard place: We are strong allies [they need our continuing support in Iraq] and we are anxious for the freedom of one of our own.

B / We will have to monitor the exchange. Any fast-ones pulled by the CIA would endanger our man's life.

C / Follow-ups: check with local DST [Ghali etc.] about information on Toumert, an accountant who Faud suspects is 'somehow involved' in Micklethwait's abduction.

Also, check Ghali. He said at this morning's meeting that—

Now Vaux had a eureka! moment. *That* was what had been nagging him.

He now recalled that Ghali that morning had talked of 'the ruse these terrorists were playing' as the possible reason for targeting Tawil. He had talked of 'the sham' of the defection by a Salafist.

What was this all about? If true, that the planned defection was some sort of trick, how did Ghali know this? Was this just a pet theory of his? If Operation Apostate was in fact based on a massive hoax and no defector existed, then how would Ghali know about the terrorists' strategy?

Suddenly, Vaux saw the events of the past few weeks in a clear but different perspective.

But did this really change anything? It was water under the bridge. Mickle had been taken, Tawil killed off for reasons irrelevant to the current operation, and the Salafists were getting their man back.

Vaux kept at the keyboard.

Major pending questions:

What role does the man Hisham Toumert play in all this?

Why has Ghali seemingly stalled at interviewing him, not yet questioning him about Faud's suspicions of his being an actor in this whole drama?

Is Ghali a coconspirator who is reluctant to expose Toumert?

Faud is doubtless playing a double game—even a triple game. Yet he has supplied valuable information and gave us a lead on the possible location of Mickle—i.e. Melilla. But that was a bum steer.

Why did Mort Cohen take his own life? Ask Greaves to monitor Spanish inquest etc.

Finally: Why was the boy Hamid in the synagogue? Was he a courier sent to find any new messages? And why was he discovered and arrested? The only persons privy to the location of the dead drop [the synagogue] are our side and the terrorist cell. Who else knows about the arrangement?

Vaux read and reread the memorandum to himself.

It was time to call on Brad Kingsley. It seemed clear now that the CIA had discovered the location of the dead drop and that Kingsley had acted in defiance of Vaux's wishes: he had colluded with the Moroccans and organized the arrest of a probable courier of the enemy despite Vaux's warning that any such action could scupper the whole deal and lead to Micklethwait's murder in cold blood.

24

'I swear to God, I had nothing to do with that boy's arrest,' remonstrated the CIA's Brad Kingsley.

'I told you, it's the worst thing that could happen. It would demonstrate to the terrorists that we were not to be trusted—that we weren't negotiating in good faith,' said Vaux.

'Yeah, yeah, I know all that bullshit. I'll have a word with Ghali and find out who's responsible. What would a young boy have to do with any terrorist group?'

'They're used all the time. The unlucky ones have a bomb attached to their bodies and have a short life.'

'Sons of bitches.'

Vaux didn't know whether Kingsley referred to the young boys or the terrorists who sent them on suicide missions.

They were in the Old American Legation building where the CIA officer had installed himself in an elegant, second-floor room with gilt Louis Quinze chairs, silk-covered Second Empire couches and, in the center of the room, a big brass, filigreed Moroccan tray whose cherrywood base rested on a multicolored Berber rug.

Kingsley had called on the services of the two skilled interrogators because he suspected that 'the mysterious case of the Arab street boy in the synagogue' seemed highly dubious. He desperately wanted to know the whereabouts of the dead drop, so he had followed up every lead he could get. But the Brits had no need to know about his abortive attempts to undermine their arrangement with the terrorists. 'Anyway, I swear to God, I know nothing about the whereabouts of your dead drop facility. Let's get that quite clear. So let's cut to the chase, Vaux. Everything's set up. The rendezvous will be in a coastal town called El Jadida. Population: one hundred forty-four thousand. An ancient port city, first settled by the Portuguese. I've done my homework.'

Kingsley picked up a packet of Lucky Strikes and extracted a cigarette. He didn't offer Vaux the opportunity to break his vows. He lit up with a wind-cheating stainless steel Zippo and inhaled deeply. Vaux waited for the exhaled cloud. It took a forty-five degree direction out of the left side of Kingsley's tightly closed mouth. 'So you're coming in our vehicle. We don't need any other Brit. These escapades have a habit of getting unwieldy—everyone and his damned dog wants to get in on the kill.'

'That's an unfortunate turn of phrase.'

'Sorry, my English isn't so elegant. Brought up in a small town in New Jersey. You know, blue-collar types—all of us, including my old man.'

'About this character Toumert,' said Vaux, raising the subject he had come about.

'Yeah, right. What about him?'

'He should be checked out. One of my sources tells me he thinks the man, an older guy and a local accountant, seems in some way to be tied up in this game. I raised the matter with Ghali, but so far he hasn't moved on him. Not even brought him in for questioning.'

Kingsley slowly stubbed out the half-smoked cigarette in a round cut-glass ashtray. 'I'll see to it, OK? Be ready this Friday—bring a weekend bag. Oh, and I've arranged for the medics to be on call—just in case your man is malnourished or badly dehydrated.'

'I appreciate that.'

'You're welcome, sir.'

***

Fifteen minutes after Craw arrived at B3's Gower Street offices, he was summoned to Sir Nigel Adair's inner sanctum. Craw, who, like Vaux, had been trying to give up cigarettes for a year or so, smelled the familiar fug—a pungent mixture of Sir Nigel's Balkan Sobranie pipe tobacco and the Black Leather cologne his wife bought him every Christmas and each birthday.

Sir Nigel, irritated by Craw's habitual air of indifference and his adherence to bankers' hours, stood at the sash window that looked out onto the white-tiled inner well of the old building. He watched the frenetic comings and goings in the various offices opposite. The building was scheduled for ultimate demolition, thanks to the landlord's assessment that the ground on which it stood was far more valuable than the building itself—only five floors high and therefore not a significant generator of rents.

He heard Craw gently close the door, but he remained looking out of the grimy window whose sill was covered with two inches of gray-white pigeon droppings. It was a depressing scene. The scores of people he saw milling around in the other offices reminded him that his department had been seriously undermanned since he had taken over from Sir Walter Mason a few years back. Now, what staff he could muster were either missing in action (Micklethwait), seriously ill (Greene), or away on assignment (Vaux). What added to his gloom was the inevitable loss—as he saw it—of control over his current pet project, Operation Apostate. 'Well, Craw, what have you got to report?'

Craw, for once, was nonplussed. He was caught off guard. He really had nothing more to report than his brief account of where Operation Apostate stood when he arrived back in London on orders from Sir Nigel himself. That was why he hadn't made a mad rush to the office that morning—preferring to wallow in the lustful arms of his new lover, a buxom, sexy lady in her late thirties who worked behind the long bar at his local pub in Kensington. 'Well, sir. Nothing more than I've already told you. I'll be getting a briefing from Vaux later today'—he didn't really know whether this was an accurate prediction—'and I should think things are moving along as planned—'

'As planned?' Sir Nigel's raised voice always indicated a degree of irritation. He now turned to scrutinize Department B3's only deputy director—this despite his constant and urgent requests to the Vauxhall HR people to appoint two more deputies to meet the number mandated in that now dust-gathering, hush-hush green paper report in the late nineties.

'Yes, sir,' said Craw meekly.

'Look here, Craw. How can you say anything is "planned" when the whole bloody circus has been taken out of our hands? "C" now tells me that the CIA have taken over hook, line, and sinker and we're just going along with *their* plans—by default, as it were.'

'If I may, sir. That is not quite as I see the situation. I made it quite clear to this fellow Kingsley that nothing should be done that could endanger the life of our man Micklethwait—'

'Yes, yes, I know. But that's not my point. My point is that we have Vaux there, who is simply taking orders from this CIA man—'

'But that's not true, sir. If I say so myself, Vaux has established all sorts of contacts within Tangier—an impressive network of assets, actually. And he's been actively involved in tracking down this terrorist cell that's responsible for kidnapping Sebastian.'

'Sebastian?' asked Sir Nigel.

'Micklethwait!'

'Yes, yes, all right, Craw.'

Sir Nigel returned to his scuffed leather swivel chair. He picked up his straight meerschaum pipe, opened a drawer and took out an old, worn leather pouch. He transferred the finely textured tobacco and stuffed it with his thumb into the bowl of the pipe. Behind him, a family-size box of Swan Vestas lay on an old mahogany credenza whose surface was scarred by numerous perfectly round, whitish circles where hot coffee cups had been parked by busy staffers. He extracted a match and lit his pipe. The process took a long minute or two. Craw inched back his chair while Sir Nigel concentrated on several strong draws. 'So tell me again. Where do we stand with Micklethwait?'

'Well, regretfully, he's still incarcerated. But as far as we know, he's alive and well. Vaux tells me the exchange will take place this coming weekend.'

Sir Nigel had been told this only yesterday. 'Then you'd better get back there, hadn't you?'

'You don't understand, sir. This CIA man says he doesn't want anyone else but Vaux in the Brit contingent, as he puts it.'

'Damn what he thinks, Craw! You're Vaux's bloody case officer. This is what I find so frustrating, man! We've been to-tally eliminated from any serious decision-making in this busi-ness—and yet it's our abducted operative who's at the center of the whole thing. For God's sake, let's show some initiative. I'm damned if we are simply going to be a bunch of "yes men." Do you understand?'

Craw knew it was no use trying to explain what he liked to call the 'situation on the ground'—a phrase he had picked up from his Israeli cohorts when they discussed the low probability of Israel's withdrawing from occupied territories on the West Bank.

Silence reigned. Sir Nigel was enjoying his pipe and thinking. Craw could see tonight's date with the barmaid disintegrating before his red-tinted eyes.

Sir Nigel got up and stood at the window again. He turned to face Craw. 'Listen carefully, Alan.' Craw knew that the use of his first name was a sign that unpleasant orders were about to be issued. 'I want you to get on the first available plane to Morocco. Get Anne to book the flight—any flight, just get there. Go home now, pack a suitcase and get in touch with Michael Vaux immediately. No resting up in a luxurious hotel or anything of that sort. This is serious business.

'I'll back you up by getting "C" to contact CIA liaison. My orders are that you should accompany Vaux on this mission in the desert, or wherever, and that you should thoroughly debrief both Vaux and this CIA wallah and report back to me ASAP. I feel I'm not getting the full story—an instinct of mine that's rarely wrong. I expect your report by tomorrow night at the latest. You'd better get moving. What is it they say in those TV police procedurals? Chop, chop!'

Craw got up. There was nothing more to be said.

'One last thing,' said Sir Nigel. 'Micklethwait's grandmother has been calling. Anne always stalls her, but I'll have to speak to her eventually. She's eighty-five now and is mad as hell at what she calls the "sluggish pace" of our attempts to find her grandson. She used to work for us—in the war. Brilliant code breaker at Bletchley, they say. Anyway, I'd like to give her some good news soon.'

Craw stood at the open door and looked back at Sir Nigel, who was smiling. 'Chop, chop!' said Sir Nigel again.

***

Hisham Toumert sipped his thick black coffee. He sat at the cluttered desk, the old Adler adding machine directly in front of him. His sausage fingers banged at the keys: he was adding up the money he had spent over the last month on what he named only to himself as 'The Abduction.'

He was not an overly religious man, but he considered himself a true Muslim who prayed daily when his workload permitted and obeyed the solemn rituals of Ramadan—the Muslims' annual month-long moveable fast and feast.

Now in his midsixties, he had always been a radical at heart. In his student days, he had joined various unfocused protest groups whose aims varied from pressuring the government to cut the price of bread to getting rid of what they saw as a corrupt monarchy whose avarice continued to siphon off the nation's wealth for its own selfish enrichment.

When Morocco won its independence from France, the world beckoned. Its citizens were told they were on the threshold of a new era: Morocco was rich—no oil, perhaps, but the world's biggest deposits of phosphates (the main ingredient of the fertilizers that a hungry planet needed to grow more food) and a farming sector whose produce would be gobbled up by the voracious appetites of their European neighbors to the north.

But, like most Moroccans, Toumert knew they had been cheated. Elections had come and gone, political parties banned and resurrected. But the pervasive poverty persisted to this day. The people had been short-changed. And the new King Mohammed VI was reported to be the richest monarch in the world—even surpassing the wealth of the British royal family.

None of this sat well with Toumert. His two sons had grown up but had disappeared into the slums of Casablanca. They had left Tangier at the height of King Hassan's clampdown that followed an aborted attempt to assassinate him there. The king took his revenge on all of Tangier's citizens: funds for public housing and infrastructure were cut, social programs for the poor shelved, and the once-colorful Paris-style street-side cafés were ordered not to sell alcohol. And so, the annual flood of big-spending Europeans dried up. Tourism, the lifeblood of the old port city, died a slow death, and the incomes of Tangier's residents plummeted to new depths.

Hassan's son, the new king, had brought in some reforms. Tangier became the favorite city of his brother, Prince Moulay Rachid. New building plans were drawn up and the laws on selling alcohol relaxed. Perhaps Tangier could regain its old glory. But Toumert's life was nearly over. He was healthy, but most of his contemporaries had died in their sixties. So he did what he could for what he liked to call the reformers—those who were bent on changing the old feudal system into a modern state with the nation's wealth more equally shared—the European or American model.

And he could never quite grasp why the Americans, of all people, propped up the status quo in spite of all the inequities. Liberty and democracy, the American way of life, seemed to be only for those who lived in the West. For all their talk, the Americans strongly supported nondemocratic regimes the world over—from South America to Saudi Arabia. He knew the rebels were a motley crowd—they ranged from moderate, liberal reformers to fundamentalist militant Muslims—but he would not refuse help to any group who fought the established order. They were on the right side of history.

So when an uninvited Driss Ghali and his partner walked into his office, he was not entirely taken by surprise. He looked up from the adding machine. 'Yes, gentlemen, what can I do for you? Your tax returns, perhaps?'

It was midday. The ceiling and table fans were humming but had little effect and it was still very hot. They could smell the fried fish oil from downstairs.

Ghali made the introductions and showed a local police ID card.

'Yes, I know you. At least, I knew your father, Yacoub, in the old days. We went to the same classes at the École de Commerce. I remember him well. How is he?'

'He died several years ago. *Yacoub, Allah yerhamah.*' May God have mercy upon him.

'*Rahemahu Allah*,' said Toumert. May God have mercy upon his soul. 'I am sorry to hear of his passing.'

A minute or so of silence to pay their respects.

'Just a few routine questions, sir. Did you hear about the missing Englishman?' Ghali believed that sudden, blunt questions often unnerved a suspect or a potential witness, and it would always show.

But Toumert showed no surprise. 'I heard something through the grapevine to that effect. Rumors swirl around this area like a Sahara sandstorm, Inspector.'

'We are just following up some leads here.' Ghali then turned to Didi Hassan to take up their gentle line of questioning.

'It's no rumor. A British man has disappeared. He was staying at the Minzah. You have your ears to the ground. We wondered if you'd heard anything.'

'Of course,' said Toumert, his habitual smile now fixed into position.

'So have you heard anything more substantial than what you thought perhaps was a rumor only?'

'No, nothing,' said Toumert. 'Was this man a tourist? There were two stabbings on the beach last summer. Could be, the man was down there late at night and you know why male tourists go to that area, surely.'

'No, tell us,' said Ghali.

'Well, you know. Our young men are short of cash. They need money to feed themselves and their families. So they sell their bodies for an hour or two...'

'But what's that got to do with a missing persons case?' asked Ghali.

'Well, use your imagination, Inspector. This gentleman from England goes on a quest for a young man, say, and he zeroes in on a thug—a good-looking thug, maybe, but a ruthless thief and killer.

Or maybe the thief never intended to kill this victim—but it happened. So this gentleman gets stabbed for his wallet and the culprit and his friends dispose of the body somewhere—perhaps out at sea. In which case, he'll no doubt wash up on our shores before too long.' Toumert sat back in his chair. He thought he had made a good point and he was still smiling. He moved the worn-out old calculator away from him toward the two security agents.

Ghali decided to come to the point. 'We heard that one of your assistants has been visiting Melilla recently. What's that all about?'

Toumert's eyes widened as if to suggest a silly question. 'I am looking to expand my client base, Inspector. I hear there's a shortage of good accountants in Melilla and I'm thinking of opening up another office there. Is that so surprising?'

'You'd be dealing with Spanish laws and tax regulations there.'

'Well, of course. But I'm not too old to learn new tricks.'

'Have you had any dealings with the British consulate there?' asked Hassan.

'No, but my assistant may have approached the people there to see if they had any knowledge of available office space, and so forth.'

'Where is this assistant?'

'He's on some auditing job, I think.'

'His name?'

'Magdi Kassim.'

Ghali got up, followed by Didi. 'OK, sir. I think that's all.'

'Let me give you my business card in case you have any more questions, Inspector.' Toumert sorted through a pile of tattered and stained business cards. He finally selected what he was looking for—his own, freshly minted, crisp and embossed.

At the door, Ghali posed the last-minute question he had rehearsed earlier. 'Do you know a boy named Hamid, Hamid Nackla?'

Toumert was still standing behind his desk. He sat down heavily. The complacent smile had at last disappeared. He had the look of a man racking his brains to remember a name. 'Yes, I seem to know that name. He works downstairs. Delivers food to customers who order by phone. Ask old Salma, the owner.'

'You never send him on the odd errand? The boy seems hungry for work,' said Ghali.

'So he should be at that age. No, I don't think I've ever spoken to him.'

When they landed at the bottom of the narrow staircase, Didi asked: 'Shall we talk to this Salma fellow?'

'*Yallah!*' said Ghali. 'Let's get out of here.'

When they got back to the small DST bureau within Tangier's main police station, Driss Ghali sent Didi Hassan down to the canteen for a Fanta. When Hassan returned with two bottles of the sweet, gassy orange drink, Ghali was busy writing notes. Hassan asked him what he thought of the short interview with old Toumert.

Ghali looked with steely eyes toward his colleague. 'He wasn't bullshitting. I remember my father and him going fishing together. They used to come back with baskets full of mullet and sardines. We'd eat off the bounty for days.'

'So?' Hassan thought this cute, historical anecdote irrelevant to the major concern that confronted them.

'So, we leave him alone. What Faud told us was just hearsay, let's face it. I'm not going to question everyone Faud thinks could be mixed up with the Englishman's disappearance. We'd have to pull in half the residents of the medina!'

'But Faud gave us the major lead—about Juhayman and the jihad cell that want to do a trade—'

'Didi, forget Toumert, OK? If anything, he's just a small cog in a big wheel. He's harmless. And my father, God rest his soul, loved him. So we drop it, OK?'

25

Michael Vaux dreaded the thought of being cooped up in some overheated official car with Brad Kingsley and his CIA crew for what would be a long journey south. But the Friday departure date for El Jadida was three days away, and, by nature a tidy man, he wondered what loose ends he could tie up here in Tangier while he waited for the climax of Operation Rescue—the name designated by Sir Nigel with Craw's enthusiastic endorsement, to embody the multinational effort to get Sebastian Micklethwait the hell out of Morocco.

It was early morning and he sat by the pool after his first swim. A low mist hung over the calm Atlantic and the palm trees and the tall planes glistened with the overnight dew. It could be another long, languid day in this corner of paradise, but experience had taught him that such blissful anticipation was an illusion. And this time, he had only himself to blame.

He picked up the encrypted cell phone he had placed on the blue-and white-mosaic tiles and dialed the number in Rabat.

'Greaves.'

'George. How are you?'

'As well as could be expected at six forty-five in the morning, thank you.'

'Are you up yet?'

'Oh, yes. I never sleep much after six.'

'I was thinking.'

'That fills me with foreboding…'

'Poor old Cohen was in your jurisdiction, wasn't he?'

'No, old boy. He answered to our people in Madrid. Melilla's a part of Spain, if you recall.'

'Anyway, would you have any objection to my going there and checking a few things out? There's an awful lot that doesn't add up—'

'You mean about his death? Don't worry. The Spanish authorities say there was no doubt he took his own life. He left the handwritten note, and the ballistics support the verdict of death by his own hand. His wife has no doubts about it.'

'Have you paid her a visit?'

'No, mate. Haven't had the time for compassionate calls, I'm afraid.'

'Then you won't mind if I go. There's a few questions left hanging in the air, that's all.'

'You intrigue me. What sort of questions?'

'I'll let you know if I make any progress.'

Greaves had known Vaux had paid a visit to Cohen to pick his brains for any morsel of information about the disappearance of their colleague, the English diplomat. But Vaux had never told him that he had gone to Melilla solely on a tip from Faud, whose diligence had uncovered visits to Britain's honorary consul by envoys of the man Toumert. Faud had suggested, without irony, that Toumert's dubious, two-faced affiliations with various 'nationalistic' groups were well known on the street.

On that fishing trip, Vaux had come up empty. This time, he thought, it could be different.

Vaux walked up to the villa, had a shower, and prepared for the trip. At breakfast, with Momtaz fussing around him, constantly offering more croissants and refills of fresh orange juice, he asked Mahmud to take him to Melilla again. It would be a day trip, and once over the border, they would head for the same warehouse as last time.

Vaux had called Rachel Cohen's small apartment on the Calle Cervantes. When she realized the man on the phone represented official Whitehall, she readily agreed to open up Cohen's office and to be there to welcome him. She would help in any way she could, and perhaps he could answer a few questions that had arisen from the sudden and unforeseen death of her husband.

Mahmud dropped Vaux off in front of the consulate. The consul's official flag still hung languidly from the forty-five degree angled flagpole. Vaux thought they might have put it at half-mast in honor of old Cohen.

Rachel Cohen was short and stout. Her hair seemed like a throwback to another century—carefully marcelled, long finger waves of jet-black hair clinging close to the head and covering her ears but not her pearl earrings. She made abundant use of mascara and deep-red lipstick that only emphasized the pallor of her skin. But she displayed a sort of middle-age sophistication that some men find attractive.

She sat in Cohen's ergonomic chair and rearranged various articles on the desk as Vaux expressed his condolences. 'Yes, well—it was all a great shock to me and everyone who knew my dear husband. But we had a good life together—never easy, but we were always happy.'

Vaux worried about her finances. 'Will you be all right—financially, I mean?'

'Morty always believed in life insurance. He saw to it that I would want for nothing if he went suddenly.'

Vaux wondered if the insurance policy excluded payouts for suicides. But he said nothing.

He said, 'No pension from the Foreign Office, I suppose.'

'Not a bean. And after all these years.'

'They sometimes arrange ad hoc payments in such cases, a lump sum for services rendered, that sort of thing. I'd look into it.'

'I will, thank you.'

Vaux then asked Mrs. Cohen if she would mind his checking a few things around the office. He said that it was just a routine exercise that Whitehall required in the sort of circumstances of her husband's death.

She invited him to be her guest. She didn't mind a bit and would he like to get together for dinner, perhaps. Vaux thanked her but said that time was pressing. When she got up, Vaux heard a low, protesting growl from under the kneehole of Cohen's desk as a small, furry bichon frise emerged, its tail wagging at the exciting prospect of another walk.

'Come on, Benji, it's time for your supper.' The small dog gave out an excited woof, its short legs moving quickly toward the door as it led its mistress out of the office.

Vaux got to work. He went over to the long window and looked out on to the Plaza de España. On his last visit to Cohen, he gave himself no time for any touristy curiosity. But now he had the time to get a better look at the old colony: the big square had been largely designed in the 1920s by Enrique Nieto, a disciple of the great Spanish art deco architect, Gaudí. This he had read in a guidebook as he sat in the back of the immaculate, black Mercedes 190E on his way here.

His earlier visit had been rushed and he had seen little of the exotic enclave. Perhaps he would wander around a bit before the trip back. He was admiring Nieto's 1940s masterpiece, the town hall on the north side of the square, when his eyes fell on a shiny, steel wastepaper basket hidden behind the heavy velvet curtain. A good place to start.

He sorted through scores of small paper receipts—lunch bills, parking and garage tickets, Visa records, and finally an invoice headed PAYMENT OVERDUE from the Or Zoruah synagogue on the Calle Lopez Marino. It looked like Cohen had pledged three hundred euros for the renovation and refurbishment fund.

Vaux picked up the bunch of keys left on the desk by Mrs. Cohen and headed for a row of steel filing cabinets. He went through every manila folder and wondered if he was wasting his time. The bills of lading revealed in meticulously boring detail the types of goods Cohen traded: from Moroccan nectarines and almonds to brass sconces and heavy Berber carpets. Imports ranged from precision-made auto parts to car fenders and Goodyear tires. Spanish perfumes and soaps were heavily traded, and Vaux was surprised to see a 'coals to Newcastle' factor in Morocco's apparent thirst for Spanish olive oil.

He looked at his Accurist wristwatch. He had about an hour left. He sat down in Cohen's ergonomic chair and craved a Camel. But he had none, so he had to press on. He began to open the drawers of the desk, one by one. There were old pocket diaries, small books with names and telephone numbers—all, as far as he could see, related to Cohen's trading business: a few souvenir ashtrays from places like Barcelona and Madrid, a small but solid iron replica of the Tour Eiffel and postcards from all over Europe. An unopened slim, cellophane-sealed tin of cigarillos sat as a solitary temptress in the center drawer.

Vaux gathered up the keys and headed for the door. He would try to enter the small storage room with the peephole in the door. Just as he looked around the office one last time, his eyes fell on a scrap of paper pinned on the leather-topped desk by an old, cracked Toby jug full of assorted ballpoint pens and lead pencils. He had noticed the old-fashioned mug before, but his eyes must have glossed over the jagged piece of paper. He picked it up. A car registration number: 77268 B 6. Underneath the seven-digit number, Cohen had written 'Jeep.'

Vaux pocketed the fragile chit of paper and skipped down the wrought-iron staircase to the main garage. There was nobody there, and he guessed Cohen's customers were observing the customary shiva. All the better. He saw that a large iron key was already in the lock. He turned it and pushed the door forward. It was pitch black. He flipped the light switch, and a dull, thirty-watt bulb hanging from the center of the ceiling gave out a dim, mellow light. Vaux saw the narrow bunk. There were no coverings, just a stained pillowcase. Then he checked out some cardboard cartons that had been pushed together in a corner: he saw several cans of Fray Bentos corned beef, six cans of Spam, cans of frankfurters and small half-cans of mixed fruit.

He looked at the upright chair beside the bed. A can opener, the practical, old-fashioned type, lay on the shiny wooden seat. Then he went through a narrow, curtained gap in the wall. A shower and WC. The smell of urine and mold reminded Vaux of his youthful days tramping around Europe and staying in crappy youth hostels.

This was surely a place where kidnappers could hide their victims. The peep hole now made sense. No wonder Cohen had chosen not to show him his 'small storage room.'

Mahmud was, as usual, spot on time. Before Vaux climbed into the rear of the car (Mahmud always insisted his passengers sit in the luxury of the backseats), he gave Mahmud the piece of paper.

'That's a car registration plate number, Mahmud. Any idea what city or town it indicates?'

'Oh, yes, sir. The last number—six. That's Casablanca, without a doubt.'

***

Najla, Bill Harvey's lithe, young assistant, clad in her usual black hijab, handed him the decoded message:

Operation Rescue

Planned day of exchange: July 10
Location: El Jadida.
Proposed site: Church of the Assumption
Cité Portugaise
El Jadida
Time (tentative): Noon
Special logistics:
Three (3) Toyota Land Cruisers on standby.
Participants: 1) Six-man team of Special Operations Forces,
(AFRICOM). Base: Agadir.
2) Diplomatic / CIA personnel (US)
3) Diplomatic / MI6 personnel (UK)

Liaison: Coordinate with UK intelligence.

AUTHORITY: SUNRISE GROSVENOR

Brad Kingsley's code name was a constant reminder that he had to answer to his London-based chief fifteen hundred miles away in the great British capital, where the ornate US embassy was located on elegant Grosvenor Square. Kingsley had assumed full responsibility for the operation to rescue a British diplomat from the hands of AQIM, and he considered this a vote of no confidence. He had done his best: drawn a blank with the *sayanim*, never found a trace of any Spanish Jew who could have been involved in the kidnapping plot, and had been sidelined by Kingsley's decision to take over the operation.

Najla's brown almond-shaped eyes rarely met his, but this morning, she looked at him with some anticipation. She was an attractive girl, but he couldn't get to grips with what he called the Muslim code of ethics and had never suggested any social get-together. He once asked her out for lunch but she'd muttered something about fasting.

'But Ramadan's not for some months, surely,' he protested.

'No, no. A diet,' she laughed.

'But you don't need to diet,' said Kingsley. He guessed she was just over five feet tall and weighed about 110 pounds. A few years back, his sister had nearly died of anorexia nervosa, but he decided not to get into it. Besides, his wife was due to fly in from the States any day now.

She still stood there. 'What is it, Najla?'

'I wondered if you had to answer the message. I can take your answer down and transmit back to London.'

'My boss is in Tangier. OK. Send an encoded teletype to the American legation offices there.'

She looked up, note pad in her hand, a pen hovering in anticipation.

'Just say, "Message received and understood,"' said Harvey. 'And use the basic book code.'

26

'You deserve a gold medal,' said Vaux. Vaux knew he was taking a risk but gambled on Faud's persistent need for cash. And it had once again paid off.

He had got Mahmud to drop him off close to the Minzah. It was early evening, and he knew by now Faud would have left the Café Central. So he made his way to the narrow, quiet Avenue des Postes and knocked gently on the door. Faud was in a nightshirt, his feet in leather babouches, and he looked tired. Vaux explained what he wanted and told him that cash would be on delivery.

Faud took the piece of paper and asked Vaux to leave it with him.

Within twelve hours, Vaux had boarded an Air Maroc flight to Casablanca. Along with many other passengers, he was just a tourist who planned to spend a few days checking out Casablanca, the storied port city made famous by the World War II Hollywood movie. He didn't feel much like Humphrey Bogart, and he doubted his chances of meeting any girl as glamorous as Ingrid Bergman, but he felt the familiar excitement of an assignment in an unfamiliar location.

Faud had used his usual arcane methods to discover the address where the Jeep's owner was domiciled (his word), and Vaux would go from there. It could be a wild goose chase, but there must have been a good reason why Cohen had written down the number on the Jeep's license plate. It suggested a need to identify one of his recent visitors who had presumably left no other traces of his usual 'place of abode.' That was enough to arouse Vaux's own suspicions, and he had decided to follow his intuition.

Vaux checked into a hotel close to the Jeep's registered address on the busy Boulevard d'Oujda. It was a seedy and shabby hostelry, offering cheap shelter to weary travelers who had just arrived at the nearby rail terminus on the Place de la Gare. The room was small, with a washbasin in the corner that smelled of urine. The stained brown carpet was pockmarked with cigarette burns. And the bedside table showed long scars where former guests had let their cigarettes smolder while they slept. For a shower, Vaux had to walk along the corridor and wait his turn while other guests washed off the grime of their journeys or their lovemaking.

But it would do. He figured he would only have to stay two nights, max—and from what he had seen from the backseat of the petit taxi that had brought him from the airport, there were plenty of small, cheap bars in the area that would provide enough booze to help him ignore the squalor of his room.

He dumped his leather holdall on the bed, hung his blue blazer from one of the three tarnished brass hooks on the back of the door, rinsed his hands at the washbasin (no soap provided) and went down three floors in a shaky, narrow cage elevator that groaned and then shuddered to an abrupt halt on the ground floor. An old Arab, who wore a fez and a shabby black western suit, took his room key—anchored by a heavy brass ball—and nodded without smiling.

He walked around the traffic-clogged square to the entrance of the Boulevard d'Oujda. From the hip pocket of his khaki chinos, he produced the slip of paper Faud had passed to him on the terrace of the Café Central: 20 bis, Boul. d'Oujda. Scribbled beneath the address:

20 bis is the flat above No. 20, a small café
(shawarma, kebabs, kofta, chicken)

Vaux walked swiftly past the small restaurant and looked into a shoe-shop window further down the street. He glanced back at the restaurant and then in the opposite direction. He observed the busy sidewalk on the other side. He didn't suspect anyone could be tailing him—his trip had been arranged too quickly for unfriendly watchers to have had time to organize. But *caution can save your life*—to quote the Portsmouth training manual Craw had insisted he reread when he was called back in from the cold. He saw no suspicious or sudden movements, and nobody appeared to be hiding behind a newspaper.

He sauntered into the small restaurant as if he were a curious and hungry tourist. Neon-strip lighting cast a harsh, bluish glow over the crowded room and a jukebox played the latest top ten from France. Kebabs and chicken legs were cooking on a hot grill and big hunks of lamb turned on vertical rotisseries. Customers, oblivious of the heat and the steam from the massive bowls of couscous, lined up at the long counter and took their meals back to the few tables that were free. A shelf that went around the whole room enabled some diners to eat standing.

Vaux ordered a lamb shawarma. He moved to the far wall and sat on a high stool, his paper plate on the shelf. He looked for an entrance to the flat upstairs. There was only one rear exit. He went back to the counter and ordered a bottle of mineral water. The younger of the two chefs served him.

'Toilet?' asked Vaux.

The young man pointed to the beaded curtain at the rear. Vaux took his water over to his unfinished meal and then went through the screen of colored beads. A dark passageway led to the toilet: it was a Turkish squat latrine, and the smell of feces and urine was overpowering. He quickly looked for other doors and some evidence of a staircase. But the passage was crammed with smelly floor mops, stinking buckets, and empty plastic bottles that had once contained detergents and bleach. He went back to his paper plate, but it had been cleared away. He swigged some water and left.

He turned left toward the big square. And then he saw it. A single, paneled door adjacent to the café: in glinting brass, about five inches high, the elusive '20 bis.' Now he would be the patient watcher. It seemed the only bit of tradecraft that could yield anything useful in the circumstances. He lingered, posing as a casual window-shopper. Every few seconds, he checked the door to 20 bis.

After three hours, the café was closing up. It was about 11:00 p.m. Vaux felt like a stiff drink. But then he had a thought. He had noticed an alley further up the street. It presumably led to the back of the building that housed the café and the flat above. It was a narrow, dark walkway littered with discarded food cartons, chicken bones and plastic bottles. The passage opened up to a wide, murky wasteland of old cannibalized cars, metal junk of all shapes and sizes, and used-up, battered plastic food containers.

Suddenly, Vaux heard the engine of a car. It revved up as the Jeep TJ bumped over a wide concrete hump, presumably a deterrent to a speedy entry. He quickly moved to hide behind a cluster of garbage dumpsters. He heard loud Arabic pop music as two men got out of the Jeep. One of the men carried a ghetto-blaster boom box tuned to maximum volume. He checked the Jeep's number plate: 77268 B 6.

'Bingo,' he said, very softly. He saw that the men were young-ish—in their early thirties, dressed like most young Casablancans in western-style blue jeans, casual shirts and trainers.

The couple sauntered toward the iron fire escape and walked up the first flight of stairs where they opened a door and let themselves in. They were in high spirits and the taller man had a hand over the other's shoulder. When they disappeared, Vaux slinked over to the Jeep. They hadn't bothered to lock the doors. He dived in under the dashboard and quickly checked out the interior of the vehicle. In the backseat, a thick sweater and some cartons of Winston cigarettes. He stretched over to the glove box. It opened with a click, and he found just what he needed—a SIG Sauer MK25. He'd left his Browning in Tangier because of airport security. He checked the chamber and put the pistol in the inside pocket of his blazer.

He reached the first landing of the steep iron stairs and saw that the front door of the apartment had been left ajar. Vaux looked down at the desolate yard beneath him and heard several clicks and clangs as the Jeep's engine cooled. He gripped the Sauer and pushed the door forward. The music had been turned down, and he listened for any movements or chatter that would indicate the location of the two men.

He moved along the narrow hallway as quietly as a cat stalking a sparrow. The first door on the right had been left slightly open. Someone moaned in satisfaction. He heard the unmistakable soft sounds of pleasure, the intimate whispers of lovers. Through a six-inch gap between the door and the jamb, he saw the two men on a large double bed. Their naked bodies were intertwined.

Vaux couldn't believe his luck. The orgasmic target of lovemak-ing, he figured, would absorb all their attention at least for another five minutes or so, maybe longer. He looked down the narrow hall-way and saw another door to his left. It had also been left open. He entered a small, cramped sitting room with a clunky, stained sofa and two scuffed leather armchairs. In the corner was a small, old-fashioned rolltop writing desk. He pulled out the center drawer. And there was the second big find of the day: a Moroccan passport. The holder's name: Magdi Kassim. Vaux quickly pocketed the passport, turned toward the door and listened. The sexual ululations were still in full swing. He trod softly as he went past the bedroom toward the front door. He skipped down the iron steps and got back on to the Boulevard d'Oujda.

Between the shawarma place and the Place de la Gare, he found a small crowded and smoky bar called the Stella. He ordered a Cutty Sark but was told his choice was limited: only the house whisky was available—J&B. He ordered a large one and fished for his encoded hand device. Curious bystanders would think nothing of a man making a call on his cell phone.

***

'Where the hell is Vaux?' asked Craw.

'All I can say is that he's working hard to free Micklethwait. Let's just say that he's chosen to be in the vanguard of Operation Rescue,' said Greaves.

'What's that supposed to mean?' asked Craw, now close to exasperation.

Greaves, finishing off his breakfast in bed, laid the small tray on the bedside table. He didn't want to tell Craw too much, even though their lines were secure. Craw had apparently flown into Tangier just as Vaux had flown out for Casablanca. Now he couldn't understand why Vaux wasn't around to welcome him and update him on the task that lay ahead. Office politics aside, he had no obligation to answer Craw's questions or pander to his self-importance. As MI6's chief of station in Rabat, there was no direct line of command between the mother institution and Department B3, a maverick offshoot that deliberately kept its distance from the chieftains in Vauxhall.

'Look, I haven't time to go into it at the moment, Alan. But I'm sure Vaux will be in contact shortly. We'll both know more then. Adios, amigo.' Greaves knew his answer would infuriate Craw, but he pressed the *off* button before Craw had a chance to reply.

Greaves's encoded handset buzzed five seconds later.

'This is Ferrari. Please identify yourself,' said the caller.

Greaves replied, 'This is Blaine.'

In their brief talk the previous evening, the new arrival had said he was having a drink at the Casablanca, the lobby bar at his hotel where the walls were covered with stills from the classic movie. They had agreed on the prudence of code names. So Greaves had suggested the bar-owning characters out of the story: he'd be Blaine (Bogart's lead role), and the other man would be Ferrari, the pro-prietor of the Blue Parrot, Blaine's competitor, played by the gruff and sinister Sydney Greenstreet.

'How are you this morning, sir?'

The caller was Lieutenant Justin Simpson of the UK's Special Forces Support Group/Counter Terrorism (SFSG), who, with a staff sergeant and corporal plus three squaddies, had flown into Morocco's military airbase at Kenitra twenty-four hours earlier.

'What's up?' asked Greaves.

'Made contact with Westropp late last night. Suspects' resi-dence now under surveillance. We plan to go in tonight, sir.'

'Report to me when you've got the bastards in custody,' said Greaves. 'What's their likely destination?'

'DST's dungeons in Casa, sir.'

'Good. And good luck, Signor Ferrari,' said Greaves.

This was getting very interesting. The Moroccans wouldn't stand for any nonsense from these two thugs. He hoped Vaux was right about the identity of this Magdi Kassim character. If he was,

the no-nonsense interrogation experts at the DST would soon uncover the whereabouts of young Micklethwait.

***

At the moment Greaves had Micklethwait on his mind, John
Keen a.k.a Omar Sala handed the young MI6 probationer a large
plastic bottle of Sidi Ali mineral water. The minivan had pulled up
at an isolated opening in a dense cedar forest in the foothills of the
Atlas, southeast of Rabat on the N6 highway to Meknes. The sliding doors had been opened and a zephyr of hot, humid air helped
mitigate the tobacco smoke.

'Just up the road is a place called Khemisset, a Berber market
town. The guys in the Land Rover have gone there to collect some
more food and stuff,' said Keen.

Micklethwait, whose legs were still manacled, had resigned
himself to his fate. He couldn't be sure if the planned exchange
Keen had told him about would come off successfully. His captors
could renege on the deal at the last minute. He didn't know who
would be rooting for him, either. He expected some Secret Service
types, maybe a small contingent from his own B3 team. What role
would the CIA play? The Americans held this guy the terrorists
wanted freed—so where would they fit in?

'Don't look so worried, mate. Only another few hours and
we'll be at the meeting point. And if all goes well, you'll be a free
man again,' said Keen.

By now, Micklethwait had got used to John Keen's reassurances. He had grown to like this Londoner's tireless good humor
and wondered sometimes if he was really cut out to be a serious
jihadist. Keen gave him regular pep talks in an attempt to persuade
him to see his side's points of view, and the nationalist parts of the
diatribe—how the West had dominated the Mideast and the Arab
world for far too long—were easy to sympathize with.

But he conceded nothing to Keen, and his obstinate adherence to the West's interpretation of events seemed to amuse his English escort. 'I'll agree with you about the colonialist powers of a hundred years ago and how they exploited the whole African continent. But the Arabs have set back their just cause by this barbaric slide into terrorism,' said Micklethwait during one of Keen's brainstorming sessions.

Keen replied: 'In other words, we in the Arab world have to lie quiescent while the West—first the English and French, and now the Yanks—push, just a little, bit by bit, the Arab autocrats toward some sort of representative democracy?

'I don't think so, mate. It's not working, anyway. Believe me, one of these days in the not-too-distant future, my friend, many of the Arab nations will rise up and overthrow the tyrants. It will probably start in Egypt, where that kleptomaniac autocrat rules the roost and then spread west to the Maghreb.'

When Keen's rhetoric soared to new heights, it often seemed to Micklethwait that he was preaching to his comrades in the minivan as much as to him. Almost as if he wished to reassure them of his total religious and political conversion.

Micklethwait said, 'That's quite a speech, John. I respect your beliefs and your faith. But what do you have in common with these militants who think nothing of killing innocent people en masse—at railway stations, bus stops, or street-side cafés? Don't expect me ever to support those crazy fanatics.'

'You're incorruptible, eh?' Keen laughed and looked over to the guard who still sat in the long rear seat of the minivan, now nursing an AK-47 in his lap. He looked bored.

But Micklethwait decided to seize the moment. Keen had been more talkative than at any time during the long drive south on the A1 from Tangier. 'Look, John. Englishman to Englishman—be fair. Where and when is this exchange going to take place? I think as a major participant, I deserve to know.'

'Be patient, young man. The meeting place is south of here. We've still quite a way to go. But everything, so far as we know, is going according to plan,' said Keen.

'So you are getting your man back?'

'Of course we bloody well are. Otherwise, this whole trip's a waste of time.'

Micklethwait had something else on his mind. 'I haven't shaved since I was abducted in Tangier. I never thought I could grow such a big, luxuriant beard. You've made me wear the usual white cotton djellaba, and my sneakers disappeared one morning to be replaced by these heavy leather sandals. So, all in all, I look like a Muslim— or at any rate like a native from these parts. No offense, please. But couldn't this confuse the parties concerned in the exchange of prisoners? We wouldn't want any mix-ups, would we?'

Keen brushed off Micklethwait's concerns. 'With those blue eyes and your auburn hair, I think everyone concerned will see you as a Brit in fellaheen garb. You'll be playing the role of Lawrence of Arabia, revisited!'

Keen had a good laugh. He looked over at the guard whose disinterested eyes remained fixed on Micklethwait. The probationary secret agent shook his head just perceptibly and closed his eyes.

27

Partly out of sheer loneliness, or perhaps a feeling that he was deliberately being left out of the picture, Alan Craw sauntered down to the Old American Legation building where he hoped to meet up with Brad Kingsley. He was asked to sit in the small austere conference room while the middle-aged English lady who dispensed coffee and note pads left to fetch the American 'guest' who had never bothered to explain to her the reason for his daily presence in the quasi-museum.

Kingsley and his Rabat-based sidekick Bill Harvey didn't keep Craw waiting. Both carried manila folders under their arms, and Harvey had a large, rolled-up map that he quickly unrolled and smoothed out on the Formica table. He stretched for the two small ashtrays to help pin it down. Craw loosened his starched collar a little and lowered the Windsor knot of his tie to acknowledge the oppressive heat of the room.

'I'm glad to see you,' said Kingsley. 'Your colleague's walked out on us at just the right moment. We're leaving tonight for the crucial rendezvous. Where the hell is Vaux?'

'I understand he's been sidetracked—'

'Sidetracked?' Kingsley was irate, but Craw was determined not to show his complete ignorance of where Vaux had got to.

'Look, he's on a special mission. It will only take a day or so. It's just that our people view it as top priority. It's just a question of a twenty-four-hour hiatus.'

'Top priority? Twenty-four-hour hiatus?' Kingsley's eyes were now bulging as his blood pressure climbed to possibly life-threatening levels. He took a small tube out of the top pocket of his white cotton shirt, emptied two small pills into the palm of his hand, threw them into his mouth and swallowed. 'Pass the water down, will you?'

Craw pushed the plastic bottle of Sidi Ali toward his perplexed American colleague. Craw and Harvey waited as Kingsley unscrewed the plastic top and gulped loudly as the tepid flat water helped flush down the widely prescribed antidotes for hypertension.

Craw finally took off his seersucker jacket. Kingsley wiped his sweaty brow with a tissue from the handy box of Kleenex that the lady had left on the conference table. 'Look, let's get down to it. I fail to see what could have a greater priority than this prisoner exchange we've finally arranged, OK? So to hell with Vaux—he's now out of the equation. All right, Bill?'

'Yes, sir.'

'Any comments, Craw?'

'If he contacts me, I shall tell him that the exchange is going ahead as planned. I presume he knows the location and all that.'

'I told him last time I saw him. But he doesn't know the precise geography of where we're going to deal with these terrorists. In other words, he knows it will be in this coastal town called El

Jadida, but not the precise site. That's top secret, and I can't tell even you—until we're right there and closing in on these guys.'

Craw took offense at this latest intelligence. 'Excuse me. Are you saying you haven't enough faith in the British side to entrust me with the details of this critical exchange?'

'You're coming with us, aren't you?' said Kingsley as though to suggest to Craw that his very presence confirmed their trust. He turned to Harvey. 'Bill, did you say that we couldn't get the three Toyota Land Cruisers that I requested?'

'Yes, sir.' Harvey slid a typewritten sheet of paper over the table. 'There's the requisition order for the substitute vehicles. The Toyota crews are on some special mission to the Western Sahara—an anti-Polisario operation, I understand.'

As he read the vehicles requisition order, Kingsley remarked, almost to himself: 'I thought we were neutral in that never-ending dispute between the Moroccans and the Polisario separatists.'

Harvey either didn't know the official US position on that long-unresolved desert conflict or didn't want to embark on a conversation about a sideshow that was irrelevant to the issue at hand.

Kingsley said, 'Here we are, then. Leading vehicle, where we'll be, is a Land Rover Defender 110. Behind us will be two other Special Forces vehicles transporting a six-man team. The men will be heavily armed and commanded by a first lieutenant, all special-ops guys from their base at Agadir. We'll be meeting them just south of Jadida. These guys will be bringing with them our star detainee, one Abdul Juhayman. And so, as you see, this is essentially an Uncle Sam operation.'

'Except, of course, that it's our man who will be returned to us in exchange for Juhayman,' said Craw. It was his claim to be a principal player who is entitled to all the facts of the situation, a mild attempt to regain the American's tottering confidence in his British colleagues.

But Kingsley was adamant. 'Vaux's sudden absence from our deliberations, shall we say, is a major problem for me, Alan. I'll be frank. I don't like these sudden course changes on my team. I like total control, and I was under the impression that it was well understood that I'm in charge of this damn caper, and that's it. If you want to know the truth, if it was up to me, we'd let the whole thing hang loose.'

'I don't follow,' said Craw.

Kingsley glanced at Bill Harvey who replied with a mild smirk. 'I wouldn't have agreed to any of this pansy dancing around the issue, if you really want to know,' Kingsley went on. 'Our Mr. effing Juhayman is providing a gold mine of info about these terrorist cells here and in Spain. Our interrogation teams know how to extract this kind of stuff. I hear the Arabs soften pretty quickly. But that gold mine has not been mined out, if you know what I mean. There's literally tons more gold in that slimy head of his, and if we had more time, we'd get it all out. Now, because some junior UK intelligence officer gets nabbed off the street because he fails to exercise proper caution and appropriate tradecraft, we are going to lose a major source of intelligence relating to this part of the world.

'That's all I'm saying, Craw. If it was up to me, then I'd say we let Micklethwait go hang in the breeze. If we refused to exchange him for this bomb builder, they might release him anyway—eventually. And we get the best of both worlds—we get to keep our mother lode of information, and you eventually get your prized man back.'

Craw, for once, was speechless. He got up, put his jacket on and headed for the door.

'Be outside this building at eight this evening, please. And bring some light traveling things,' shouted Kingsley as Craw left the room.

Craw didn't answer and silently cursed the American cousins, as well as Vaux for his absence.

***

Vaux checked out of the hotel at about 6:30 a.m. By rising early, he had avoided the lineup for the single shower on his floor. Once outside the hotel, he checked in with George Greaves on the encrypted phone.

'Christ almighty, Vaux, can't you ever get up at a civilized time?'

'I just had to get out of that fleapit of a hotel. I'm already scratching the bites from the bedbugs. What's new?'

'A hell of a lot, actually. The good news is that they broke this fellow Magdi Kassim. The other guy was just a sidekick or a lover—whatever. Kassim says our man's in transit. A team's on its way to meet the Americans at El Jadida on the coast, about one hundred miles south of Casa. But you'd better get in touch with Lieutenant Simpson—he's got all the dope and his team is preparing to leave. His code name is Ferrari, which I said you would use to identify yourself. He'll probably use my code name—Blaine—just so that you know.'

'Mad about Ferraris, I presume.'

'It's a long story.' Greaves didn't have the patience at that time in the morning to explain the connection with the movie.

'So where do I find him?'

'They're all staying at the Hyatt on the Place des Nations Unies. Just get a petit taxi there and meet up with the boys for breakfast.'

'Thanks.'

Greaves called Simpson and told him to wait for a Mr. Westropp in the lobby. Vaux would use Simpson's code name for identification.

'The boys are in the pool,' said Simpson as they sat down at a low square table and ordered coffee. The lobby, furnished with 1930s-style white leather-covered arm chairs adorned with big red cushions, contrasted starkly with the slum where he had spent the night.

'Ministry of Defense do you guys proud, it seems.'

'Only on a super-short mission like this,' said Simpson. 'Anywhere else, we'd be conspicuous. This must be the biggest hotel in Casa. While you're waiting, why don't you go into the Casablanca Bar just over there? Unbelievable: stills from the film, the old posters, and even movie cameras hanging from the ceiling!'

'I'll do that. But hadn't we better hit the road as soon as possible?' Vaux was surprised that the SFSG team, sent over from their base at Saint Athan in Wales, weren't ready to go.

'We're leaving at noon. We had to requisition two vehicles from the DST guys on the Place Mohammed. They promised delivery around noon. You know what the Moroccans are like.'

'I heard from "Blaine" that Kassim spilled the beans pretty quickly,' said Vaux.

'Yeah. They don't pull any punches, these DST guys.'

'Literally, I imagine. Where did they take him?'

'They've a place under the old cathedral on the Boulevard Moulay Youssef, not far from here. Pretty forbidding place—torture chambers in a cold, damp basement on sacred ground. Not so sacred to them, I suppose.'

'So what's the game plan?'

Lt. Simpson produced a small road atlas. He turned to the page that showed the west coast of Morocco. 'It's simple: first, we go about one hundred kilometers north of here before we turn east on the N6 just after we hit Rabat. It's on the road to Khemisset, where we should find our prey. It's a small campsite in a cedar forest where our friends often find refuge, according to Kassim. The owners of the tourist campsite are, shall we say, sympathizers. So they should be staying there tonight before the scheduled early morning rendezvous at El Jadida. If we draw a blank, then we turn around, get back on the N1, and hightail it south again to El Jadida. We'll have special police number plates, so we can speed south at a good clip and hopefully overtake the two-vehicle convoy that's taking your agent toward the rendez-vous. The bad guys won't be speeding; it would attract police at-tention—and that's the last thing they want.'

So the backup plan was to be a hijack, plain and simple. But to Vaux, it all sounded a bit tenuous. 'And when we overtake them?'

'We stop them. We'll have a DST observer with us. He'll be armed like the rest of us. Obviously, he speaks Arabic—and then either all hell breaks loose or it will be a peaceful surrender and your man Micklethwait will be freed.'

'So we simply force them to stop on the motorway and give us our man back.'

'Yes, but I left out one important detail. An armed DST team will be following us for backup, and they'll have the means and the authority to arrest everyone. We understand our quarry consists of a couple of terrorist baddies in a vintage Land Rover followed by a Peugeot minivan where you'll find your man.'

'What if we don't catch up with them?'

'Worst-case scenario: we show up just in time to meet up with the CIA Special Forces team in El Jadida who are making the hostage exchange.' Lt. Simpson seemed to have everything under control.

A young man with a bush cut came up to them. He was wear-ing camouflage fatigues. 'This is John—our main driver. Seconded from the Logistic Corps. Now he's seen the way we live when we're on a quickie, in-and-out job, he wants to join us!'

Corporal John Swift blushed and told Simpson the crew was waiting for him in the basement garage.

'Are the Moroccans there?'

'Yes, sir. We're ready to go.'

Both men got up from the low armchairs. Vaux leaned down to pick up his holdall.

'Can I take that, sir?' said the corporal.

'Oh, thanks,' said Vaux. He unzipped the holdall, pulled out Kassim's SIG Sauer pistol, and tucked it quickly into the inside pocket of his blazer.

'Oh you've got a handgun,' said Simpson. 'I was going to loan you a Glock 17 for the trip. There could be some fireworks.'

Vaux was still troubled by something. 'Last but not least, Justin. Do we know the exact place where the Americans have promised to release the AQIM captive in exchange for our man?'

'Our DI guys tell us they've chosen a place north of the center of the town—an old Portuguese fort overlooking the sea, all battlements and ramparts. Apparently, there's an ancient disused church there, too. It's where the Yanks want to do the exchange—if we don't get your man first.'

Vaux's respect for the British Army's low-profile Defense Intelligence (DI) outfit soared to new heights. They seemed to know more than he did about Operation Rescue. But he'd been out of touch and for once could hardly blame Kingsley.

He thought about Simpson's hijacking plan, and he did not feel at all confident that it would work—the difficulty of finding AQIM's small party of desperados in such a short space of time and in the depths of a dense forest seemed obvious. But there was always the possibility of catching them up on the highway.

So he didn't worry much about the politically unpleasant repercussions of apprehending the AQIM team. Stealing the Americans' thunder by freeing the English hostage before the officially arranged exchange of both men at the same time could only exacerbate any strained relations with the cousins. In any case, he reassured himself, Brad Kingsley, et al would be secretly delighted with such an outcome: they would be able to hold on to their high-value prisoner indefinitely.

28

Abdul Juhayman had been in captivity for almost three months. Thanks to multiple, well-rewarded tip-offs from Juhayman's erstwhile and erratic comrades, the Moroccan intelligence service had finally learned that he was the mastermind behind the Casablanca bombings.

When they had established his location in the notorious Casablanca slum of Sidi Moumen, they called in the US Special Forces teams based at American Forces Africa Command—AFRICOM—headquarters in Agadir. In the firefight that followed, two militants were shot dead, and only Juhayman, a lithe twenty-eight-year-old, came out alive.

At the US-Moroccan 'black site' detention facilities near Temara on the Atlantic coast, the expert teams of special CIA interrogators got to work on Juhayman. It was three years after 9/11, the earth-shaking terrorist attacks in New York and Washington, and few people were then concerned about the ethical niceties of harsh interrogation techniques.

Now Juhayman was a broken man. He had spent the last six weeks in a military medical facility at Essaouira, but his condition had not improved. Punctured kidneys (due to blunt trauma), a collapsed lung, and a broken pelvis were among his more severe medical problems. But the CIA teams gave him little respite. The physical torture had ended, but the verbal third degree continued through the long hot nights. They had found a now-broken but willing and pliant informant. The immediate and longer-term terrorist strategies of Al-Qaeda in the Maghreb (AQIM) were now an open book—at least until AQIM's leadership revised its plans in the light of Juhayman's probable collapse of will.

Brad Kingsley and his Rabat-based colleague, Bill Harvey, sat in the back of a Land Rover Defender 110, built and modified to the sporadic and often lethal needs of Special Operations crews. In an uncomfortable side jump seat, Alan Craw, in his usual tropical-seersucker suit, quietly watched the arid countryside flash by while he wondered where the hell Vaux had got to.

Directly behind them, keeping a polite distance, was an M1161 Light Strike Vehicle, an enclosed armored Jeep ready for armed combat at the shout of a command. Its occupants included Juhayman, hooded, handcuffed and manacled; accompanied by Lieutenant Andrea Puzo, head of Operation Rescue's military contingent; his number two, Chief Warrant Officer Joe Frayn; and the driver, SPC Peter Brown.

The third vehicle in the small convoy, a Mercedes Benz Wolf 4x4, was driven by SPC Henry Franzen with passengers Sgt. Jack Bennet and Cpl. Seymour Erdman. Following Kingsley's requests, the specialist anti-terrorism squad was appropriately armed for any contingency, and all wore DPM-camouflaged jumpsuits and green berets.

The vehicles made their steady way northward on the R301 coastal highway, and they had just passed a fishing village called Safi, about 150 miles south of the El Jadida rendezvous.

***

As Vaux had feared, the AQIM team was nowhere to be seen. The campsite was about two miles into the thick cedar forest and the old man at the booth said business was very slow. The week-end tourist rush, he said hopefully, would get underway tomorrow. Lt. Simpson, on the pretext of checking out the site for future use as tourists, sent Sgt. Duckworth and Cpl. Swift to search for any evidence of recent arrivals. But if the militants had spent the night here, they had been thorough, and there were no signs of their pres-ence. And anyway, the old guard was a suspected sympathizer.

So the small convoy headed back to the N1, turned south, by-passing Casablanca, and finally began the last phase of the trip to El Jadida. Cpl. Swift thought the highway's smooth surface and long curves were comparable to any UK motorway, and his driving abili-ties were soon evident—even if Vaux watched anxiously as the ana-log speedometer swung almost 180 degrees toward the 220 kph mark.

'Keep your eyes skinned for a blue minivan, Corporal. That's where we'll find our Englishman,' said Simpson. He turned to Vaux. 'That's another nugget they squeezed out of our captor.'

Vaux looked at the long road ahead. No minivan of any descrip-tion was in sight.

Lt. Simpson, Vaux, and Sgt. Duckworth were in the lead vehicle, a Land Rover 4x4 driven by Swift. Following them, an HMT Jackal 400, described by Swift as a 'covert assault vehicle,' was driven by Sgt. Durrell. In the back, two 'other ranks,' both expert marks-men, lovingly nursed their medium-range sniper rifles as carefully and tenderly as newborns. Keeping a long distance behind the two

SFSG vehicles was a large, unmarked Peugeot 37 saloon transporting three Casablanca-based officers of Morocco's Direction de la Surveillance du Territoire, the DST.

***

Since his school days, Micklethwait had rarely prayed. But in the last few weeks, he had turned to his God more than once. He had prayed for his deliverance and made certain pledges about his future behavior. And now, silently, he was praying again—for the successful outcome of the planned and imminent exchange of prisoners. He looked sideways at John Keen: he carried a frown on his face, his worry beads clicked through his fingers, and Micklethwait could only assume that his prayers for a safe outcome to the operation were as strong as his.

Meanwhile, in the Land Rover Defender, Craw flipped through a tourist guidebook. He had zeroed in on the page devoted to El Jadida. He saw that the proposed exchange site was not all Kingsley had probably expected. 'Brad, you do realize that this church you've chosen as the rendezvous is no longer in use as a church, don't you? It's now, according to this guide, a community center—showing films, putting on plays, and so on. Might that tend to put a spanner in the works—lots of tourists and whatnot milling around?'

Kingsley looked at Harvey in disbelief. 'Trust a Brit to spread doubt and despair. Look, Craw, my best local scouts checked this place out, and they said it's an ideal spot. It's closed to the public this morning—we made sure of that. Let's get there first before we start to worry about last-minute changes.'

Craw ignored Kingsley's answer and continued to gen up on the location of the planned exchange. Kingsley's observation about his nationality spurred him on. But he would try not to be negative, only constructive. 'Anyway, if the Church of the Assumption proves unavailable, I've found a backup site nearby,' he said.

Kingsley again threw a 'God save us' glance at his partner. 'And what might that be?'

'There's a place at the northwest of the old Portuguese compound named, believe it or not, the Bastion of Saint Sebastian. Appropriate, don't you think? Perhaps a good omen.'

Bill Harvey didn't know what the hell the Brit was talking about. 'Why so?'

'Well, our man's name is Sebastian—Sebastian Micklethwait,' said Craw, suddenly and uncharacteristically taking pride in the very Englishness of his junior colleague's name.

Kingsley sighed in frustration. 'I want to stick to Plan A—which is the old Catholic church, OK? Let's not get too complicated here. One of my agents checked the place out, and he said the old sacristy would be the ideal pre-exchange meeting place where we work out the logistics of the operation.'

***

As the subsequent investigation would uncover, communications modes between the various parties to Operation Rescue had chosen to ignore the recommended technology and procedures then found in military manuals and had fallen far short of any clandestine methods recommended in contemporary treatises on CIA tradecraft.

Kingsley had a phobia about voice or text messages, electronic chatter and ciphers similar to the older generation's general dislike of new computer technologies. He suspected all verbal contacts were subject to detection, no airwaves were secure, and the newfangled, much-ballyhooed Wi-Fi technology probably the most vulnerable to enemy eavesdropping. So, once he had given man-to-man orders, he preferred not to talk about a planned operation.

In a strange, strategic coincidence, the rebel militants felt the same way as Kingsley. Nothing more clandestine than a conventional cell phone played any role in their sparse and usually coded conversations.

The British contingent had also seen no reason for a sophisticated, encrypted chain of communications: the mission was clear and relatively simple. The CIA had assumed command because they held Juhayman. The time and day of the planned exchange was known to all participants. They just had to get there on time.

So when the three negotiating teams drove up to the precincts of the sixteenth-century Church of the Assumption on the southwest corner of the Cité Portugaise, the participants were playing everything by ear.

The only exception to what Kingsley later termed the vital necessity of a total communications blackout were the radio messages from the rear-guard DST contingent to the local police. They were commanded to stand by in case of an unruly public presence at the historic site once word got out of a major interchange between US officials and local militants.

29

At noon, Brad Kingsley and Bill Harvey entered the sacristy of the Church of the Assumption on the southwest corner of the Cité Portugaise. Built some five hundred years ago, it sat just behind an imposing stone bastion that was part of the ancient defensive wall that protects the coastal settlement. It had been closed to the public since the evening before, and the old stooped caretaker, who preferred visitors to call him the sacristan, busied himself with the placement of eight chairs around a long wooden table.

Craw had remained outside the gray stone building so he could have a moment of reflection. He took a forbidden Gauloise from a tattered blue packet. He was getting anxious. The opposition hadn't arrived. He hadn't heard anything from Vaux or Greaves, and he felt isolated as an official bystander with no power or authority to justify his presence. Still, he assured himself, he would soon see Micklethwait, and he knew that the anticipation of witnessing the final outcome of this unprecedented deal between the CIA and the jihadists was the cause of his apprehension.

He looked to his left, where an ancient mud-and-brick wall separated the front courtyard from the road that led to the nearby Place Mohammed Ben Abdullah. Kingsley had requested the road be closed before positioning the Land Rover 110 behind the wall. The M1161 light strike compact Jeep was parked parallel to a third vehicle—the Mercedes Benz Wolf. The anti-terrorism teams were ordered to wait in their vehicles in watch and wait mode until further orders.

Through the shimmering waves that rose from the hot surface of the approach road, Craw now saw the slow progress of a blue minivan. It was followed by a gleaming black sedan, and then by an early model Land Rover. The vehicles crawled toward the forecourt, bouncing on the uneven cobblestones. They stopped about fifty yards from where he stood. He threw the cigarette butt on the floor, stubbed it out and headed for the sacristy. 'I think our friends have arrived,' he said.

'Good,' said Kingsley. 'Now, if you don't mind, you can make yourself useful.' The comment was semijocular, so Craw decided not to take offense. 'A high-powered lawyer will alight from the car first—he should be in a black limo. He's the guy who will confirm the preliminary steps we have to make to effect the exchange. He's big-time, from Casablanca. So could you go out and meet him? He'll be wondering what to do.'

Craw knew that the church was no longer a place of worship, but he could smell a lingering odor of incense as he left the stuffy sacristy. Perhaps, he thought, some undercover Christian sect still practiced their rites here when the social center was closed. He strode down the long nave of the church and emerged on the porch that led to the forecourt. Nothing was happening, so he walked cautiously toward the great car. The lawyer sat far back in the rear seat. He was heavily built, with short, salt-and-pepper hair and dressed in an elegant navy-blue western business suit. His white shirt was open at the collar.

Craw heard the locks click open, and the lawyer heaved himself out of the car. The young Moroccan driver, also in western clothing, turned off the ignition. Craw explained the logistics, and as they walked past the minivan he shot a quick glance into the tinted side windows. No Micklethwait: all he saw were four Arabs in white robes and the traditional Moroccan *ghutra* headdress. But he knew he could have been mistaken. It was a quick check and he could have missed someone—especially if he had been told to lie low on the floor of the vehicle.

In the sacristy, Bayjan Adid shook the hands of the three representatives of what he remembered from his school days they used to call the Western powers. 'Your man is here. He is healthy and in good spirits. On my orders, my clients will release him, and he will be told to walk straight into the church, where I presume you or your appointed officials will take him in hand,' said Adid.

Kingsley then asked Bill Harvey if the medical team had arrived. 'We would like to give him a thorough examination, Mr. Adid.'

'This was not in our agreement. He is in good shape; don't worry. A medical exam would prolong this exercise inordinately. I can't agree to this. Let's get on with the exchange.'

'But surely it's reasonable for us to check the condition of the man who has been held in your custody for over a month now,' said Kingsley.

'And what about Juhayman? Do we have the right to check his state of health after three months at the Temara black site? Where is he, by the way?'

Kingsley nodded to Harvey. 'He's patiently waiting at the nearby Bastion Saint Sebastian. But he will be escorted here just as soon as we give the go-ahead,' said Harvey.

Adid acknowledged the implied insult. The nearby Bastion Saint Sebastian was an old synagogue with a restored Star of David emblazoned on its rear wall.

Craw felt compelled to break the apparent deadlock. 'Look, gentlemen, I think we'd all agree that at this juncture, time is of the essence. Let's agree to shelve each other's demands for medical examinations and go ahead with the physical exchange of the parties.'

Kingsley looked at Harvey, and Adid nodded agreement. Kingsley said, 'Very well. Bill, please go now and bring our detainee to the forecourt position.' He then explained the mechanics of the exchange. His eyes seemed to cloud over, as if he was looking back to the past with some nostalgia. 'We want it to be like those old classic Cold War exchanges. Remember? The spy swaps over the Glienicke Bridge in Berlin. So we will release your man from the portals of the church. Simultaneously, we will expect to see Knight, the man you are holding captive—'

'Monsieur Kingsley. I am holding no man captive. I am the agreed-upon intermediary, the legal representative of your antagonists. It is a mutual agreement, no? And actually, I'm sorry to say I have never heard of this bridge in Berlin.'

'Oh, well, all right. I don't want to haggle over legal niceties...' said Kingsley, as if such details were too insignificant to matter. 'But to get back to what I was saying: the two men will be released simultaneously. They will walk toward each other, pass each other on their left-hand sides, and both return to their respective support group, more or less at the same time. Do we understand one another, sir?'

***

At the very moment the four men rose from the long table to get the operation underway (some have since called it the prisoner exchange, others the hostage exchange), the contingent from Britain's Special Operations base in Saint Athan, South Wales, slowly made its way toward the ancient Gothic church. In the leading Land Rover, Vaux looked anxiously at the queue of vehicles that had lined up before the church. He observed the three AFRICOM desert-tan vehicles parked on his right behind a low brick wall. The crews were not visible.

He told Cpl. Swift to drive very slowly and to stop about one hundred yards from the aging Land Rover at the rear of the black Peugeot C4 sedan. Then, in front of the limo, he saw the quarry that had got away—the blue Peugeot minivan. Waves of shimmering heat rose from its rust-spotted roof as the midday sun blazed down on the eerily silent scene.

Vaux tapped his large side pocket to check the presence of the SIG Sauer. He opened the Land Rover's door and asked Lt. Simpson to stay put while he checked things out.

'If you're going to do a recce, let me come with you,' said Sgt. Duckworth. 'I'll cover your back.' Vaux didn't argue. The two men got out of the Land Rover and walked slowly in single file toward the church. As they passed the minivan, they saw four men in Arab dress. They appeared to be smoking, the windows lowered slightly to let out tendrils of blue-gray tobacco smoke.

Abdul Juhayman, supported by two uniformed medics, walked hesitatingly toward the front doors of the church. The medics had their hands planted firmly underneath Juhayman's armpits, and at times, it looked as if his feet weren't making contact with the ground. His beard was long, he wore a loose-fitting *kuffiya*, and his scuffed leather sandals were unstrapped. His feet looked bruised and scratched.

Vaux had been surprised that no one had yet challenged him. He wore khakis, a blue shirt and a green safari jacket, a last-minute purchase in the lobby of the Hyatt in Casablanca. Sgt. Duckworth, in workhorse camouflage fatigues, had probably immunized him from suspicion on anyone's part. But then he saw the pathetic image of a broken man, propped up by his helpers, all three staggering toward the doors of the church. He stopped walking and stood in place.

Sgt. Duckworth knocked into him from behind. 'Sorry, sir.'

'All right, Sergeant. Our friends must be in the church. Let's go.'

The prisoner had been led to a bench in the church porch where he had sat down. Vaux passed in front of him and heard voices and loud footfalls as Kingsley, Harvey and Craw made their way down the stone-floored nave toward him. An overweight man in western clothes and carrying a leather briefcase followed.

'For Christ's sake! You've finally arrived,' said Craw. He felt relief as well as anger. He had missed Vaux's presence, but he was annoyed that he had remained in silent mode for so long.

'It's a long story,' said Vaux. 'I guess we got here just in time to witness the recovery of young Micklethwait. Where is he, by the way?'

Kingsley, irritated by this diversion, replied curtly: 'He's in that battered, old minivan and I would ask you people to kindly make yourselves scarce. We can't risk anything to go wrong here, Vaux, so please remain as passive as you've been up to now.'

Lt. Simpson, who had finally decided to catch up with Vaux and his sergeant, refused to let the put-down stand. 'I don't call the apprehension of Magdi Kassim particularly passive, old boy. We wouldn't all be here today without the information the DST got out of him.'

'That's debatable,' said Kingsley. 'I'll see you at the inquiry. Meanwhile, let's get on with this. Bill Harvey, please go to the minivan and tell them to release the English hostage now. And don't forget to tell them about the agreed protocol: he is to walk slowly toward the portals, and he is to pass our detainee on his left-hand side.'

Bill Harvey glanced at Juhayman whose head was bowed as he clicked through his prayer beads.

Kingsley nodded to the medics, and both men put their hands under Juhayman's arms and hoisted him up. They shuffled toward the open double doors of the porch. Vaux and Duckworth followed them.

Bill Harvey walked behind Juhayman, still supported by the two medics, across the forecourt. They were about fifty yards away from the minivan. They heard loud talk in guttural Arabic, doors slamming, and finally a quiet that seemed only to heighten the tense atmosphere.

Sebastian Micklethwait, tall and thin, emerged from the sliding door of the minivan. He was accompanied by Omar Sala a.k.a. John Keen. Both wore flowing white djellabas and white *ghutra* turbans swathed their heads. Their beards were long and thick.

Kingsley, just behind the church's double doors, looked through his powerful Steiner-Optik daylight binoculars. 'Where the hell is the Englishman?' he shouted.

'I think the taller one is Micklethwait. He has a light-brown beard. I'm pretty sure that's him. It matches his hair color,' said Vaux.

'We'll soon know,' said Craw. 'The one who walks will be our man.'

The man with the long, auburn beard and white robe started to walk toward them. Kingsley ordered the medics to release their patient.

The men walked toward each other. Juhayman's step faltered. He fell to the ground. One of the medics rushed up to him and helped him stand upright. He then gave a gentle, encouraging push to urge him forward.

Micklethwait had slowed his pace when he saw the other man fall. He waited as Juhayman got back on his feet. Then they resumed their slow walk. As they came close, both men looked into each other's eyes—a sign, perhaps, of respect for a fellow captive.

Seconds later, a muffled shot rang out. It came from the low wall where the US Army vehicles were parked. Juhayman fell to the ground, a fountain of blood spouting from his neck.

The man who had always sat in the rear seat of the minivan as one of Micklethwait's watchful, sullen guards, slid open the rear door with a resounding clang, dropped to the ground, and aimed his AK-47 at Micklethwait, who had turned around when he heard the shot that hit Juhayman.

John Keen, a.k.a. Omar Sala, who had been standing close to the minivan to watch Micklethwait's progress toward the church, quickly drew a Glock 17 from under his robe and shot the guard before he could pull the trigger. The short-range impact ripped open the man's skull. Micklethwait was now running toward the church's entrance.

The minivan's driver, a quiet, young Casablancan who had never uttered a sound during the long trip from Al Hoceima on the Mediterranean coast to El Jadida, now jumped out of his seat. His AK-47 was equipped with a long telescopic sight. He knelt down and carefully focused on the running man—the man he knew his comrade had tried to kill to avenge the assault on the crippled man they had come to rescue.

But then he saw Keen closing in on him and he jumped up. Instantaneously, he lashed out with a karate high side kick. Keen's Glock spun away from his grip onto the gravel paving.

Vaux had been standing behind one of the stout concrete pillars that supported the sheltering porch and he had felt useless as he watched the bloody scene unfold. He had seen the minivan's driver, a young Arab in jeans and T-shirt, jump out of the vehicle with the AK-47. He saw Keen move toward him, but the driver had jumped up and high-kicked the handgun out of Keen's grip. Then he quickly knelt down again and pointed his telescopic AK-47 at Micklethwait's back, just as MI6's probationary secret agent got within two yards of the safety of the church's portals. Vaux carefully aimed his SIG Sauer at the gunman, pulled the trigger and saw him topple as he clung to the side of the minivan while a stray shot ricocheted around the forecourt.

Vaux's concentration on the tragedy that played out in the forecourt and his careful aim at the second would-be killer blinded him from the silent stalker who ran down swiftly, low and bowed, from the left side of the minivan, directly opposite the US combat team.

Vaux was looking to see whether his target showed any signs of revival when he heard a loud, reverberating bang from his right and felt a searing pain in his shoulder.

The last thing he remembered was hitting the ground and looking at a carpet of small, white stones as they faded into a foggy range of snow-capped mountains and then a total blackness.

30

'Where am I?' asked Vaux.

He was looking into the deep, blue eyes of a beautiful English girl whose straight ash-blond hair hung down to her shoulders. It was Anne. She was leaning over him, a broad smile on her full lips, a look of triumph on her pretty face. 'Just rest, darling, you've been through a lot.'

Vaux's shoulder ached, he was forcing his gummy eyes to open more fully, and he couldn't move his neck. He felt he had come back from the dead. 'What happened?'

Before Anne could reply, she was gently pushed aside by a young man in blue scrubs. 'Please, Miss, we'll handle this now.' He looked at Vaux whose eyes were fixed on the ceiling. 'You're doing well, mate. We've called up your doctor, and he'll be here in a jiff. Just relax; don't strain yourself.'

Vaux had no option. He wondered if he could get a pillow. 'Do I have to lie like this?'

'Yes, very still. Your wound's healing fast, but you mustn't move too much.'

A big man in a white coat shuffled the male nurse aside. He had a large head and thick, black hair—and a bushy, salt-and-pepper handlebar moustache that reminded Vaux of Spitfire pilots in World War II movies. 'How are you feeling, old chap?'

'Well, at least I'm conscious. How long have I been under?'

'About sixty hours. You've been in an induced coma since you were operated on in Agadir. They rushed you there to some US medical facility, took the bullet out of your clavicle, and put you on an RAF transport back to London.'

'What's a clavicle?'

'Collarbone.'

'And the prognosis?'

'Excellent. Another week here, and you should be all right to go home. Someone will have to be with you for some time. But you're headed for a full recovery.'

'Thank God for that,' said Vaux. 'Or perhaps I should thank you and everybody else for that.'

The surgeon responded with a nod. Then he reached for Vaux's arm and took his pulse.

Twenty-four hours after regaining consciousness, Vaux had an official visitor. Alan Craw, in a dark-blue Savile Row suit, highly polished black oxford shoes, and a striped, blue-and-white shirt that clashed with his usual diagonally striped Worcester College tie, proffered a bag of grapes and a paperback novel by Andrew Camilleri. 'I noticed you reading a Donna Leon novel at the villa, checked it out and saw it was based in Venice. So I bought this for you: it's a thriller, too, and set in Italy—or is it Sicily? Anyway, you'll have plenty of time for reading from now on.' Vaux thought this sounded ominous. So he lay back to listen to Craw's undoubtedly rehearsed report. 'Is Anne still around?' asked Craw.

Vaux knew Craw had the hots for Anne and could well be preparing an array of invitations for dinner and cocktail parties while Vaux was laid up and out of circulation. But he also knew he had more urgent things to worry about—like getting out of hospital and back home to Hertfordshire.

'No, she's gone home to daddy—in Hatch End. I can't expect her to stay here all her nonworking hours,' said Vaux.

'She's doing very well at the office, and Sir Nigel's very happy with her.' Vaux ignored this gratuitous piece of intelligence and popped a white grape into his mouth with his free left hand. 'So, here's my version of what happened. The official version, of course, is weeks away. The US authorities are conducting your usual official inquiry on the balls-up, and our friend Kingsley could well be disciplined—at least, that's the scuttlebutt.'

Vaux sighed. He was bored with being helpless. It was the impatience of a lame duck. He felt that if he were up and about, he could make some useful contribution to Department B3's inevitable inquest into what went wrong at El Jadida. 'Get on with it, Alan.'

Craw helped himself to a grape. 'First off, it's not what you're probably thinking.'

'How do you know what I'm thinking?'

'I think you suspect, as we all did just after the incident, that it was a setup: that Kingsley had given the order to his snipers behind that wall to shoot to kill his loathed terrorist. Kingsley never really wanted to give him up—especially not just to please his English allies. He had a fanatical hatred for these guys and was loath to send this one back to making bombs that would kill his American comrades as well as innocent civilians—'

'Don't put words in my mouth, Alan. I thought no such thing. I'm still in shock, and I haven't been able to collect any such cogent thoughts, believe me. The coma has effectively wiped out my memory of the debacle. Fill me in, please.'

'Very well. This sharpshooter, it turns out, took it upon himself to kill Juhayman because just two days earlier, he had learned that his brother, also in the US Marines, had been killed by insurgents in Iraq. The chap went quietly berserk, I suppose, and he took it out on a man whom he knew to be a terrorist. He had decided that Juhayman would get the same kind of justice that the Iraqi militants meted out to his brother. He'll face a special court of inquiry, of course.

'Well, as you know, this is what sparked the subsequent fracas. The guys who had been in the minivan with Micklethwait—'

'How is he, by the way?'

'In great spirits.'

'Good.'

'So this apparent guard who had driven with them all that way to the meeting place lost his cool at seeing his comrade Juhayman cut down by the Americans, who were supposed to be making sure nothing like this happened. Understandably, they saw it all as a trap and a betrayal of the American pledge to see a fair exchange carried through. So, not too surprisingly, he thinks he'll avenge Juhayman's death by shooting Micklethwait in the back as our colleague is making his way toward the church.

'But here's the intriguing part: this chap John Keen, in full Arab attire and supposedly a member of some Salafist extremist offshoot of AQIM, the very guy who had closely guarded Micklethwait almost since the day he was abducted in Tangier, turns out not to be Omar Sala, an English Muslim convert, but a mole planted among the extremist fundamentalists by a new, very hush-hush subgroup at MI6. I understand it's in fact a joint MI5-MI6 operation whose task is to monitor Brits who succumb to the temptations of following the prophet Mohammed.

'So, Keen shoots the guard before the man has a chance to pull the trigger, and our purported Muslim convert saves Micklethwait's life.'

Vaux said, 'Let me get my head round this. You mean that it was an inside job—that Mickle would have been killed if it hadn't been for this double agent John Keen—who shot the guy who had Micklethwait in his sights?'

'That's precisely what I mean. Can I continue?'

'By all means. Who shot *me*?'

Craw relished Vaux's surprise and impatience. 'I'm coming to that, Vaux. Patience, please.' Vaux flipped through the pages of Camilleri's *Voice of the Violin*. The count was 239, not too overwhelming.

'So far, we have two people felled—Juhayman, shot by the maverick Special Forces guy; the guard—killed by our planted mole, to save Micklethwait. This is where you decide to take action. I'm sure you remember. You observe the driver of the minivan get out after he sees his comrade, the guard, shot by Keen.

'He's got poor old Micklethwait in his sights as he's just making it to the porch where you happen to be standing. You see him raise an AK-47, but then he sees Keen close in on him. He drops the rifle and aims a sudden karate kick at Keen's handgun, which goes flying into the blue yonder.

'Vaux, it was like a scene out of a Bruce Lee film. Did I tell you I took karate lessons in my twenties? Didn't quite make a black belt but it was damn good exercise. OK, so you now see that the baddie has the upper hand, and you whip out your trusty SIG Sauer and hit the target. Miraculous shot. So now, it's three men down. But there's another assailant—in the old Land Rover that had led the minivan on the trip south but had parked behind the van for some reason.

'He's making his slow, surreptitious way down the field to your right, stalking and taking advantage of the mayhem. He gets close enough to see your shot that took out the minivan driver and decides to give you your just rewards. He has you in the crosshairs, and you go down with a severe wound to your shoulder or collarbone, and the tragic episode draws to a close.'

Vaux said, 'But where were all of Kingsley's backup boys? He had three trucks full of special forces types armed to the hilt with sniper rifles and what have you. I even saw two light machine guns mounted on a Jeep. Where the hell were they when all this was going on?'

'Frozen. Lieutenant Puzo, the commanding officer, said something about the 'fog of war' and had ordered his men to hold their fire during the whole fracas. I think the shock of seeing one of his group defy orders and kill Juhayman shook him up so much, he couldn't function. But we'll never know.

'At any rate, Kingsley defended the officer's restraint to the hilt. Says if they had intervened with their overwhelming firepower, there'd have been a bloodbath. As it was, only two deaths on the baddies' team and two casualties—you, old bean, and the guard you shot.'

'What damage did I do to him?'

'You winged him. He dropped his weapon on impact. The DST, hovering in the background, took him in. He's hospitalized, of course, and no doubt due for a long and arduous interrogation about his comrades and affiliations.'

'And the guy that shot me? What happened to him?'

'Unfortunately, he got away—disappeared through that dense stand of eucalyptus trees.'

'Were there any more survivors among the terrorists?'

'We think two who were probably in the old Land Rover with the guy that shot you ran for their lives. They disappeared into the bushes and probably hid out in the old medina. It's not far away from the church, and it's a veritable labyrinth.

'The DST are very upset, of course. They stayed back from the fray for diplomatic reasons, I suppose. But they're on high alert for any terrorist threats that could arise from the incident.'

Craw took another white grape from the bag. Vaux placed the paperback mystery novel on his cluttered bedside table. 'You do realize that if my plan to waylay Micklethwait and his captors on the road to El Jadida had worked out, the body count would have been nil.'

'Yes, *if* you had been successful and Micklethwait's guards had meekly surrendered on the highway. Given their AK-47s and their fiery loyalty to their cause, that's a big if.'

'And what about our sterling contingent—where the hell were our British Tommies when all hell broke loose? Did they just come along for the ride, nursing their L96 sniper rifles like babes in arms?'

'Sgt. Durrell, who was in the Jackal, told his men to hold fire until the scene clarified. They were right at the back of the line, if you remember. By the time they got a fix on what was happening, it was all over,' said Craw.

***

It was a Sunday morning, and England's long hot summer lingered.

Vaux sat on the flagged terrace that overlooked his long garden and, beyond, the rolling hills of Hertfordshire. It was the green belt, and Vaux, as he knew when he bought the place, had a guaranteed vista of green English meadows and copper-beech copses that no private or public developer could ever spoil. Unless, of course, the politicians decided they needed more land to build houses for Britain's bulging population.

He heard the tinkling of ice in a big glass jug of lemonade as Anne walked through the french doors and placed the tumblers on the marble-topped bistro table. She poured the pink fizzy liquid (Vaux preferred the bottled variety) and sat down on the canvas director's chair beside him. 'I think I should roast the leg of lamb for lunch. After all, it's Sunday,' said Anne. She was still dressed in a light, cotton blue housecoat; and she had cleaned up the breakfast things while Vaux showered and shaved.

'Nonsense,' said Vaux. 'I'm taking you to the local. Their Sunday lunches are as good as your mother ever made. And besides, now I'm more mobile, I want to show my face there. Get reacquainted with my neighbors, that sort of thing.'

'But you bought the lamb only yesterday, darling.'

'Just relax. Sunday's a day of rest. We'll have the bloody lamb later in the week.'

'Do you like it like that?

'Like what?'

'Bloody.'

'Sorry, I know I shouldn't swear in front of a lady. Especially a Roedean girl.'

Anne thought the remark didn't deserve an answer. She gazed into the distance. The midmorning heat was visible in the shimmering waves that rose up from the fields that were now more a faded straw color than green. The meteorologists said the drought would likely continue until autumn.

'Is that settled, then? The Pig & Whistle for lunch,' said Vaux.

'Yes, if you like. Cooking's no fun in this heat, anyway.'

Vaux folded the *Sunday Times* into a neat package and placed it under the table. Anne knew he was getting bored with this domestic existence. His recovery from the gunshot wound was complete and although he always maintained his only aim for the rest of his life was to live in semirural tranquility, enlivened occasionally by visits to the West End and perhaps Paris, she recognized the signs of restlessness. 'Did you ever see *The Mousetrap,* darling?'

'Centuries ago—with my mum.'

'John's got six complimentary tickets, and he's trying to get a group together. The play's run nonstop for over fifty years, and he thinks we should all see it before it dies a natural death.'

'Which is more one can say for the Agatha Christie characters that get popped off, I seem to recall.'

'We could all drive up to London in the car.' Anne referred to Vaux's recent purchase of a glossy black Audi A6, financed from the ex gratia payment from Department B3 'in appreciation of his efforts that contributed to the successful conclusion of Operation Rescue.'

Vaux wasn't too surprised that the note that had come with the check made no reference to the ill-fated Operation Apostate. As Craw had remarked before he finally quit Tangier for home, the initial operation that had sent them to North Africa in the first place had been based on 'an ill-conceived and false premise.' No terrorist defector ever existed.

Vaux took a swig of lemonade. He felt like a cigarette but suppressed the urge. 'You're referring to John Goodchild, I take it.'

'Yes, your old school friend.'

'Where did you come across him? I haven't seen him since I got back. That's one reason I wanted to go to the Pig.'

'I met him walking his dog on the street.'

'And I thought he'd been avoiding me. Funny guy, old John. Well, anyway, it sounds fun. Yes, we'll certainly go. Meanwhile, I have to finish the mystery Craw gave me in hospital. Haven't felt much like reading anything but the newspapers recently.'

Vaux's Nokia mobile chimed the first few notes of 'Lullaby of Birdland.' Anne stretched over to pick it up. 'Hello?'

'Ah! Anne, I presume.'

Anne's heartbeat quickened a little as she recognized the cultured but slightly gruff voice of her boss, Sir Nigel Adair, the enduring head of Department B3, a subgroup of MI6's Middle East and North Africa desk. 'Yes, Sir Nigel. Good morning.'

'Is Vaux there?'

'Yes, he is. I'll get him for you.' Vaux thought he'd wait a minute or so since Anne had given the impression that he was not sitting right there by her side. But he was impatient to find out what the old boy wanted. 'Sir Nigel, how are you?'

'More to the point—how are *you*? You're the man who was wounded in action, serving queen and country, what?'

'Fully mended now, I think.'

'Happy to hear it. Now, here's the point, Vaux. We haven't had the opportunity to talk since you got back and went straight into hospital. So naturally, I'd like to see you and basically debrief you, if you like, on our successful completion of Operation Rescue.'

'Are we on a secure line, Sir Nigel?' Vaux asked out of habit more than any real concern.

'No, as a matter of fact. I doubt if any listener would know what we are talking about. But while we're on the subject, I trust you remember signing the Official Secrets Act—many moons ago. So I just want to remind you that the Apostate caper will never be mentioned again by you or anybody else who was involved in that complete waste of time. I hope we understand each other.'

Sir Nigel Adair thus relegated Operation Apostate to the deep archival dungeons at Vauxhall Cross. But as the true believer in what proved to be the chimera of a top terrorist's defection to Britain, Sir Nigel's ability to recover from self-made fiascos, seemed to Vaux to be truly daunting. Vaux said, helpfully, 'Yes, of course. Name the day and time you want to see me, and I'll be there.'

'Very well. I'll call tomorrow from the office. Anne will be there, I hope.'

'As far as I know, sir.' He looked at Anne. She guessed Sir Nigel's question and nodded yes.

'Good. One more thing. Something's come up, and I'm buggered if I know who to send. You're the obvious candidate—if you wish to work for us again.'

Vaux did not want to commit himself as quickly as Sir Nigel had pounced the question. So he thought he'd use some ammunition— information leaked to him from Anne during one of their pillow talks about the office. 'I hear John Keen is joining us,' said Vaux.

'Oh, you heard, eh? Yes, they didn't know what to do with him. He lost his cover, of course, and MI6 passed him on to us. A bit rough around the edges—a Maida Vale boy, born and bred—but I think we can smooth him out,' said Sir Nigel.

'And Chris Greene. I hear he's fully recovered and back on the job,' said Vaux, exposing Anne as his obvious source of intelligence. But with Nigel in a good and solicitous mood, he didn't think it mattered.

'Yes, yes. A good man. But I need someone with your experience, Vaux. We can talk about it. Craw's now your biggest booster, by the way. He thinks you'll be bored in the suburbs.'

'He doesn't know me,' said Vaux. He pressed the off button and sighed.

'I got the gist of it,' said Anne. 'He wants you on another job.'

'Something like that,' said Vaux.

About the Author

Roger Croft is a former journalist whose reports and feature articles have appeared in numerous publications, including the *Economist, Sunday Telegraph* and *Toronto Star*. He also worked in Egypt where he freelanced and wrote editorials for Cairo's *Egyptian Gazette*.

Visit www.rogercroft.com

Made in the USA
San Bernardino, CA
15 October 2017